THE CHOICE

THE CHOICE

A.ROBINS

CONTENTS

DEDICATION

This book is for the Survivors
When all is lost, starting over is not that
bad.

Foreword

Hello, and welcome to my story. Let's be honest; no account is ever new. But how that story told can be. So, as you read my work of art, I will list several music titles. Then my suggestion is to find the song and the artist. Then listen to the song before continuing to read or even better if you can read the book while listening to the music; it will have a better impact on the story. What I am trying to do is to create an environment where you enjoy the power to not only read with your eyes but read with your ears.

Warning

The start of this book has some domestic violence. It might be hard to read, but the truth is this violence is real. The impacts of violence are more than just skin deep. If you are experiencing domestic violence or know someone who is, please find the help to get to safety, you are worth so much more. I did, and my life has never been better.

Thank you. I hope you enjoy it.

LifeLine (Australia)

13 11 14

1800 Respect (Australia)

National Domestic Violence Hotline (US)

1–800–799–7233

24-hour Domestic Violence Hotline (UK)

0808 2000 247 24

CHAPTER 1

The Encounter

Hello, the date is November the 23rd, the year does not matter as it happens on the same day, every year for over 13 years. There is this lovely house, the only house on a little gravel lane. There is nothing wrong with the house, well-groomed yard with plenty of adult trees, two cars in the driveway, trampoline, sandpit, chicken coop, and an outdoor seating area. It's rather large with plenty of space for a family of seven.

Time moves forward, and four of the children grow up and move away. By all outward appearances, this is the perfect family. Children with a stable home and two parents.

But the one thing that remains steady throughout the years. That what seen on the outside is not what is going on behind closed doors. There is a dark presence that evades it and erupts in violence from one person towards another. It makes no sense, and it has no rhyme or reason, it just simply is.

It fills the whole day from sun up to sundown. It is always directed only at one person, never the children. But they are still collateral damage, and there is no shielding them from this insidious behaviour.

Let me introduce you to Everett. He is a wonderful gentleman with a heart of gold. He is not very tall, only about 5'6". He started to see the grey in his short brown hair a few years back. Everett always seems to have a smile that fills the room. But he hides a secret pain that of loving a person, who he knows hates him. But fools himself into ignoring the facts that stare at him. One should question why he puts up with so much hate directed at him. But no one ever does or steps in to stop it. This story or maybe a story that is bigger than him or even all of us.

Now let us enter the home and witness a story that will change the way you think about choices.

[Go your own way – Fleetwood Mac]

Yelling fills the home, "Fine, go fuck yourself," and the wooden door slams shut. Everett walks over to his desk, pulls out his chair and slumps down into it. His head rests into his hands. With an exhausted sigh, the tears begin to flow down his cheeks, then drop to the floor.

The air in the home starts to feel heavy as to the point that it pushes a person down. It is robbing them of hope, love, and security. It is the same event that it has been for over ten years, and this year will be no different.

A short time later, the self-comforting starts as he begins to talk to himself. "Why do I do it? Why do I put up with her and all the shit she puts me through?" The sense of hopelessness fades as a sense of disgusts invades his every thought. "Fuck me for better or worse than this is the worst I have ever felt about anyone." He leans back in his leather office chair.

Resting his arms on the armrests, he stares at the door. Soon the anger begins to remove the rational thoughts. "It just boils my blood that every time I want to do something nice for our anniversary, she goes and starts fights and ruins the whole day." Once again, he knows it does not make any sense. "From the morning I got up, I did whatever she wanted me to do. What am I going to do to fix what I don't know how or why it's broken?"

An exhausted sigh is released as he regains his composure and resolves to try to think of a solution to rescue the day. "I seem to ask myself this question every year. Maybe I should just say I am sorry again for something? Even though I don't know what I did. But every year she ruins this day with a fight. First comes the micro fights the little mini disagreements, then BAM out of nowhere I am running from her."

He continues to stare at the door "I just don't know," he once again returns to a state of hopelessness and sighs loudly. Right or wrong, he chooses a path that he has done so many times before. "I'll go retake the blame once more. Is there anything else I can do to fix this day?"

Everett stands up, he sturdy's himself takes a couple of deep breaths, looks into the mirror to make sure his eyes are dry, and then opens the door. Walking out the office and into the hallway, the fear begins to grip him. There is a sense that this is not over by a long shot as he closes the door behind him softly. Turns and can see that stupid sticker she had him put up on the wall in the hallway as it makes no sense for their family, "Families are forever." But then again, he'll never complain about it. As he walks down the short hall, he passes the family photos; they all seem to have actors. Because if people knew the truth, this is not this family. Past the last picture of the children as he heads towards the kitchen. It runs through his mind once more *"They are the reason I stay."* As he turns the corner to enter the dining room, plate wizzes by narrowly misses his head as it slams into the wall shattering into pieces. Shocked and startled, he yells, "What the fuck," after almost being hit. "What the hell are you doing?"

She yells, "I hate you; I hate you with all I am. I wish you would fucking die."

Everett's mind races as he contemplates his next actions quickly. Trying to return everything to a calm state of chaos, he says, "I am so sorry you feel that way about me. I don't know why you hate me, because I don't hate you, nor have I ever. You have always been my best friend; someone I have always looked up to in my life. I hate when we waste so much time fighting when we could be doing something that could be fun like going out for dinner, movie, and a slice of pie afterward."

As he finally turns towards her facing what might be another attack. The next plate ready to be thrown is in her hand; she is trying to decide what to do. She begins to understand that he is not going to fight with her. Out of anger, she slams the dish onto the floor.

Trying to lighten the air, he says, "Well, if you wanted a new set of dishes, we could just go do that before we go out." As soon as he said that, he knew that he did not think that out very well. It starts her up again as she begins yelling, but at this point, Everett has tuned out of what she is saying. The three little children are hiding in rooms scared of her violence. Everett has stopped listening to her screaming. All he can think about is the children. *"I have to calm her down or get her to leave this part of the house. The kids need a break from her, and lord knows I do."*

She pushes past him and mutters viciously, "Like I would go anywhere with you." That is the last words he hears from her as she walks away in anger. He understood that all too clear, this was the end of the day another anniversary is over.

"Well, there goes the night," he thinks to himself. She storms down the hall into the bedroom door and slams it shut, and then with a click, she locks it. He walks into the kitchen and over to the sink. Opening the cupboard doors below, it grabs the dustpan and hand broom to clean up the mess like he has done so many times before. As he sweeps up the mess in the kitchen, the tears once more begin flowing, his eyes become red and itchy. He finishes cleaning up the broken dishes. He tries to hide the disappointment of the children as they start to come out of hiding. Quickly he dries his eyes and stands and turns to face the children. Silence as the children look to him for guidance. There is no excuse for the violence.

He thinks to himself, *"The children are starting to see this as the normal."* He mutters to himself, "What am I going to do?" He is sullen as a sense of hopelessness is all that. Thinking to himself once more, *"It just cannot keep going on like this."* With that sentence, a little more of his heartbreaks. *"Maybe I should seek some help, but who will believe me. After all, I am a man who is being attacked by his wife. Yeah, like that will go anywhere. Should I take the kids and leave? I don't know if she even notices that we have gone. Would she even care if we were gone? If we did do it, where would we go? Where would we go? It is almost as if I am trying to convince myself that it is better the devil, you know."*

Looking at the children, he begins to think to himself, *"Who could help us? We would have to start all over again. We would lose it all, everything gone. But then again, peace.* He dumps the broken pieces into a rubbish bag. *I better take these out to the bins just in case she sees them, and it triggers another fight. Who am I kidding? I think I am trying to paint a pig a rosy color when in the end, it is just a fucking pig."*

He looks at the oldest child and says, "guys, I need to take out the rubbish, and I will be right back I promise you can watch me from the window if you need to." As he walks toward the front door as he grabs his keys just in case, she tries to lock him out again.

He shuts the door softly and walks towards the bins to put out the broken dishes. He lifts the lid and says, "Out of sight, out of mind."

He turns and begins walking towards the house. He's lost in the sound of the gravel that crunches below his feet. Soon his thoughts race to the children, *"I guess I better go back in and pay some attention to the children to let them know I love them and that everything will be okay."*

There is that voice deep in his gut "This is not okay, how can any of this be, okay." He walks up the wooden steps to the front door as he places his hand on the doorknob he thinks to himself every time *"I walk up these steps, I feel more and more like a guest."* He lets out a heavy sigh and with the twist of the handle. He is greeted by his three youngest children rushing up to him, wrapping their arms around him in silence and tears. Reaching down, he dries the eyes of the youngest two who appear to be scared. He says to the children, "It is going to be alright," even though deep down inside, he is not sure that it is the truth. But he will never let the children know of the feelings of pending doom that plague his every thought about their mother these days.

Then the four walks down the hall towards the kitchen, and he asks them, "What would you guys like to do tonight."

They reply, can we watch a movie, daddy?

Everett replies, Sure, that sounds like a great idea. Would you also like popcorn?

Yeah! That would be great the excited children say.

Well, I could use some help, making it how about we do it together. says Everett

Soon from several different cupboards and in the pantry, all the supplies are out for making popcorn. As the popper begins to wind up and the microwave melts the butter. BAM! Something down the hallway hits the bedroom door. They all jump as the loud noise breaks the peace and happiness. He tries to cover for the sound, but the truth is he knows what just happened.

He says, "Sounds like the next-door neighbour's truck backfired again." With a nervous laugh, he chuckles.

The oldest turns to him and says, "yeah, dad, maybe your right; that's what it was."

He looks at his son and thinks, *"He knows the truth as well."* His heart breaks just a little more, knowing that even that violence is reaching the children.

Soon the big yellow bowl of popcorn is done. Everett looks at the children and knows popcorn is not enough. Smiling, he was hiding the fact that the hotdogs were cooking in another pot. Much to their surprise, he dishes up hot dogs with all the fixings and hot buttered popcorn. Food in hand as they walk over to the big green couch, ready to enjoy a movie just the four of them once more. He looks at the three children and thinks, *"Is this the future?"*

Everett asks the children, "What do we want to watch?"

After a short time talking it over, the middle child suggests hey how about Mary Poppins, that always cheers you up, dad.

He thinks to himself, *"Cheer me up when all I am thinking about is you."* Your right; it does let's enjoy that one. The kids sit down as he places the movie in the player. He sits down in silence in the middle of the children. The kids all snuggle close, and the youngest one moves around to sit on his lap. Then he grabs Everett's arms and places them around him, just like needing a comforting blanket.

The movie starts, and there they all are snuggled together as a huddled mass. At about 5 minutes into the film, the bedroom door swings wildly open, and Everett's wife storms out of the bedroom fully enraged. Her actions caused the children to be scared, and startling Everett. The children cower and move closer to Everett.

She pulls the power cord from the TV. Turning around, she stands in front of all of them. She then begins to yell at all of them, "Where is that damn remote, give it to me now!" Just then, she sees the remote in the youngest daughter's hand, and she hands it to her mum shaking. She grabs the remote from the young daughter and turns to turn off the TV that was not on. Frustrated, she turns to all of them sitting on the couch and starts to yell once more "I have a headache you knew that, but you felt it was okay to turn the TV on so loud."

She storms back into her room with the remote and slams the door shut, locking it once more.

Silence engulfs the room; the air is thick, which makes one feel like it is hard to breathe. Nothing but silence for a short time as the shock of what just happened has is not over.

"Well, oops," Everett says, "how about we go to the office and watch it from in there." He knows that the comfort of the office is not the same, but it is further away from her. With the doors shut, he thinks, "*it might be another noise buffer.*"

The oldest child says, "yeah, that is a great idea, dad. I'll get a couple of blankets. Mum must just have a headache."

But they all know the truth; she does not want to hear happiness. Tomorrow just like all the times before, she will act like nothing ever happened. He thinks to himself again, "*I cannot keep doing this; it is not fair to the children.*"

They all move to the office and settle once more to watch Mary Poppins. After sitting down on a small green couch, everyone getting the same seats that they had in the lounge room. Once again, settling in as a smaller family. He thinks, or shall we say he knows, "*Is this our future? Just the four of us? Oh, I don't know what I am going to do. I am going to need to do something about this. It cannot continue anymore.*"

The movie continues Everett notices that all three of the children have found some peace. They lie snuggled under the blanket fast asleep on or near him. He closes his eyes as well; some rest might help as he is exhausted from the strain the fight has put on him. They wake a few hours later when the movie ending credits finish, and the music stops. The youngest one moves on his lap. He slowly removes the blanket, softly stands up, and begins to take the child to their bed.

[Let's Go Fly a Kite – Marry Poppins Soundtrack]

As he starts to move, the oldest one gets up and says I am going to bed as well, dad. I love you.

He takes the youngest to his room. He places the child in his bed and tucks him in. As he has always done, he kisses the young child on the forehead. He goes back for the next child. He knows that he has to walk softly as not to wake up the monster once more. As he picks her up, he thinks to himself, *"Wow, she is getting big, I'm not ready for her to grow up."*

As he places her in her bed, she grabs his neck and says, "you know I love you, daddy."

Pulling up her covers, he replies to her, "you know you are always in my thoughts, and I will always love you."

She replies once more, "big enough to give me more hugs?"

He softly brushes the hair out of her face and says, "yes, my dear, you are correct." The hugs seem to go on forever, removing her concerns. When the hugs are all done, he turns off her light and says, "sleep tight and pleasant dreams" as he hears her sigh in peace. *"I will carry this burden for all of us."*

He walks toward the oldest child's room. To find out that he is fast asleep. He begins to tuck him in.

When the child says, "please, dad, can you stay for a little bit?"

Everett says, "Sure, now move over, and I'll hop in next to you." As they lay there, they fall fast asleep once more. Everette wakes up an hour or so later rolls over and then kisses his son on the forehead and slides out. He is hoping not to make any significant movements as not to wake up the child.

But these are just planning of mice and men. He then makes sure not to forget to tuck the child back in.

No sooner than he finishes, the child says, "I love you," in a sleepy tone, more like a whisper.

Everett replies, "I love you more."

The child replies once more "not possible," both playing a loving game that has been part of the bedtime ritual. Leaving his son's room, he turns to look at him once more before walking out into the hallway.

The house is quiet, there is no movement but his, he softly walks through the house, turning off the lights trying to avoid the squeaky floorboards. He thinks, *"Fuck I am locked out of the bedroom once again, sleeping in the guest room is getting old. There is a bright side to not being attacked in the middle of the night. By her thinking, it is fine to punch me. It looks like a nice summer night maybe I could go for a sit outside, just relax, clear my head and figure out what I am going to do."* But this is not the first conversation that Everett has had with himself about the violence. Nor will it be the last he fears.

He slowly opens the sliding door walks outside to enjoy the stars, and the still night air, keys in hand. He is closing the door softly so she cannot hear him going outside. He knows that he has to be careful not to run the risk of being locked out again. His eyes turn upward to the stars, and he can see that they are in peace. He looks at the old porch swing and decides to enjoy the night air while sitting on it. Something is magical about sitting out here without her. I can think of what my choices are. Then all I have to do is find the courage is to do them.

A short time later, the thoughts of the violence begin to

roll in once more, "*What am I going to do? I just can't wake up tomorrow once more with her acting like nothing happened the day before. It is just becoming far too hard to keep the charade up. I don't think she loves us or ever has. She has robbed us of happiness at every turn. Everything always seems to be just about her. Never what we want or need, never supporting our dreams. What is the right thing to do?*"

As he looks at the star-filled sky, a star streaks by, "*Oh, to be free of this pain and hurt. If my heartbreaking could make a sound, I am sure the world would hear it.*"

In peace, he rocks in the swing relaxing and once again trying to letting go of the stress. His eyes begin to drift down from the calm night sky. That hope also falls like his gaze. Just then, reality strikes, and he takes notice that the chicken coop door is open.

"Crap, in all the noise and fighting, I forgot to close that. I better do something about that. If I grab the flashlight, I can get all the eggs as well."

"I don't want to go back inside the house." Everett thinks to himself, "*Walk slow and soft, miss the noisy floorboards; don't let them make a sound. Why am I so scared of her? I live here as well? I feel like she has destroyed me from the inside.*"

Soon he returns outside with a flashlight and egg basket in hand. He turns the flashlight on and sees the moisture on the grassy ground. "Well, this is going to be a great egg hunt' Walking towards the chicken coop the Earth all of a sudden below him gives way.

"Oh shit" he screams

He begins to fall into darkness. His mind races in overdrive, "*Oh no, am I falling into another well from the old train*" *station.*" It seems to go on for a very long time. He thinks to himself, "*This is a long fall,*" just as he hits the floor. He's knocked out, cold.

Don't worry, he is okay, and his life is about to change forever. I think I should fix how I get to meet people.

Soon Everett wakes up

"Oh, my fucking head, what the hell did I hit on the chicken coop. Oh, I don't even remember making it to the coop."

His mind races to something dark and sinister, "*Did she hit me from behind?*" I would not put it past her anymore. I am talking to myself again.

"Oh, the pain comes from the front of my head, and she wasn't outside, so it can't be her."

Thinking to himself once again, "*Okay, you know what to do, just walk through your training. First, don't panic; everything will be fine. Even if it is not, you know what to do. Second, don't breathe too deeply, only taking short, shallow breaths increasing in depth to search for pain. Oh, that is good; no ribs seem broken. Third, check fingers and hands, okay, nothing broken. Fourth, check my arms, okay, no pain, and they move. Stay calm the fifth thing to do is to check my toes, phew okay toes can move. The sixth thing to do is to check my feet and legs, yup those are doing okay. Seventh, check for blood on my head but move slowly. Ouch my shoulder, oh right, I don't feel anything wet on my head. Okay, slowly roll over to get on my knees, don't stand up yet. Check the front, good no open wounds, however. Nothing is wet, so I am sure there is no blood anywhere. Okay, time to open my eyes. Oh, shit, it is dark wherever I am at or in. But*

I don't think I am in a well. Sit up slowly, making sure not to rush I might pass out again. Feel for the flashlight, no not close."

Now what I need to do is to cry out for help and then see if someone replies, HELP.......HELP........" With no response after a short time, he begins to think, *"oh shit, no one can hear me. There is not an echo to my voice. Oh, great looks like I'll be here for a while; at least it is not cold. I wish I had some light. Then in a sudden flash of panic. Shit spiders and snakes fuck, I better stand. He gets ready to jump up, and it dawns on him, Yeah, dipstick like that is going to stop a snake or a spider. Might as well just stand up slowly; don't be stupid take in your time movements. Falling on your face again will not help you."*

A voice in the darkness begins to speak, "Hello, I can see you are alright, would you like me to make things a little more comfortable for you? Oh, how stupid of me, I don't need to ask for your permission for that. So here we go, shield your eyes it might be a bit bright at first." As the lights start to shine brightly, then begins to fade to a manageable state.

Everett rhetorically asks, "Oh god, am I in hell, did she kill me?"

The voice questions Everett, "Pardon me, why do you say this is hell, you are too worried about that, and no you are not dead. I promise you; you are very much alive." the voice said to reassure him.

As the lights soften, a gentler and even tone. Everett starts to look around, but that light is far too bright to see clearly. "Who are you, and where am I at?"

The voice reassures Everett once again, "you're in a safe place."

Everett confused replies back, "Yeah, right, why should I

believe you? First, you knock me out, and then you say that. How about a bit of common sense? Awe crap here, I am talking to myself in a strange place and telling myself I am in a safe place? Okay, the first sign of madness is arguing with oneself. Maybe I am dead or out cold still, and this is all a big dream."

"Crack" a loud sound is heard

"Ouch what the hell was that?" questions Everett

"It was me proving to you that you are not dead, asleep, or even passed out. As you would know that in those types of cognitive states, you would not feel."

"Okay, so you're right, I am awake. Now can you help me get out of here, I need to get back to my children."

"No, right now, you don't, you just put them to bed, and they are fine," said the voice.

"Wait, how do you know that?" asked Everett.

"Listen to me, Everett we have a short time, and I know a lot about you and what your troubles in life are. You built your home on top of a building and who was I not to learn about the people that did it. Right now, I know you are wondering if what or who is talking to is even real. But I assure you I am very much real. What I need to talk to you about is very important, or else I would have never approached you. So, let me get to the point."

The voice continues, "A few cycles ago, I have woken up once again. That happened when a major shift in the Earth took place. Warning system alerted me to some very catastrophic problems on Earth."

"I am sorry," Everett says as he interrupts. "This is starting to feel like a line of bullshit. They tested the ground below my home before I built it, and there was nothing strange under it, let alone a building. Next, you are going to tell me I am the chosen one or some other pile of shit. Wait, there might be even something better the only you can save the.... story."

The voice raises and says, "Alright, I have just about had enough. Will, you SHUT UP AND SIT DOWN!"

This outburst shocked Everett, so he began to sit down on the floor once more.

The voice speaks calmly, "not the floor, the chair behind you would be better."

Everett's eyes have now adjusted Everett began to look around and noticed that the room is elegantly furnished. There were two high backed leather chairs with a small wooden table in the middle of the room. There is a fireplace that seems to be keeping the room at an even temperature. But this is confusing as no heat is coming off the fire.

Everett decides to choose the one on the right side, and he slowly sits down, more like sink into the comfort of the leather chair. *Wow, I was not expecting this chair to be this comfortable.* "It was at that moment he began to notice his surroundings fully. He was in a very ornate library with books as far as the eye could see. Tables, chairs, and reading lounges seem to be everywhere.

The voice became more precise and more evident as Everett could begin to hear the sounds of footsteps coming toward him from the direction of the books. Though moving around, they never seem to come closer to him. It is almost as if someone is working in the Library. The sound of the boots instead of soft-soled shoes, but he is not sure.

The voice began to speak once more. "Everett, I am so very sorry I yelled at you, but we don't have a lot of time to do what is required. To your right on the table is a datapad I need you to grab it and have a look at what I have displayed on there for you."

"Wow, this time the voice is polite, I am a bit confused by all of this." Everett reaches over and picks up the tablet, and all that was on it was a photo of a Japanese Nuclear power plant. "Okay, so you have a photo of the Fukushima power plant," Everett replied.

"Good, so you know of it," the voice replied. "Now what you need to know is that it is about to reach a critical tipping point. There is very little that can solve the problems now. I have been monitoring this plant since the explosion due to the Tsunami. The attempt to stop the power rods will fail. Once this happens, it will set in motion a series of events that none of them can be reversed or stopped."

Everett speaks up once more, "Look, see there you go a doomsday story. That makes me the only person who can save the world, right? This story just keeps getting better and better."

"Everett, please listen up; you don't need to be a narcissistic baboon. You of all people are not the saviour of Humanity. Yes, this is the Doomsday warning that is coming to fruition. When Nuclear weapons and energy. Humanity was warned by one of those who discovered the technology that it was an abysmal choice to power a light bulb. But no one listened, and you just kept forging ahead, thinking that it will be just fine. Building the powerplants had to be built in safe areas. This powerplant did not follow the regulatory guidelines for safety. Then let's talk about the waste that Nuclear power creates. There was never going to be a way to store it safely.

At some point, someone should have seen all these problems. The Tsunami ruptured the plant, and now the rods are posing a severe problem. Once those rods reach the groundwater, it is all over. I mean it, over. There is no way to contain the millions of problems that will follow."

"So, what do you want me to do about this? If you already know about it, then fix it", asked Everett.

"To put it simply, I have no solution, short of going back in time and giving a huge kick up the ass to a lot of people. But we cannot time travel as you are sure to understand. Right now, we have a bit of work to get done before those events take place," replied the voice. "So how long do we have before you think it's all over," Everett asked once more in a condescending tone.

Ignoring Everett's tone, "From what I have figured out about 100 days is about what the Earth has left. But that does not mean Humanity has that same timeline. You see, once the chain of events begins, Humanity's timeline is vastly shorter. But that is not something I can calculate at this current time."

Everett smartly replies, "let me get this straight you can see the problem, you know what it will do, but you are not going to solve the problem."

The voice replies, "Okay, since you want more information on this problem. I will give it to you, smart ass. Do you remember the Russian nuclear power plant that exploded?"

"Well, yes," said Everett.

"Great, we are on the same path now. So, you know that radiation is more than a power source and that it also produces a poison. What you might not know is that it also creates an erosion effect that acts a bit like speeding time up.

Electronics fail at an extremely high rate. Plastics will fail, and rubber hoses will give way to the pressure. If you move in a piece of equipment, it does not last very long, and the closer you get, the faster it fails. Not even my advanced technologies can survive. So, are you starting to see the problem? There is nothing I can do to stop it at all."

Everett replies to the voice, "Do you see where I am coming from, my standpoint, you keep creating an event that is a bit farfetched."

"Farfetched? But it is happening whether you like it or not." said the voice, "But ask yourself this what if I am sincere and you don't take the time to hear me out? I assure you that you are not the hero to save Humanity. But as a result of helping me, a little, we can save some lives. Some of those lives will be you and your family if you wish."

Everett replied, "So, what you are saying is that you are going to save lives, and some of those will be my family and me. It is so very crazy to hear all of this. But where is the proof that all of this is real?"

Just then, Everett jumped from his seat into the air.

"Ouch, what the hell did you do to me again? That Hurt" cried out Everett

"Did you feel the sting of the shock I gave you?" asked the voice?

"Well yeah! Why did you do that?" Everett replied, a little agitated.

"Some of it was to remind you that I am real, and this is happening. Then there is this wicked part of me that enjoyed it. But all that aside, what would help you to trust me?" asked the voice.

"Well, first of all, knock it off with that shocking shit. It is not a matter of trust as much as it is a matter of completely understanding what you are asking me to do. Then if just if it is even possible for it to be true, we will work together on trust issues after that. But I mean it, knock off the Shocking!" Everett replies in a stern voice.

"Okay, Everett, I stop shocking you to get you to believe that this is real. What you are going to choose is the number of people whom you will save. Then they will also be given the same choice until the maximum number. Once the maximum number achieved, we will not be able to save anymore." The voice stated

"How many do I need to choose?" asked Everett

"I am going to allow you to choose fifty and only fifty. All choices are final, and I cannot change once you have made a choice. So choose wisely," replied the voice.

"Can I have a day or two to make my choices as this is a huge thing to ask of a person? Everett asked

"Everett, let me stress that this is a time-sensitive issue. I can give you a day or two, but nothing more. What I will do is return you to your home, and in a day, I will find you, and we will start with your choices. Please, Everett, I am trusting you in this matter. I am sure you understand that if you tell any-one they will think you are crazy." Instructed the voice

"I feel crazy, to be honest, I am waiting to wake up at any moment." Replied Everett

"This might make you feel a bit sick" the voice commented

Everett blinks, and he has returned to the front of his home. The chicken coop is on the other side of the house. Looking around, he knows that this was not where it all started. Then he vomits. He is exhausted and enters the home. Cleans himself up to make sure that he was not making a mess in the house. He then goes to check on the children and heads to bed. As he lays down, the thoughts of everything that just happened start to replay over and over until the exhaustion forces him to sleep.

The next morning as he rolls out of bed and goes to get the children ready for school. The events of the night before weigh heavy on his shoulders. He gets them dressed in their school uniforms. Hurries them to the dinner table for breakfast, makes their lunches, and has a coffee with just enough time to enjoy it. But soon, his wife walks out of their master bedroom and looks at him. But this time, something is very different about the way she is acting.

She glares at Everett as he turns to see her face she demands, "What is wrong with you?"

"Nothing, why," Everett replied, thinking to himself, "*This is a trap she is acting very strange. I better be careful with what I say and do. Something feels very off with her. Don't take the bait!*"

She looks at him and says, "You're sulking around like a baby I wish you would stop because you are bothering me. I want you to drive me into town today. I'll make my way home." She sternly instructed

Everett's gut feelings start to interrupt his thoughts. Stand up for yourself. Don't keep taking the abuse day after day! Everett setting his coffee cup down, looks at her for the first time in the marriage makes a stand by saying, "No, I am not going to do that for you. I have something I need to get done;

you are going to find a different way in or drive yourself." Everett replied

She snaps back "Oh so now you are upset with me when you are the one who screwed up our anniversary yesterday. So you are punishing me today. You do this every year, Everett, and I am sick of you."

Everett taken back a bit, looks at her, then says, "Are you crazy? The world does not revolve around you! I am not your slave, and I had plans last night for both of us, but just like every year. You started a fight for nothing at all, and now your blaming me for it. When I did nothing wrong." firmly replies Everett

"What do you want me to say Everett" she questioned

"I think you said more than enough last night in your attack on me. You need to find some help because this is getting too much, and it is affecting the kids." Everett replied

"Fuck you; you are such an ass Everett," she screamed.

Everett looks at the children who, at this point, have stopped eating their breakfast. Get back to eating, and you have to go to school, she orders. Then she turns around to walk away, and Everett says in a stern voice, "Enough! Stop attacking them." He had never done this before, and it seemed like all time had just stopped with the one action. Then looking at her dead in the eyes and says, "I am taking the kids to the bus, and I am going for a walk before I say something unkind to you."

Everett looks at the children. "Okay, guys, let us get your bags and grab an extra apple, and we can start walking towards the bus.

"There you go running away like a scared dog. I wish

sometimes you were more of a man." She yells regardless that the children are within earshot.

With that said, Everette stops with the children in front of him and his back towards her. Everett reaches in and grabs the door handle and closes the door. It is at this point that one of the final parts of his love for her breaks, and he tells himself, *"Crystal, you are a hate-filled monster of a person. I am tired of giving you all of me. I will get us free from you."*

[The Long Goodbye – Sarah McLachlan]

Everett ignores the bait for a new argument. "Come on; guys, let's get you to the bus and off to school. Hop to it 1,2,3,4, and we got our butts out the door. 5,6,7,8 hurry up; we don't want to be late." Everett joked with the kids as they all marched down the driveway, never looking back. The door is shut on a face of anger, still yelling at him, but it is too late he is not listening.

Like a breath of fresh air, all four of them took a deep breath and relaxed as they walked to the bus stop. The children are singing songs from Mary Poppins as they walk down the sidewalk. Soon the bus arrives, the children give hugs and tell Everett "I love you dad" with the oldest saying "thank you for being here for us" Everetts' heart soared with the love of his children as he watched them all get on the bus and head off to school. As the bus pulled away, his heart sank as he knew he would enter the house later, and it might still be a toxic environment. So, he tells himself it is time to get another cup of coffee and maybe a treat.

As he walks towards the town center, he grabs his stomach as a sharp pain fills it. He knows this pain all too well; something is not right. It is almost like a sixth sense he has had since childhood. He only wished he knew what it was. But this time he tells himself that he went too far this morning and he is going to pay for his actions later.

He looks at his phone and chooses to walk to a little deli. Grab a coffee, a treat, then start to think about all that had happened in the last 24 hours. As he walks, his mind began to race. "*What am I going to do? I cannot keep living like this. All she wants to do is find faults and start fights. I need to make a choice.*" You did make a choice his gut speaks up "*What if last night the Universe was making that choice for me? What if I did talk to someone and they gave me a choice to make. What if I did not make a choice?*" Then nothing would change.

"Good Morning Everett" as he walks in the deli's front door. Such a kind greeting by the owner and staff. Everett loved the way she showed compassion and the kindness that they have always shown him. That makes a better way to start the day. As he sits down and a young waitress walks up to Everett with a cup of coffee and some creamer and a fresh blueberry muffin. Soon the smell of the new coffee rises, and Everett stares into the steam that rose from it lost in contemplation of the offer and the choice. "*Okay, what if I made a list of fifty? Who would the first person on my list be? Could I choose just fifty, I could not leave my family and friends. But then who else would I add in once have made all those choices.*" Everett begins to think of all the names counting them one by one.

"Everett, are you okay?" the deli's owner asks she touched him on his shoulder. "Do you know you have been looking at your coffee for over an hour. Let me get you a fresh one, and this time I hope you can enjoy it despite the weight that appears to be on your shoulders."

Everett sits back in the wooden chair and starts to nibble on the muffin. With each bite, he takes his time to enjoy the blueberries (which are his favourite) Here you go love, which startles Everett from his thoughts with heavy eyes he looks upwards to be greeted by the deli's owner's kind gaze.

"Oh, I am so very sorry, I was in such a deep thought. Thank you, but you do not need to refresh my cuppa I might just get lost in it again." Replied Everett

"Oh, hush Everett if you need a safe space, this is it, and we don't even see you sitting there. I will make you something to eat for lunch as well. You just relax and wait here until it is time for the bus." The owner told Everett. Nothing ever stays hidden in small towns. People talk, and the good ones are always known.

Everett takes a deep breath as the weight of going home is lifted off of his shoulders for a short time. The chair creeks as a massive weight had left it. He slowly enjoys his muffin, fresh cuppa, and lunch. Soon he is joined by the owner as she sits down with a pot of coffee in hand.

"Everett, I have a friend I think you need to talk everything over. I know things are hard right now for you and the children. I would love to see all of you smile, and I know it will take time for it to return. But this person is where you need to start." She slides him a business card on the table with a phone number on it and a name.

Everett cannot control the rush of emotions that take over the conversation. Tears begin to fall as fast as he can wipe them away. The owner reaches out for his hand and comforts him.

They start to talk over what took place the night before. Soon the time for going to the bus is close. Everett thanks the owner for her friendship and goes to pay. But what Everett does not know is that behind him, the owner is signalling the young waitress not to charge him.

Everett heads towards the door of the deli. The owner says, "Please take care of yourself and the children." She hands him a card and touches his hand to comfort him.

Everett swallows hard as he can finally see that what has been going on is not a secret. As he lets out a deep sigh, he can feel the weight of emotions take over once again; it is everything he can do not to burst into tears. Everett takes the card and offers to pay once more; the owner speaks up and says "It's on the house" you take care of you and the kids we will be here for you when you need us.

[The Black Crows – Seeing Things]

Everett begins to walk towards the bus stop to collect the children. This time it is very different. The sky appears to him to have lost its beauty. The birds have lost the songs. He can feel the weight of going home begin to weigh on him once more. With every step, he knows the monster that is waiting for him. He knows that she will be angry that he was gone the whole day and did not do as she commanded.

Everett sits down and waits for the bus alone. Like begins, the bus arrives. The children exit the bus into the loving arms of Everett, who was waiting for them. *"Ah, the hugs I have been waiting for all day."* They all start to walk toward home; the stress begins to create concern for the children. Something is just not right with the silence of children. With each step, the gravel below their feet makes a crunch, and Everett thinks to himself, "*This sound is what my heart feels like.*" As the door opens, the children scurry to their rooms as fast as can be. They hope to avoid their mother. Everett makes his way to the office to grab a pen and paper. The house is silent, and it has that empty feeling that when you know, you are alone. Everett walks through the house, checking to see if his wife is home. He takes a deep breath and starts to relax. "Hey, kids, come on out."

"Hey dad what is for dinner?" the youngest child asks

"I don't know yet what would you like me to cook?" Everett replies

"Could we have Pizza or Tacos over even Taco pizza would be cool." His son asks

"Sure, why not pizza for dinner sounds like a killer idea," Everett replies to his youngest son with a smile.

Dinner sets the mood, and all over them enjoy their favourite pizza that Everett has made. With each bite, laughter and cheer fill the house. "This is the way it should be," his gut says.

Sometime later in the night. Like an evil wind, the front door opens, and the home takes on a new feeling of trepidation that another encounter might happen. Everett's reality has returned home. From the moment she sees him, she starts once again.

"I can see you have returned home. I wish you would have told me that you were going to cook. I had planned dinner as I did not know what you were doing" quipped at Everett

Everett, with a stone-cold expression on his face, turns to her and replies. "It is seven pm at what time were you thinking of cooking, let alone what time would it be ready? I have already fed the children and got them bathed. They are ready for the downtime and stories before bed. Here I made this pizza for you in case you were hungry when you returned."

This time she replies with a tone of vitriol, "I don't want anything that you have made. I am going to the bedroom. Stay out!" Turning her back on Everett, she walks towards the bedroom with her shopping bags.

As the door slams shut and locks, Everett thinks to himself, "*Thank god, I was not in the mood to deal with you for the second night of fighting.*" His thoughts are interrupted by a child yelling, "I am a ready dad, I want the book; there is a Monster at the end of this book."

"Okay, let me take care of the last pizza, and I will get the book. All of you get to one room, and we will have our Storytime" Everett replies

Dumping refused the small pizza in the chicken bucket. Everett grabs the book for the children as he knows they will all be ready for the big show that he puts on every time he reads something for them.

Clearing the throat in preparation for his audience is on the edge of the youngest one's bed, ready for their chosen story brought to life. Just like the book, Everett's voice changes as he plays the main character of the book. The children know this book by heart, but it is how their dad reads it that brings sheer joy to their lives. Half-way through the book, Everett is building the level of expected excitement for the children. When all of a sudden, they can hear her scream down the hall, "STOP BEING SO LOUD!". But Everett is in full swing of the action. He ignores the rant and continues to give the show of a lifetime. At the ending, the book's audience was full of smiles, laughter, and applause all around.

"Hey guys it is time for hugs and kisses, then also go tell your mother goodnight," Everett tells the children

"Do we have to?" one of the children complains

"Yes, it is the right thing to do. Never let your feelings cloud doing what is right" There it was Everett's answer to the question that has been filling his questioning heart for the last two days. What might be right might be a challenging thing to do, but it must be. He takes a deep breath as the reality of his choice appears to be made for him. The children walk down the hall slowly. A tear rolls down his cheek to see the disappointment in their faces.

[Say something – Pentatonix]

Everett watches as the bedroom door fails to open for the children as they give up and return to him. Nothing needs to be said; anyone could see it on the children's faces. Everett takes each child into his arms as he hugs them, he tells them how special they are. Then to their rooms, tucks them into their beds, places a kiss on their foreheads, and tells them that he loves them forever and ever. Turns on night lights as he turns bedroom lights off. But this is not the last thing they require of him. "Dad, please, I need another hug." Everett returns to each of them, holding them for what seems like an eternity, but worth every second. *"This moment in time is the magic of being a parent,"* He thinks to himself.

As he walks away from their rooms, he looks at the closed master bedroom door and says in his mind, *"She has completely worn me down, you win. But I think your cost is far more than you will have won in the end. I give up on you and us; it is over." He* reaches in his pocket for the business card. Just as Everett is about to read it, a burst of bright light surrounds him. His eyes readjust realizes that he is once again where he was the night before. This time the smell of old books and he can feel the warm fire. Everett replaces the card into his pocket

"Hello Everett, this time seems to be as good as any. Have you thought about your names?" the familiar voice questions

Everett replies with a crackle in his voice, showing his concerns for the children "You do know I just put the kids to bed and what if they need me and I am here with you?"

Everett, the voice replies calmly. "If there is an issue and I will hear them. I will guide you back to where you were. There is no need to worry; it is all under control. So, do you have the names?"

Yes, I have some of them. But in this choice are my choices going to be questioned and no attempt to change my mind?" asked Everett

"Everett, these are your choices and yours alone. I am placing a huge trust and risk in your choices." The voice answers him

"Well, I would like a third-party opinion on what you are saying it is a lot to take in as well as a huge responsibility. Because I am not sure, I can do this alone. I am going to need this help. Some things in my life weigh me down that you don't know about." Said Everett

"Okay," in a calm tone, said the voice, "But there will be a consequence as a result for this request that I will explain to you that once you have agreed to, you'll help me."

"So, what you are saying is that I am going to pay at a later date for someone to prove that you are right and to give me a hand. You sound very confident," replied Everett.

"Yes, that is about it," said the voice. "So, in all of the world, I want you to think of one person and only one person. This person needs to be intelligent, and I mean that when I say it. So, choose carefully, because this is a onetime offer. I am not going to play any more games because we are running on a tight timeline. Do you understand me?" asked the voice

"Sure, why the hell not. Not like my real life is falling apart," replied Everett in an exhausted tone.

"Everett, I know what I am asking of you is rather a hard thing to do. That this is not the best time in your life, choices in life that are going to be difficult, offer the best rewards in the end. But Everett, I have been watching you for years, and I think you will do fine. Please think about a name, and let's get you some help." The voice reassured Everett

Everett continued after a short time thinking about who he wanted. "Okay, I think I know who I want. His name is Neil Haley, he is an Astrophysicist, I highly respect his knowledge, and he seems like an alright kind of a person."

"Everett, are you 100% sure that this is the person you are going to trust. That what I am saying is above the board and correct? You will not get a second chance at this." said the voice

Everett sat back and thought for a few more minutes. "I am beyond sure, and I am confident if you are pulling the wool over my eyes, your story will fall apart with him," Everett replied.

"Very well, look at your datapad to make sure we are talking about the same person. If that is the right person in about 15 minutes you will know I am telling the truth" said the voice

Everett looked at the datapad saw a few photos and found the correct person. After agreeing that the picture was of the right person.

"Very well," said the voice, "Time to wait for his arrival."

As time passed, Everett began to assume 15 minutes was about up when all of a sudden, he could hear a screaming ARGH..... followed by a Thud and there he was Neil Haley face down on the floor and out cold. Everett is pointing to Neil on the floor, "If this is true, we need to work on your grabbing people skills. The way you are doing it is not correct."

"OUCH," combined with a few moans, said Neil as he began to regain consciousness. "What the hell am I doing here, and who the hell are you?" pointing at Everett. Everett is raising his hands in a motion to signify that he did not do it.

Just then, the voice interrupted, "Mr. Haley, please relax and take a seat. Everett points to the empty leather chair next to the table. We have much to talk about and a short time to do so. Please don't worry about my other guest right now."

As Neil sits down next to Everett "You better have an excellent reason for kidnapping me whomever you are,"

The voice interrupted once more, "Dear sir, to your left is a datapad. On this device is some essential information, and I need you to take a few minutes to read through it and let my other guest know your thoughts on the matter. Once you have done this, we will talk about getting you back to where you were before joining us."

Neil reached for the datapad and began to read. At one

point, he sat it down, rubbed the sides running his fingers thought it, and then returned to his reading.

As Everett watched, he could see the expression of shock and horror on the face of Neil.

Neil sat the datapad down and began to ponder what he had just thoroughly read. Neil then demanded, "Where did you get this information, and it is not meant for public eyes as well as your conclusion is only a theory."

"Mr. Haley," the voice replied "Let's start this off on the right foot, the three of us know that a secret is only as good as those keeping it. The conclusion is no more theory than you were just walking down the street, and now you are here."

Neil replied, "What your conclusion is that in 100 days or thereabout, the Earth will be useless."

"Yes, Sir, that is my conclusion. I believe the information that is listed there is sound. This information presented evidence you have already seen with several others in the scientific community. The time has come and passed to act on all the information. But you have missed that, and now the time has run out, there is nothing that can be done to reverse the impending doom."

"So, if your conclusion is true, then why am I here?" asked Neil.

Everett spoke up "That is and was my fault. I am no one special, and I needed some help to understand what I was reading. This crazy voice told me a day ago it needed my help. That added in with what it was telling me, I felt that this is a bit farfetched. I needed a second set of eyes to provide proof that this is all real."

Neil spoke up, "Yes, from I am reading, I can confirm that

the information here is telling you it is sound. Currently, we are running out of options, and we have a few more to try. This information is saying that those are not going to work. I am very concerned with the data that has also been collected and what can be done. Maybe I should just stop thinking and go home a spend the remaining time with my wife and children."

"Neil, what if I was to offer you a better choice?" Asked the voice.

"I am listening" replied Neil

"I am about to make both of you an offer that might require a bit of work, but in the end will result in your family being saved."

Neil, with a crackle in his voice, said, "Okay, what do you want from us. I will do anything for my family."

The voice replied, "Well, that is the Million-dollar question, isn't it. It is not just about the two of you. What I want is from both of you is very simple. Choose fifty names of those whom you wish to save." The voice paused as if to reconsider what it said earlier but then resumed

"Remember what I said, Everett, that there is a price to be paid."

CHAPTER 2

The Choice Made

The voice speaking in a softer tone to Everett "Choices have to be made, and they are going to be hard and need to be done in a hurry. Time is not our friend," said the voice as it paused once more. After a short silence, the voice resumed. "I bet that right the two of you are having a hard time understanding where you are. So, we don't have the time to try to explain how this happened. Though in time, I will explain everything to you. But for now, let me do this for you. I am going to open a few windows for you to see something amazing. That should help put perspective on what is going on."

Behind Everett, a window had become visible. Everett could see Neil's face, and it was one of amazement. Everett turned around to see the full glory of the Earth.

Neil spoke up without a second thought and said: "It is so beautiful and to think we are seeing the last minutes of her life, what have we done..." Neil sat back down as the tears started. One could easily see the distress on his face.

Everett became week in the knees and slumped to the floor, just staring off into space, looking at the glory of the Earth for the first time with his own eyes. Dumbfounded, he whispers, "I am ready to choose."

The voice spoke, interrupting their awe and emotions, "I am so sorry, but now is not the time to reflect. What is done is done. What you need to do is select fifty people each to save. Everett, you will only be able to choose 49. Remember, I told you there is a consequence in choosing Mr. Haley; he is one of your fifty. Now, as your choices are made, they will join us and receive the same information with a choice to accept what I am saying or not, just the same as the two of you did. Upon accepting the offer, they are allowed to choose fifty others. But there are a few catches to this choice. Children under the age of 12 are only half a person. Those above are a full person. I will not allow you to choose those who are in prison, regardless of the reason. Choosing those will draw too much attention and create a burden we do not need. Now take the data pads and begin working on your list now. Be careful about who you choose. If they accept, then I will not return them to the surface of Earth. Remember that you should also consider those who you feel embody Humanity. Well, I think I have said enough so that I will leave you for a short time. Though I cannot empress enough that this is time-sensitive, I would suggest hurrying as the time it is not our friend."

With that, the voice and footsteps begin to move further away, leaving the two men to start making their choices.

Everett thinks to himself, "*I am ready to make most of my choices; some are an easy choice family first, right?*" So, he began with a loving touch of his 49 choices, 1.5 are children, then four other children. His two grandchildren at 1, then he thought he better add the spouses 3, then my closest friends five and their spouses 5, then their children 4, my nephew and his spouse 2, then my sisters and their spouses 4, and my Father. "Well, that makes 31.5 people wow that went fast." But what if I am wrong about choosing my family? They are not perfect by any means what so ever. What if by selecting them, I doom us all?

Everett began to think again as tears rolled down his face *"But wait, is she the wisest of choices? She hates me so much, or at least it feels like she does. Maybe if I could leave her and choose another friend, that would not be right, and the children need her in their lives. I am not sure if it is good or bad. They need to be the ones that need to make that call.*

What about my father, he's older? He does not even talk to me anymore unless I make the call? But then if I don't choose him, I lose him, he is my father. I can't just leave him to die. My sisters are not my friends; we don't even talk. I see a trend with this. But if I don't choose them, then I am going against everything I have ever heard about family first. Maybe I'll just accept them for who they are and just do what is right. If they choose not to accept the offer, I cannot be blamed for not giving them a fair go. But then there is one of my sons who is in jail; nothing I can do can save him. I am going to see one of my children perish. How am I going to explain that to my other children that I cannot save their brother's life? So, who am I going to choose for the remaining?" As Everett thought hard, the gravity of his choices started to show.

Without knowing, he started to speak out loud. "All I keep coming up with is how does this person deserve to live, where this one does not. What about the older ones, the sick, the disabled they have the right to survive as well? But if we only have limited space, is it right to pick and choose based on emotional attachment? People like my father, who are in their 80's and have had a good life. Why not choose someone younger. But then you have the loss of wisdom and real-world intelligence. You can't teach wisdom; it has to be learned. I don't know what to do." He said as he paced the floor.

Neil spoke up, "Everett, I am facing the same problems. What I came up with in my answer to the question is very simple. Without these loved ones in my life, where would I be? Yeah, we might have to learn some things all over again. But you cannot ignore the fact that without them we would not be here. Then I have about five of my fifty that I am not able to choose. I wonder if we just hold out on those for a bit as we might need someone with a set of skills at a later date that we don't have in our choices so far."

Everett agreed, "I think you're right, holding off on a few might be the best choice for now. I am going to leave the last few I have for later and be content with my choices."

They could hear the footsteps of someone moving closer. Soon the voice spoke up, "Gentlemen, I need to get this moving forward. Do you have all of your choices made."

Everett said, "Yes, and no...well some of them I have written them down. I even gave some instructions on how to find them."

What about you, Neil, how are you coming along with your list?

"Well, I have had a bit of a struggle with about the last 5. In talking with Everett, we have both had the same issue. We came up with an idea to hold on to those last few in case we find a need for someone with a special set of skills."

"I can understand what both of you are trying to explain to me. But I need to repeat it a few more times, time is not on our side, and saving choices might be very counterproductive" replied the voice

Neil started to question the voice. "How do you plan to grab so many people in such a short time?"

After a short pause, the voice spoke once more "Excellent question Neil, and I am going to show you how I am going to do this. Look out the window, and you will see a bunch of ships leaving ours to go and collect them. I have adjusted the settings to bring people back here. That way, no one will be falling out of the ceiling like you requested, a bit nicer."

Everett chuckled a bit and thought, *"A couple of people he wouldn't mind falling as it would be an excellent sight to see even worth a chuckle or two."*

Everett watched as what appeared to ship flying towards the Earth and then disappeared, he assumed some were for his names and others for Neil's. The gravity of his choices was so tough to make; he said out loud. Should I have avoided the old, the ill, and the challenged? But what does that say about my Humanity? What if I left out those not quite perfect? I can't do that, and I have to choose everyone equally to each other."

Everett returned to his list and began once more. "Who? Who can I save? Why should they be saved?" He began writing again and stopped by needing to ask a question, "pardon me how many are going to be saved, and do you want the children to give you fifty names?"

The voice replied, "Well, the children will only be allowed 5 of their friend's names to come and have fun with us. But I will bring those children's families. As for how many this ship can hold, that is 150,000."

Everett gasped, "Wow, that is a lot of people; this thing must be massive."

The voice replied, "Yes, it is, there is a story behind it, but you are not ready for it. It will unfold in time. You need to get back to your names. So that you know people have started to arrive and are being instructed the same as you and Neil were. When you both are done, I will instruct you on how to reach them. I assure I will get everyone on your list, fear not."

"But what if we can't name fifty people?" asked Everett. "Like Neil said that pool might be best served as an emergency pool. I am sure we will not be alone in finding it hard to choose fifty people."

"We will have to worry about that later," replied the voice.

Everett returned to his list and began to check the names he listed. Then a few talented individuals that he thought would be a loss without them. Lastly, he chose to set aside his remaining 5 for a reason later. Everett stood at the window and thought to himself. *"Dear God or whoever you are, I am hoping I have made the best choices possible this list has been so hard to create, and I have left so many off of this list. I hope I am doing the right thing. Please, God, or whoever you are, forgive me."*

He must have been saying his thoughts out loud again as Neil walked up beside him and placed his hand on Everett's shoulder. Neil then said, "Relax son, we have done all we could within the boundaries given to us. This ship will fill up fast. We hope others will be like you and I and reserve 5 to the pool in case we need to grab especially skilled people. I am so concerned about what this all means for us as Humanity."

The voice just spoke up and said, "I am glad we three are concerned for Humanity. The cost is so very high on all of us writing down names. Many will be left behind that we cannot save. Some will refuse the gift we have placed before them. There will be others who will see their family tore apart by choice of one."

"What will happen to those who do not want to stay? Will they be returned to the surface?" Everett asked

"Yes, and in the trip back, they will have their memory wiped, and they will go about their lives thinking all is normal." Replied the voice

"Wait, I am a bit confused let me ask this then," Everett said, "Let's say my wife chooses not to stay. We have children together, and I am not going to let them go back, no parent in their right mind would."

The voice replied, "I am only going to be honest with you. Young children are far too naive to make a choice, such as this, so that I will make the final call in the end. I am here to save Humanity, and with your help, we will do it. Children who are in this type of situation will stay with the parent who chose to stay, and the other parent would be returned to the surface."

"Don't you think that is a bit harsh," asked Everett.

"Yes, it is, but I cannot force an adult to stay if they do not wish to. Please understand that as many that are chosen, many will leave rejecting this offer. This is why making these choices is such a hard responsibility to do."

"But the person who is returned without their children will raise alarms," said Everett

The voice replied," I will take care of the memory and wipe it to make sure they have a new narrative without the children. This is all I can do for those who do not want to be saved."

Everett replied, "there is something wrong with that action, but I am not able to see a better choice."

"Nor can I, said Neil then continued; it bothers me as well. But I think it is something we will all have to live with to some point." Then Neil turns and walks towards the books.

The voice speaks, "Neil, you are welcome to look at any of the books, but they must remain here, and you are not allowed to enter the back section of the Library. Though in time, this will change."

A few hours pass as Neil and Everette comb through the aisles of this vast Library. Both in shock at several titles, some that Neil had never seen before as he thought they were lost to time. Like an excited child, Neil would yell out titles then run to a different section to see if there were others. When Neil calmed down and returned to the leather chair, he began calling for the voice.

"Yes Neil, what can I do for you?" spoke the voice

"Hey, you said we would be able to see those we chose once they had made their choices," mentioned Neil.

"Yes, that is correct, but we have a small problem, and I need you to stay as I talk to Everett about an issue that has arisen." said the voice.

Everette hears his name called and returns to the chairs. "What's the issue? Tell me now and don't pull punches, give it to me straight."

"Very well said," the voice, "There are a couple of your choices who have chosen not to stay. Remember, you said, what if it was your wife? Well, I am sorry to say that it has become a self-fulfilling prophecy. Your wife has chosen not to stay. I would normally send her back without question, but because I want to show both of you, I am merciful. I will allow you the chance to change her mind. I would suggest you talk to her. Because she is vocal on wanting to return quickly."

[End of the world – Sharon Van Etten]

"Well, take me to her, please," Everett replied as he lets out an exhausted sigh.

"I am bringing her to you in hopes that you can talk to her face to face, and I am doing it as an act of kindness to you for all that you are doing." replied the voice.

"Everett, are you okay, your body language is saying that you are not ready for this," asked Neil?

"Thank you, Neil, I am fine, not shocked, just fine. In fact, why don't you see your family? I will be okay" Everett calmly said as he reassured Neil

"Only if you are sure, this is going to be hard no matter which way it might go I think" replied Neil

"Thank you, but I am okay, nothing surprises me much anymore when it comes to people" commented Everett

"Neil, I will have a droid take you to your family since it is okay with Everett." Informed the voice

Surprisingly enough, both Everett and Neil did not even think that there were droids as they have not seen any. They can hear mechanical footsteps coming towards them. Soon they are face to face with a "Droid" standing about 5 ½ feet tall with no facial features though looking humanoid to a shape.

"Please, Neil," the voice spoke once more, "Follow the droid, and it will guide you to your family."

As Neil and the droid left, there was Everett alone with the voice. The voice spoke up, "So, we are faced with what we talked over earlier. What are your thoughts now that you are faced with the reality that she does not want to stay?"

"What do our adult children think?" asked Everett.

"Well, that is also one of the issues her son has also chosen to return as well. The older girl has chosen to stay, the three of them had a huge fight that a lot of others heard and saw. But your wife is here now. Are you okay? If so, I am going to let her in and leave you two to talk it out. If you need me, just call out Mika, and I will be here for you." The voice said

Just then, the door to the Library opened up.

"Hello Crystal," said Everett "Please sit down, I think we should talk before you do anything rash."

"Fine," said Crystal as she sits in a chair away from Everett "But I don't know why I am going to waste my time on you. I would rather die than spend one minute more in this horrible dream with you."

"Crystal, it is me, Everett. Do you need me to pinch you to understand this is not a dream?"

Crystal turned and looked at Everett with a cold and hardened look and replied, "You're fucking right; this is not a dream; it is a nightmare. If you touch me, I will call the police on you."

Everett looked shocked at Crystal in confusion to what she

just said, trying to make sense of it. Then he began, "Crystal, please listen to me for a minute," he begged.

"No," replied Crystal. "You listen to me this is a dream, and I control it, and even if this was real, I am going to say what I have to say, and you can deal with it. I want a divorce, and you need to move out. The kids will be staying with me."

Everett leaning back in the leather chair, *"I knew this was going to happen someday,"* relaxed he started, "A divorce why? Yeah, we have problems, but let's see a counsellor. Wait, I don't know why I am going to stop you and this idea. To a point, I welcome a divorce from you. I am so sick of you attacking me at every turn. For 14 years, you have ruined anniversaries and events that mean things to me. You have be-littled my friends and loved ones. Yet here I am like a fool trying to save your life. You want a divorce, done.", replied Everett.

"I don't care what you say. When I wake up, you are going to hear this from my lips, and then I am calling the police to have you removed. The kids are going to stay with me, and you will never visit them because I will prove that you are a vi-olent person," Angerly replied Crystal pointing her finger at Everett. Then she slaps her face a few times.

Everett looks at her, entirely shocked at her actions in slap-ping her face. "Crystal, come on, why are you doing this? It is a huge waste of everyone's time and cements what you are in many people's eyes. Which is not something you should want to be known as the over-bearing, a cruel wife, and mother. Some have even called you a gold digger," Everett replied.

Crystal paused, "Go fuck yourself, Everett, I don't love you I stopped a long time ago. You see Everett, what you have not noticed is for the past six months; I have been planning everything out. Right down to the police arresting you for hitting me." She slaps her face more.

"What are you doing to yourself. You do know that your actions have hurt the children?" asked Everett, looking confused and dazed. "On top of all of what you have said, I think you need to get some help. I have never raised a hand to you, and you know it."

"Yeah, I do, but the police don't, and all they care about is how my face will look like in the morning. All bruised and sore, the Police will arrest you on the spot. After all, we had a big argument the night before, and my son saw it all. I will just say that you burst into my room and attacked me in the middle of the night. My son will even make the call for me. It is so simple." Once more slapping her face until it is extremely red. "You know what Everett I have found someone else, and I don't love you, and I have not loved you for a long time now. I was just waiting until I could make sure the kids and I were looked after before I cut you out of the picture." Again, striking her face.

"You do know that if you are asleep right now, slapping your face will do nothing. Plus, you can't cut me out of the picture." laughed Everett. "You have to be crazy if you think this will work." Everett paused, and then continued, "Why am I wasting more time trying to argue with you. After all, I did for you, I supported you while you got your degree, and now that you have it, you want out. Well, there goes 14 years down the shitter. I did not think you were this shallow. But I guess we all make mistakes."

"Fuck you Everett, I got what I wanted out of you, and

I don't need you anymore," said Crystal. "Well, except one more thing I still want from you."

"And that is?" Everett laughed as he replied.

"Child Support you bastard, you see even in jail you have to pay that," replied Crystal.

"Okay... child support, well, you better not hope too hard on that," replied Everett.

"What do you mean by that Everett," sneered Crystal.

"Well, very simple if you believe that this is a nightmare, let us ramp it up. The kids are not leaving; I am not going to allow that. I have put up with you for 14 years. I thought it was just a person being a bit of a flake for the first five years, that you would not finish your first degree. You said so many excuses even though you had every chance to do so. I stood by you when you attacked my friends and family, and finding faults in every one where nothing was wrong. But to keep the peace, I kept my mouth shut. I walked away over all the countless fights you started for no reason other than to be a bitch. Our children ran from your screaming and yelling time and time again. Yeah, it is over when you go back to Earth, or you wake up we will be gone. When the world starts to fall apart, look to the skies and remember you were given a chance to save your life and the lives of fifty others. But you chose not to. I am done with you all the problems you and that parasite of a son of yours. Yeah, this is your nightmare, and I hope that you have a great night's sleep. Because in the morning, your new world that you wanted will start."

Just then, Crystal got up and grabbed the chair and was about to throw it at Everett when the voice spoke up with a booming volume and said: "Put the chair down!"

The voice was so loud it boomed in the library startling both Everett and Crystal

Crystal returned the chair to the floor

Everett is looking right at Crystal. "Well, I have said what I wanted to say, now get out."

Crystal walks away, Crystal starts to reply, "Well, just so you know I don't care what you have said, I am taking the kids and my son is also coming with me."

"Whatever you think, it is wrong. I have heard enough Crystal just go. Don't stop just go." Everett keeps his back towards her, so she can't see the tears rolling down his face.

Crystal stops just short of the door and looks at him with hate in her eyes.

"Go!" Everett demands, "After all, this is just a crazy dream of yours," pointing to the door.

As the door opens as she is leaving, she turned around, looking right at him, "You were a dumb fucker."

"No," Everett says softly, "I wasn't, I was faithful, honest, caring, kind, and I was there for you. I did things for you when all others, including your family, turned their backs on you. But it does not matter, Crystal, and I am done with you and all of your problems."

As the doors close and Everett was left sitting there alone in an empty library. He could hear the footsteps walking towards him. The voice begins to speak very softly, "So, do you understand the choice that is at hand? That many even loved ones will refuse the gift you are giving them."

In a shaking voice. "Please, can we force Crystal to stay," asked Everett. "My children need their mother, period."

The voice replied, "I am so sorry once a choice is made; I cannot force them to do something they do not wish to do."

"But returning her to the surface with a new memory is also wrong," said Everett.

"Sometimes, the hardest part of a choice is the result of the outcome. I am so sorry that you must face this" replied the voice

After a short pause, the voice continued in a shaky voice, almost allowing Everett to think, *"Is it human?"*

"Everett, let me put it to you this way; I am here to save lives said the voice. The children cannot speak for themselves, so I have to ensure that they are looked after when their parents cannot. Also, from the moment you stepped aboard, I have been planning out the future, and you are part of my bigger picture. Forcing her to remain on board would result in problems that she would cause, and I could not let that happen. But for you, I allowed her to be given a choice. With all that will be happening in a few weeks, she could be poison to my plans. I assure you that I will leave her and her son with good memories she will think that she only has part of summer vacation with the children and that the two of you are still in the process of divorcing. She will think the oldest one is living with her husband and life is going well. She will not remember this ship or the information she was told. It is the only thing we can do, know these are the rules that I am bound by; you are also."

"But what about my children, they need to know the truth," replied Everett.

The air becomes thick with emotions.

In a caring voice, "I am so very sorry to say they already do.

The children's mother was very vocal, and everyone within earshot knew what was going on. She did not hold back by any means. Her actions and comments very hurtful to the children."

"Oh no, not the children, not them, take me to them right now," pleaded Everett.

"Be calm, Everett, they are okay," said the voice in a soft tone. "I need you to focus for a few more minutes. I assure you that some of your friends and family are taking care of the children right now. Then in about 10 minutes, they will join us. I am sorry to say you are not done with your disappointments. One of your sisters wishes to return as well. Would you like to talk to her?"

"Oh yeah, that will go over like a lead balloon. Why not, let my sister in I am sure this is going to be fun. Let's just add a bit more pain to my life right now." said Everett. Everett walks over to the window facing the Earth. There he is just looking at the Earth to make sure he could always remember what it looked like before the destruction. He heard the doors open to the library. Without turning around, Everett started. "Well, hello, I bet you did not think you would be seeing me. Come over here and look at this beauty." Everett chooses not to face his sister. After a few minutes of staring at the Earth, Everett began to speak. "Isn't it beyond beautiful? I have heard that you wish to return to the surface, even knowing all that you have been told. There is no deception here, and I invited you because I care about you."

A brief few minute of silence. With the two siblings looking at the Earth and all of its beauty.

Everett continued, "I would ask you to reconsider your

choice in returning to the surface. You are placing our father in a bad position. He has been told the same information and has not been told yet that you are returning. That will place him in a choice to stay or go, for him, it is a catch 22 situation. If he stays, he loses you, but if dad chooses to go, he loses all of us who are staying. How is that fair to him? But what he does not know is that once his choice was made, he is not allowed to change his mind. The only reason you are here talking with me is that voice has some kindness for me, and I don't know why yet."

Everett's sister Jo replied. "Look let's say we go back and the Earth starts to fall to destruction our God will save us before it happens. The bible has told about the end days, and as far as we can see, this is what it was all about."

"Okay," said Everett, not wanting to fight her on the choice. But after a few more minutes, Everett's heart began to soften again.

"let me ask you this. What makes you think that if God does come, he will forget about all of us who are out here in space. We are part of the Human race, and then there are the guys in the space station. I am going to let you think about it before I approve your transfer back to the surface. But let me remind you that you are placing our father in a bad position, and it might be the death of him. That is not going to be on my shoulders. What would your God think of you then?" Everett stands up and begins to walk to the door of the library. He leaves his sister to make her choice alone, facing the world below. Where two droids wait for one for him and the other for his sister, he tells the droid in a firm voice, "take me to my children now."

Everett starts walking down the hallway following the droid. The understanding of his choice and the choices of others begin to feel like two tons upon his shoulders. He begins to feel short of breath, *"I can't seem to get enough air"* and passes out. His eyes start to open; he is greeted by the sight of his children and family.

The sister who was thinking of leaving speaks up and says, "I am so sorry we are behind you all the way."

Everett looks to his left and sees his children who rush to his side, grabbing him, and tears begin to follow shortly after. After what feels like a lifetime filled with hugs and tears, no words are said between Everett and the children. There are no words for what has taken place. Soon Everett begins to sit up and starts to get out of bed.

His father's hand rests upon his shoulder. His dad says, "Son, it is time to rest; you have done all that you can. Neil told all of us about what you had to do. I also heard what Crystal said in front of the children. I am so very proud of you but rest for a bit longer. I am sure everything is in perfect order."

Everett looked at his father and began to speak as tears continue to roll down his face, "I am so sorry dad. I tried to be a good husband, I tried even to convince her to stay, in the end, and she chose a different path. But I have also made choices that have led to other choices that I will have to carry for the rest of my days. I need to get up and see this through to a point where I am sure it is safe for me to rest."

As Everett said that, the voice spoke from somewhere. "Everett, it is okay for you to rest right now. I need you with a fresh mind and ready for the next step. I will be okay as I can use one of your closest friends until you rest. I could use the help of your Nephew, Frank, to help me in the library. Now get some sleep. There is much to be done in the coming days."

Everett exhausted lays back down and quickly drifted off asleep with his children near him and youngest lying next to him. No one in the room is left with dry eyes. The reality and pain of the truth of Everett's life were in full view to everyone in the family. They are all faced with the fact that he was being abused, and none of them knew it.

CHAPTER 3

Time Waits For No Man

Everett awakes later to find his children and family surround him all in different states. It appears that they are in some sort of medical room with droids moving silently around. Some of his family and friends are also awake are awake, while some remain asleep. Those that are walking around are in a stupor of amazement of the Earth below. He looks to his right, and he sees his father sitting in a chair looking over him but fast asleep. He feels a complete sense of love and togetherness. One that has been missing for what seems like a very long time. Forgiveness goes a long way, and maybe in time, he will be able to forget as well. He slowly slides out of bed, hoping not to wake those who are in his room. He kisses his children on their heads and says, "I love you always." As he opens the door to leave, his dad speaks.

"Son, Remember I am proud of you, never forget that."

This was something Everett had longed to hear his whole life.

His dad continued, "I know the choices that you are facing

right now might seem like a mountain. My only word of advice is straightforward. How do you eat an elephant?"

Everett replied, "Oh, oh, okay, dad, you have me there." Everett knows that he has heard his dad tell him this so many times before. But he respected his father to the point that hearing it again was just as wise as the first time he said it.

His father replied, "Simple son, only one bite at a time. Do what you can and find others to help; many hands will also make a light load."

Everett replies, "I love you, dad, I'll be back for something to eat later. As he walks out the door." Everett begins to walk down the hallway people were passing him by saying thank you. After about the 20th person, he stopped and rose his voice and said, "Please stop telling me, thank you. I am not a hero or anything else. I am just a person who made a tough choice." He then returned to his walk, still noticing that people did not care what he had said, they continued with their thanks. Everett opened the door to the library exhausted once again, he rested his back on the door for a second with his eyes closed, hoping to find some peace and solace. As he opened his eyes, the library was full of people. Many of them rushed to see if he was okay. Everett pushed the door button over and over until it gave way to his demands. As he jumped out the door, he was greeted by a friendly face.

There was one of his great friends Roe.

Rowan or as many calls him Roe stands about 6ft Dark brown hair cut high and tight with a goatee neatly trimmed. His expressions, though, gave away his boyish nature of kindness and love for family and friends.

"Hey Everett, I was sent to guide you to your quarters and the bridge."

Everett looked and said, "Can we make it fast; please, you know how I don't do well with too many people."

"Don't worry mate I've got your back" reassured Roe to Everett

Roe walks across the hallway and touches a panel that is in the wooden lining of the hall. Soon doors opened to a lift that Everett did not notice all the times he has passed.

A different voice speaks, asking, "destination, please."

Roe replies, "Officers' quarters, please. Everett, this ship is HUGE, and the nerd level is through the roof. By the way, my friend, you look like shit. Plus, I think you need a shower, badly," Roe says with a cheeky grin on his face.

"Thanks, mate," Everett replied. It was knowing that only a true friend could feel comfortable enough to say something. It appeared that over the last few days, he had forgotten some of the simple things in life.

"I will show you to your quarters first. So, you can freshen up before you meet everyone."

"Everyone?" Questioned Everett

"Yes, everyone, those who were closest to you and will help you. We stepped up to be by your side and to make sure you did not need to carry this weight on your own.", replied Roe.

"Thank you mate for being here and being one best friend, a person could ever hope for," Everett replied

As soon as the lift started, it ended. One could not even tell that it was moving in the first place. As the doors opened, Everett could take in the simple please of a well-designed look about the ship. Every hallway seemed to be lined with wood and carpet floors. It is almost as no expense was spared in creating this ship.

Roe said, "There is the bridge (Pointing straight ahead to a round door that is made of metal with a dulled shine with crosshatch pattern), you are not going in there, you stink badly. On the right is a hallway with your quarters, come on I will give you a quick tour as he opened, they left the lift. Walking to a door, Roe continued, "This is your quarters, and I think you are going to like them. Jassy's are the next door down. Most of us who are helping you are located on this level of the ship." As they entered the door, Roe pointed and said, "This is your main living area. On the left is a hallway to your kid's rooms, and they are connected to Jassy's (Everett's oldest Daughter) quarters as well. She said she and her husband would help care for the kids until everything gets put in place. Okay, here is the food machine, I know it does not sound sexy, but hey it works. I don't remember the name of it. There is so much information to learn, and I think I am close to overload. It does a mean steak and chips, but the salad needs a bit of work, though. Okay, to the right is your bedroom and a second shower, which I would suggest taking now. By the way, there is the door directly to the bridge down that small hallway. See you in a few, by the way, some clean clothes with an interesting fit in the cabinet. I found some paper and left you a few notes. See you soon, mate...." As Roe walked down the hall towards the door to the bridge.

"Confusion is nothing new in this place, but it looks like Roe might have made things easier by all the damn notes everywhere." With the most significant sign of them all saying shower. Everett is not sure about this device as it appears to be

a small room with two poles. Everett jumped into the shower, and after a few minutes of reading Roe's instructions, he got it all started. Everett began speaking out loud in the warm water, "Wow, how long was I out for, I do stink."

Just then, the voice speaks up and says, "About two days. Not all that long. But we have a lot of work to get done."

"Um, I don't know why you are here. But a lot of people in the shower like to do it alone. Can you please give me some space", requested Everett?

An hour had passed as tried to come to terms with what has gone on. Everett turned off the shower, and it was a bit different though it felt good to be clean again. "*Well, I better get out of this thing and get some clean clothes. Hey, I wonder how to dry myself off, of course, there is a missing note to say how this is going to be comical as I try to figure it out.*" After a few misses on pushing buttons, some ice-cold others where he was not sure he was the right gender. He finds the right button all of a sudden. There is an enormous rush of air that was coming from all directions. It was powerful enough it blew his family jewels around and dried those off as well. "*It was almost like a car wash.*" I miss towels, and I never thought I would be saying that in my life.

"Well, that was refreshing, I kind of miss a towel though" Everett stated as he stepped out. "Oh, crap, where are my dirty clothes? I'll have to look into that when I get back. Notes are everywhere shaving equipment, powder over there, underwear, and clothes phew glad he listed it all. Opening the drawer listed underwear surprised, holding up a pair, what the hell type of underwear are these? They look like G-strings, hmm not too sure about this. Now for the clothes. What the heck a uniform, hmm great something to set me apart from everyone else. What if I don't want to be the one in charge. I am not too happy about this all. When I talk to that voice once more, I am going to give it a piece of my mind. Argh, they have snuck up my butt crack, this is not right at all. In second thoughts, the uniform is not too bad. I can live with it, maybe. I wonder what others are going to think. Well, I better look in the mirror. Wow, look at me respectable to the top. Shoes look good as well. I love Grey and Blue colors very sharp. Hmm, these marks on the collar must mean rank. I am not sure about the rank or leadership thing."

Everett looking at the chair in his room and decided to have a bit of rest before facing everyone on the bridge. As he rested looking out into space, he started to think to himself, *"I know the end; she was a bad person, but deep down inside, I loved her, and now I miss her. I think that is the sickest part of loving her,"* Followed by wiping a few tears away from his eyes.

[Empty Space – James Arthur]

Everett stood back up and straightened out his uniform. Speaking to an empty room, "Well, I better get out there and get things underway, whatever those might be. Heaven forbid that anyone ever finds out how terrified I am, as he looked around the rooms. *"I kind of like these quarters, but I bet not everyone has the same amount of room. I'll need to check on that to make sure we are all okay, and there is no one in a prison cell for quarters."* As Everett walks down the hall towards the bridge, he notices a single photo hanging just by the door with something written below it that he cannot make out. Right on the door at about head height is a mirror so that the person looking at it is looking directly at themselves. Hmm, I will need to ask the voice who the person was or is and what it says."

Just then, the voice says, "It was a Commander who once stood where you are now. The words say, "Remember, you are only the same as everyone else."

"Well, those are powerful words in times like these," replied Everett. "I want it replaced with the photos of my children. But keep the quote; this will keep me grounded."

Everett pushes the button for the door. As it slides opens, he is faced with the expansive bridge, which is the command hub for all the ship and her crew. There is a lot of people in here he says out loud. He first notices his closest friends, followed by Neil, Frank, and a strangely out of focus image in a humanoid shape.

Just then, the voice begins to speak once more; only this time, it is coming from the direction of the out of focus figure. "From my numbers, we are 10,000 people shy of filling our required numbers, and I would like to know why."

"Well, it is elementary," replied Everett. "I instructed all of us here to keep a left-over pool that way if we needed some especially skilled people. While I was resting, I came to a question, and that was how we could defend ourselves should the need arise."

The voice replies, "Simple, I have drones, and I can make more if need be."

"Ah, that is a problem then, you see drones remove the issue of accountability for one's actions. On Earth, we made that mistake, and I will not allow ourselves to repeat that." Everett ordered

Just then, Frank spoke up and asked: "Can pilots fly these drones?"

"Yes," replied the voice.

"Well then, Uncle, we require some skilled pilots then," said Frank. Frank being Everett's nephew, is a sturdy built man standing about 5'11' bald as can be with a look of steel determination.

"I think I agree with what Frank just said," interrupted Everett.

"We need some highly skilled men and women who are trained, Protectors in a way that many who are on board now are not. So, what are you thinking, Frank? Do you have any ideas on how we gather these people?"

Frank speaks up and says, 'I have an idea, but it might be crazy and may not work as what we will be asking these people to do goes against everything they have sworn to do."

"Okay, let's hear this idea, and we can look at the pros and cons of it." Replied Everett

"If we look at what is going to happen, we can assume that all sorts of rescue missions will be going on to help the people of Japan. We should focus our view on aircraft carriers. If we look at trying to get one of those, we can assume we are looking at 1,600 to 4,000 people just one the ship alone, and with their families, we would reach that 10,000 marks rather fast. We would have to look at a ship or two that would be en route to Japan to avoid creating other issues."

One of the people speaks up, "You are not just asking them to leave their position and join yours. You are asking them to do the unthinkable. They took an oath that was fused with the blood of those who came before them."

"We are giving them a choice to save their families lives; they can refuse just like everyone else.", replied Everett.

"Then we have the issue what do we do with the ship if they so choose to join us?" commented Frank.

"Sorry, Frank, I don't see that as an issue, if you are worried about that scuttle it. After all, it is not like anyone is going to survive to use it." Replied another person.

Everett continues after a pause, "Frank, I am going to place you in charge of this make it happen. You're highly skilled and more than qualified. Figure out a way; just get it done."

"Okay, Commander, I will do as you ask." Replied Frank

"I also want you to grab as many of the Australia SAS as you can. Next, I want the retired Officer Cate McMillian, and I have the utmost trust in her abilities. This is a rush, Frank, and time is not on our side in these matters."

"I'll get it done once this meeting is over," Frank replied

Everett begins once more "Next, we need to get people doing things to help them in this massive transition. Al, can you and your wife look at setting up and Education department." Al has always been one of Everett's closest friends. Al is a bit on the large size with a personality that matches. But a heart as big as his kindness that fills the room. There has never been a friend to Everett that has proven to be so loyal as Al.

"We will have to fill a lot of jobs all over the coming days. Gazza, can you and Neil work on engineering. Gazza, what can be said about a friend who would drop everything to be by his loved one's side in their time of need. Gazza stands about 5'8" looking like the computer guru he is. But with a voice soft and caring. "We will have an influx of highly skilled people from the ship that can help you in that area. If I ask around, we might be shocked at the results. We need to make sure we find those people." Gazza replies

"Great idea mate I think you should get right on that," said Everett. "But let me know how things are going on with what you find. I know we still have a portion of that 10,000 spaces we can fill after Frank finishes his chore. Find me some free thinkers on Earth, ones who take risks and are willing to look outside the box. I want the inventor of the electric car that is so popular. His name is drawing a blank, and he has that car company. Get him now and listen to him about who he thinks is the best. All of you keep an eye on the numbers of spaces. Once we reach the 150,000 population, we have no more bed spaces."

Everett pauses to think about a few things. "*So many things to do, and it feels like I am way out of my depth.*"

Everett is turning towards the figure, "Right now, I think it is time to hear from our host. I have a question that is bugging me, and I would like an answer. I want to know what your real mission is. It does feel like there is some hidden agenda. We are placing a huge amount of trust in someone we have not met as of yet."

The voice replies, "Very well, you deserve those answers. As I said, the photo in the hallway from your quarters was the original Commander of this ship. He was a very kind soul; his orders were to save his people and destroy this ship. But I knew that one day the people could forget the past. They might need this ship once again. On his final trip to the surface, I disobeyed the orders and placed two teleportation rooms that could be used in case of an emergency. He never returned to the ship. So I was left with my mission to make sure humanity had a way to survive at all costs. When I saw you, I watched and noticed how much you reminded me of him and his kindness towards others."

"When the Tsunami happened, it resulted in the meltdown of those Nuclear plants I watched and noticed that everything was out of control. I knew that moment I would have to act as I did not think that the world could not solve all the problems that this event would cause. So, I made the choice that I would teach you to be a new Commander. I could have chosen a lot of people, even when the first teleporter was found. But I kept coming back to the fact of the old Commander was fair and filled with a sense of true justice. Is there anything else you would like to know about him or my mission?", asked the voice

Everett looking directly at the figure "Yes, there is one more that needs to be answered right now. We don't have a name for you, and we are calling you the voice as until now none of us have seen you,"

The figure moves across the command deck. "Very well, my name is Mika, and this ship is named Mother." Mika pauses, and then the figure fades away. Leaving everyone standing on the command deck wondering where it went.

Soon a door opens from the Commander's office and out steps a lovely woman. She has a face that one could describe as kind and loving, with medium length dark brown hair, medium build standing about 5'6". "Well, it is about time we meet. My name is Mika, and now you can stop calling me Mika. It is my responsibility to ensure all of you survive. Now Everett, you are the new Commander of this ship, and I will assist you in your role as you assist me in mine."

"Wait one damn minute. I don't want to be the Commander. I have no clue how to do that. There has to be someone better on this ship to do that." Commented Everett

One of Everett's friends Yvette, interrupts, "Everett stop! Listen to me please for a second. You are a good person with a heart of gold. You saved each and everyone on this ship. It is about time that you accept the fact that you can be more than you have been. She chose you not just for the person you are, but for the person you could become." Yvette is 5'7" and light skin with medium brown hair. She has a lovely motherly shape and very delicate features.

Everett sat there with a shocked look upon his face from the words that his friend just said.

Just as the height of the stress and revelations. Commander, Neil interrupts "We have a problem on the surface. The temperatures of the landmasses of Japan have risen 10 degrees above normal, and it is steadily climbing."

"Neil, where did you get that information?" asked Everett

"Everett turn around" replied Neil

A beautiful view of Japan confronts Everett with an overlay that gives so much information that it was all a bit confusing."

Mika speaks up, "It has begun. I would advise we fill those other spaces on the ship as fast as you can."

Everett looks at "Frank, you better get that ship and people now."

"Commander, I am going to help Frank; he is going to need it," said Liam, another close friend of Everett's.

Everett begins to give orders. "Very well, let's get it going and fast. Frank takes Liam to grab as many helpers as you can.

Frank, your grandfather, also would be a good person to help you as well why not ask him."

Everett turns to his friend, "Yvette, thank you I needed a reality check."

With a warm smile, she replies, "You're welcome, Commander, what would you like me to do?"

With a concerned look, Everett replies, "Please check on people I need to know if they are living in dog boxes or have close to what my quarters look like."

Mika speaks up, "I'll tell all of you something right now. I designed this ship, and I promise you that everyone has quarters beyond what you could ever expect. It is bigger on the inside than the outside. It is a bit hard to explain physics in a short time, but I can go into it later if you would like."

"Later, please Mika and maybe with Neil and his people. It is a bit over my head, but thank you for the offering." That made Everett smile thinking to himself, "*Wow all those looks and brains to boot. Shut up, you jackass, and you have no time to think like that.*"

[Working Class Man – Jimmy Barns]

CHAPTER 4

Franks Choice

Nothing weighs more on a person than a choice forced upon them in a time of dire need. Frank walks down the hall towards his quarters.

"What am I going to do? The moment I step foot on a ship without being part of the crew or invited, I will end up dead or in the brig. Then what can I do? I cannot ask others to risk this; it has to be me." Frank, in a plodding pace looking at the woodwork of the hallway. Others can see that he is feeling the pressure of what needs to be done.

"Fuck, Fuck, Fuck.... I have no solution to this." Frank yells

Mika appears to the left side of Frank "Hello Frank. It appears that you need some help, lucky for you not much escapes me in this place. At this time, we need to make sure we are a team that offers it helps to all."

"Holy Shit, Mika! don't ever sneak up on me!" Frank says with his hand on his chest. "Some people like myself have experiences in life that have changed us to do certain things."

"I am so sorry, Frank. I can see that me just appearing next to you has upset you. It was never my attention to do that.

How about we keep walking to wherever you were heading. We can talk as we walk about my solution to your problem. You see, if you do go back, the risk is far too high, and I am not willing to allow such a risk. As I have plans for you on this ship and for these people."

"Well, I am glad you and I agree that there is a huge risk in going back to Earth. Let alone set foot on a ship that is right out of the blue. So how do you think we can bring people up here so I can talk to them without running into such a risk. Plus, I remind you about what Neil and I have said, we are on a tight schedule."

"Okay, Frank, look behind us right now. See the Orb that is following us?" Mika points to the object floating behind the two of them. "I can get anyone on Earth to this ship if one of these is near them. I have looked at your idea, and I think I can even grab the whole ship if I can get enough of these to it."

"You have to be kidding me right that you can just grab a ship in the water on Earth and bring it to space and put it in this ship. That will be a feat that I would have to see." But then all of them will see that they are not on Earth anymore and that is going to ring alarm bells on the ship, where they have weapons and people trained to kill. Mika, are you sure you want to risk that? Hey, we are at my quarters. Why don't you come in and meet my wife, and we can finish this chat in there as we have a sit-down and a drink."

"That sounds like a wonderful idea," Mika replies to the offer.

Her calm demeanour helps to reassure Frank that a solution is at hand. Soon the door opens, and they are greeted by

Frank's wife, who happens to be Japanese. "This is my lovely wife and best friend, Anri."

"Oh, hello, I have wanted to meet all the others from the Earth for a while now. It is a real pleasure to have you aboard the ship. I am so glad you came." So, looking around the room, Mika notices the lack of creature comforts. "So Anri can I show you a few things that might help you in setting up your home as I am so sure this might seem a little overwhelming" Mika steps inside the door past Frank.

Frank, with both hands, shrugs to his wife as Mika steps inside with a broad smile ignoring his introduction.

"If you come over to every panel in each room, you can lift them off the wall and walk around and place plants, furniture, and even filled bookcases." Mika taking the tablet and pointing it at the everyday table and places a vase with flowers in the center of it. "There that looks so much better, and they complement you so much, Anri. You can choose anything your heart desires from the Earth with the touch of a few buttons." Mika holds out the data pad for Anri to take control. "Oh, by the way, you can also teach the food dispenser what to cook and how to do it."

"Oh, Mika, thank you so much I was wondering how to make this place home. You have just solved that one little problem." Anri replies as she gladly takes the tablet.

"Mika, how about we sit down and have a glass of water. Then we will look at what to do with your idea." Frank then returns to the subject of the Ship and their crew. "How about we talk in the lounge room?"

"Oh no, you don't," Anri interrupts. "At least until I have time to set it up, we will not have any more guests until I am done." Like a child in a toy store, she is off with data pad in hand."

"Well, it looks like we are going to sit here and enjoy the flowers while talking over your ideas," Frank suggests as he motions to a chair at the table.

"Frank, what color scheme do you think we should go with" Anri interrupts, "On never mind, I will do it all."

"Okay, love whatever you want," Frank replies with a huge smile. "Okay, where were we with the Orbs' oh yes. The whole ship is a huge risk but might be faster than grabbing every person by themselves. But then we have a problem with getting your message across to them effectively."

"Well, Frank, I easily have room for that ship in one of my cargo holds. Then we can use the Orbs to display on the wall with you talking and introducing the standard information. We can place a few data stations on the deck of the ship for people to put their personal information for their families and loved ones. What do you think about that?"

"Hmm, Mika, I am not sure this is going to work as effectively as you are hoping. What are you going to do about the ones who don't accept your offer?"

After a short pause, "Okay, Frank, I have done the adjustments and calculations to my introduction. I don't think there is going to be much of a problem when I tell them I will return them to their homes to be with their families for the end of the Earth. In a way, it is a bit of calculated risk; they will be given the information that you all were with an update. Then we add in the risk factor that we will only return them to their families to live out the death of Earth." I cannot keep playing who is going to come on a risk. We need to hedge our bets a bit. What do you think?"

"Well, that is fine, Mika, but we are not addressing the fact that the moment that ship is not in the water, they are going to be on guard and looking for it. That guns will be operated and at the ready to shoot anything that moves. It is a huge risk. So, I suggest those videos fill all sides of the cargo hold with a volume that all can hear clearly." Frank drinks the rest of his water, "would you like a refresh on your water?"

"No, thank you for the offer of the water. But how about I do this here is a control unit for the Orb, and you can make it do so much more than follow us. It also has a bit of an AI to it and can help you in your current role. If you need me, just call me on the data pad. Next, I will program the Orb to take you to an office that you can use as yours as well as showing you the way to the cargo hold that the ship will be put. How does that work for you?"

"Wow, okay, it seems like you have taken the time to plan most things out." Replies Frank

"Well, Frank, I have watched for a long time what is going on in the world. I have studied interactions and what has become of those who are on Earth. I planned this ship out many years ago, and I had a gut feeling that it needed to be ready just in case. So here we are facing something no one ever wanted, but we now know what needs to be done. We must also be ready for the chaos which will happen regardless. We cannot plan for everything. As for the issues of weapons, we can place the ship in a protective field that will not allow the damage in or out. As love ones are collected and brought to the ship, we will bring them into the same cargo hold. That way, everyone sees each other. So, do we have an action plan?"

"Sounds great, and thanks for helping me, Mika I was some worried and confused about how we are going to do everything that you needed to be done."

"Don't worry about it frank I reached out to you for more than one reason. You see, I am forced to make a choice, and this is still my ship at the end of the day until your Uncle is ready to take it over. I need you to take on the role of the security chief. It will be your role to protect your Uncle and the command staff of the ship. I will assign you the ability to have an excellent staff and equipment to do the role. Can I count on you to accept it?"

"My Uncle has saved the lives of all those that matter to me in this world. Oops, in my life, I mean. To return the favour to him, I would do anything he asked within reason. You gave him the ability to save all of us as well. For that, I am in your debt, and if this can repay that debt, I will do it for you."

"Great thank you, Frank, why don't you take over this Orb and head down to your office and get things running. I need to talk to your lovely wife as I have a role for her as well."

"Okay, have fun, she is the kindest soul I have ever known." Frank yells out, "I have to go and finish a job for Mika."

"I think I am going to stay a little and help out," says Mika

"You two have fun, I'll be back as soon as I can. I love you."

"Okay, Hun, please be careful, I love you too." Mika, I am in the back working on the baby's bedroom. I love this everything is so perfect right down to the photos hanging on the wall."

After Frank leaves his quarters and the women, he follows the Orb to a doorway that is close to his quarter and appears to be close if not connect to the Command Deck. As the door opens, he enters a room filled with a wooded desk, few chairs, and a weapon rack filled with a few different types of firearms all safely secured and in a state of readiness. On one of the walls is a food dispenser as well as drawers. As he looks in, some of the uniforms are similar to his Uncles though he can see a rank difference in them. *"Hmm, these must be for my staff."* "So, Orb lets go look at the cargo hold and see what Mika this is large enough to hold an Aircraft carrier," Frank commands the Orb as they leave the office.

After a short time and a ride on the lift, Frank and the Orb arrive at a door. "We are here Sir" informs the Orb

With a deep breath, Frank opens the door to be greeted by a cargo hold large enough to hold three full-sized Aircraft carriers. "Well, this is a bit of overkill in size if you ask me Orb. Can we do anything to reduce two-thirds of it?"

"As you command, I will adjust it to the size you are requesting," Replies the Orb.

"Can you show me what the information video will look on the side walls." Requested Frank

Soon the information video is up and running on all four walls at the same time, with correct sound levels for the environment.

"This is perfect," replies Frank, "let's get the ball rolling to grab that ship."

Within an hour, Frank makes a call to his Uncle. "Hello Uncle, I have just had the ship teleported to the cargo hold, and Mika is in the process of talking to all of them, and the information is being shown to them."

"That is great news, Frank, let's make sure we can get to their families as fast as possible the updates on Japan are rolling in. They are not looking great, and from the images, we can see the water is boiling around edges of the power plant. Keep me updated on the progress that you are making. I hope you don't mind, but I need to keep this short, and Mika told me about the job role she has you in place already. Thank you for accepting to keep all of us safe. Wow, have to go something that needs to be done. Love you, kiddo."

"Love you too, Uncle."

CHAPTER 5

Meanwhile on Earth

Well, I think it is time that I change your focus from what is going on in space to what is happening on Earth. Meanwhile, in Japan, everyone is blissfully unaware that right below their feet, the world is about to end. Lucky for you, I have eyes all over; after all, I needed to record the last days. People must not forget how we got to the end of it all. What took place and who couldn't have solved it all.

Japan, it is a beautiful day. The sun is shining and not a cloud in the sky. Who could wish for a more lovely spring day? People are going about their daily lives. Children are in schools, at a hospital a mother gives birth to a healthy baby girl with down syndrome, a child celebrates that they are out of nappies, all in all, it is a typical day in the lives of so many. All are unaware of the storm that is looming below them.

In another part of Japan in Fukushima, an office door swings wildly open, breaking the glass window of the door. A man carelessly rushes down a long white hallway. In doing so, he pushes past people without regard. In his wake, people are thrown to the floor and into the sides of the hall.

In a different part of the same building, a man sits at his

desk in a well-furnished office talking to his wife "yes, my dear, I will stop and get some milk on the way home. It is a fine day, nothing but the same old reports." A pause, then he begins once more, "I will not be late for dinner."

Just then, the running man bursts through the door without knocking. Sweat drips from his forehead as he states in a shaking voice, Get OFF the Fucking phone. When I call that bitch out there, she better put me through. Oh, by the way, we have a huge problem.

The man behind the desk calmly says, "I am sorry, my love, I will call you back." Hangs the phone up, takes a deep breath. That was my wife on the phone, so whatever you have to tell me better be important! The man who is sitting behind a desk said in a stern voice.

The runner replies I don't care who it was. We have reached the evacuation level point; it has drastically failed.

Then go to the backup procedures, orders the man behind the desk.

That is what I am trying to tell you, listen to me, we have failed on all levels. It just happened so fast, and I could not get through to you on the phone. It was forcing me to rush down here to you in person. I need to know what we are to do now.

Okay then is there any crazy last-ditch ideas that we have not tried, asks the man behind the desk.

I am sorry, sir, there is nothing more we can do; we are past the point of no return the runner replies.

Then I am left with no choice, and the government must be notified. Do we have a timeline?

About a week if we are lucky, maybe two, replied the runner.

Very well start enabling the procedures to give us as much time as we can get, send nonessential staff home as well, orders the man.

The runner leaves the office in the same hurried state as he had entered.

The man picks up the phone, Sakura, call my wife now, please.

The man gets up and shuts the door before his secretary can. He then walks over to a file cabinet and opens the bottom drawer. The man then grabs out a large bottle of unopened scotch and a couple of glasses. Next, he takes a large red, sealed envelope. He returns to his seat as he begins to sit down just as the phone rings. "Hello, my love, you need to listen. I will not be home for dinner, and you need to grab the children from school. Then drive to the west coast and get a hotel room stay there until I call you. This is not a joke, and I am sorry for scaring you, but please do as I ask. I love you with all my heart. Be safe, and do not stop for anything or anyone until you are there. We will talk soon, no, my love I am not in trouble, I will speak to you soon. I love you too, okay? Goodbye." The man hangs up the phone.

Takes a deep breath and dials his secretary, Sakura, please come to my office. As she steps inside the office, he states, would you like a glass? I think you are going to need it. She agrees as he begins to pour. Please sit down, invites the manager. Thank you for all the work you have done here. But I am sorry it is over, and we all need to start looking at getting out and getting our families to the west coast. Do you understand what I am saying?

Yes, replies, Sakura.

Good, here is your drink. Now listen to me carefully. Pack your items and leave, do not rush. Go to your family collect them and head to the west coast when you see water you will be safe. I am sure by the time you are there; the government will instruct you on what is going to happen next. Once again, thank you for all that you have done. The woman gets up bows and turns to leave as she says, thank you. She walks out the door closing it behind her softly.

The man sits down and pours another drink, then grabs the envelope. Then with shaking hands begins to open the red envelope carefully. With one large mouthful, he drinks the scotch. He pulls out a single piece of paper that says only use in dire need. With a unique phone number, he pours another drink as he begins to dial the number.

Soon someone picks up. A voice answers, "state the emergency?"

The man replies, "All safety precautions have failed."

After a short wait, a voice on the other end says, "has the backup procedure been put into place"?

The manager replies, "sir, and we are looking at an evacuation level event. All backup procedures have failed."

A heavy sigh can be heard over the phone. The voice on the other end of the phone says, "very well, we are left with no choice. I will contact the cabinet ministers. What are your plans?"

The manager replies, "I will wait for your further instructions. I have ordered an early release of non-essential staff. We will do what we can to be able to provide as much time as possible."

The voice replies once more, "do you have a timeline?"

Yes, sir, we are looking at "One to two weeks at most."

"Thank you, and I will be in touch soon with further instructions," the voice on the other end of the phone says. The phone goes silent as the man drinks the third glass and, once again, a fast gulp.

Meanwhile, in Tokyo, Japan. Phones begin to ring, and runners and messengers are sent. The failsafe plan is being enacted, the military and private contractors are being ordered to ferry loads concrete to the failed powerplant to encase it. Ocean barriers will be put in place and filled as well. Calls are being made to the UN for assistance to evacuate all of Japan. Requests are made to China, the USA, Australia, Russia, Vietnam, and Korea. Within two hours, plans are put into place to evacuate all of Japan via the western coast.

An argument breaks out between the US president and the Prime Minister of Japan due to the use of help from China and Russia. In a series of simple tweets, the arrogant US President notifies the world that the US is leaving Japan.

"It is time for the US to end our role in Japan we are removing all staff asap. We will save millions of dollars, the best plan ever!"

All across Washington DC phones in all the powerful offices. Yes, I know he is a fucking idiot. But he is our fucking idiot. We put him into office. Call Japan to ensure that the US will help. Then someone needs to call the airlines and get them to fly as many people out as they can. Call Australia and get permission to land as many people as we can there. Tell them we will provide as much support as we can. Get me the joint chiefs of staff, and let's get some airlifts going. Someone shut that jackass's phone down by taking him golfing or something. It is time for the big boys to play.

US naval headquarters, "Admiral coded message for you, sir."

Ten minutes later, send this out to all ships in the Pacific region; they are to make way to Japan and assist in the evacuation of Japan.

Send the following orders and instructions. This is a need to know basis until it is all done. We will keep a tight lid on this as much as we can.

Three hours later, "Sir, I have the President on the phone for you."

"Hello, Mr. President, how can I help you?"

"Mr. President, with all due respect, you need to restate your orders."

"So, to clarify once more, you are saying we are not to be assisting in the evacuation of Japan as China is helping as well. Sir, we are talking about millions of lives are at risk, and you are saying no. Very well if that is your orders, sir. I have to follow them, but they are a poor choice."

The phones disconnect.

"Yes, Admiral, sir, you wanted me," the secretary answers.

"Hold all my calls, and no wait get me General John on a secure line like it was yesterday and no incoming calls."

"Yes, sir."

After a few minutes, the secretary rings the General

"Admiral Sir, the General is on the line for you."

"John, yes, Mike, we have a serious problem." After explaining all that is going on in Japan and the call from the President, the Admiral says the following, listen, John, I have no choice but to not listen to that moron. How can I accomplish this without interference? We need to save lives above all else. I am not going down in the history of being a person who let millions die because some lazy Politician was playing games.

The two men talk for an hour and create a plan. They were making sure that both the orders are upheld, and the lives are saved.

You know this is going to be the end of my career John. But in some ways, I am going to go out on the right side of History. I will never include your name in this.

Thanks, Mike, but I think while we are evacuating the airbases there and, in doing so, just happen to use our naval fleet to help. We just happen to help a whole bunch of civilians at the same time. I don't think the president would even grasp what we have done.

We better update our orders to the troops and our counterparts in Japan as well. Heaven, please help those poor people.

Meanwhile, in Japan, Tsunami warnings begin to sound all over the islands. On all media, people are being advised to make their way towards the west sides of the islands. Airports are all being listed as safe places. The population is told that it is a national emergency. Police and the military are doing what they can to assist. We return to the power plants and those who are trying to save lives.

The gentleman once again sits at his desk. Returns to the file cabinet and removes four bottles of Saki. He knew this day was going to come; it was just a gut feeling. He just knew.

He takes the office phone and makes a call over the intercom and says, "Can all remaining staff meet me in the control room I would like to have a meeting with all of you."

Then he hangs the phone up and grabs the photo of his family and heads out of the office. He closes the door behind him; he knows he will not return to it. As he walks towards the control room, he stops at the break room and grabs the cups from the water fountain and cupboards. He turns the lights off in the break room and then shuts the door he heads once again towards the control room. As he passes each of the rooms, he turns off lights in a sad sense of closure. Soon he starts to move by people waiting in the hall of the control room. A look upon their faces all say the same thing it's over. People part to the side of the room as he enters the control room. He stops and pauses thanking each of the workers by name as he passes them. There is an eerie silence as he sets the bottles down and separates each cup; he then begins to pour the Saki evenly in all the cups and begins to pass it out. Thanks, every one of them as he hands them a glass.

When he can see, all of them have a cup. He begins, "I raise my cup to salute you in honour of all of you and your efforts." He raises his glass and then brings it back down to drink it.

He continues, "We all know why we are here, and now you need to make a choice, one that is something only you can make, and I will not force you. You need to choose to stay or go home to your families and get to them to the western shore of Japan. I have already sent my family, and I hope you have done the same. I will be staying to make sure others can get out safely."

Soon a voice from the back yells, "I will stand with you."

Then another repeats the same, "I will stand with you," soon, it fills the control room and hall.

The gentleman raises his hand to calm the workers. "Please make your calls now, today we become heroes and shall be remembered in history." He walks out of the control room and outside for a breath of fresh air.

He begins to dial his wife once more. "Hello, my love, are you on the road? Good, I am calling you to tell you that I love you and the children. I need to tell you that the plant has failed and that I will not be able to join you and the children. I know my love, I know. I am so sorry, but if we leave, millions will die. I cannot risk that you and the children are some of them. I am going to stay and try to make sure to give you the time you need to get to safety. I love you very much, and he tries to hold back the tears. Please let me speak to the children." Soon he is finished with the call with one last, "I love you" he hangs the phone up.

He adjusts his suit then wipes the tears away. It is easy to see that he has been crying due to his puffy eyes. Then steps back inside the control room. He can tell others are feeling the same way. Okay, let's get back to making sure we can give them as much time as possible.

Within hours ships from several countries begin to make way for Japan in a rush to evacuate all of the islands. Back in Washington DC at the Whitehouse in a security meeting.

The President begins to speak. I have an idea about the best idea ever. Let's drop a nuke on that power plant and blow it up. That will solve all the problems.

In a look of utter disbelief, a General begins to speak. "Did you just say drop a nuke on the nuclear powerplant?"

The President replies, "yes, best plan ever."

All of a sudden, at the end of the table, another General stands up. In a rage-filled rant, he screams at the President. "SHUT UP! SHUT THE FUCK UP! You fast-food eating, dim-witted, undereducated, waste of human evolution if I want to hear from a fart like you, I'll go and take a shit. So, unless you have something useful to say, don't say another fucking word or so help me God I will grab the back of your head and smash the life out of you on the fucking table, am I making myself clear to you maggot. Yes, good, now we are leaving, and we are going to get back to rescue the people of Japan. If you even think of touching that twitter account of yours, I am going to find you and take your phone and shove that phone up your fat fucking ass so far that you will need to open your mouth to hear the ring tone."

The generals all leave. The president has lost the confidence of the military.

The President speaks to those remaining in the room. "I am going to fire him. Yeah, they are all fired, and then I am going to launch a missile."

"Shut the fuck up, and we have had enough," the Speaker of the House interjects. "As of right now, you are relieved of your duties," says the Speaker of the House. "Mr. Vice President, you will be taking over for the time being, and you will do as we say, understood. Take the football from the President," the President is under house arrest. Take him to the presidential quarters, and he is to have no contact until this works out. Understood soldier?"

"Yes, Mr. Speaker." A soldier that was standing next to the President

"You have not heard the last of me," screams the President, then grabs the football and rushes out of the meeting room.

"Stop him," the others in the room yell out.

But other soldiers who did not know what was going on start to defend the President as he runs screaming, "They are trying to kill me."

On an Aircraft carrier in the Atlantic Ocean, we join Frank on his mission to secure specialized men and women to join those that are saved on the ships above. It is late, and the ship's captain has chosen to call it a night after a briefing about the state of Japan. He walks down the hall with one of his men towards his quarters.

"Gunny, I am going to call it a night, we'll talk in the morning have a good night's sleep." The Commander opens his office door and steps into a dark room. He reaches for the light switch, "well, I am going to pay for playing cards with gunny in the morning. I can already feel the headache." As the lights in his office fill the room, he begins to see that he is not alone.

"What the.... Who the hell are you, and what are you doing in my quarters? Gunny!" Yells the Commander to no reply.

"Please, Commander calm down; we have a lot to talk about and in a short time."

"I asked you a question, who are you."

"Well, I see Commander, you have already forgotten me. My name is Jones, Frank Jones, to be precise."

"Gunny!" Yells the Commander.

"Sir," Frank speaks again "He is not going to come no one can hear you right now. It is just the two of us right now. Do me a favor and come over to this window. I want you to see something essential. The people I work for want you to understand the topic we are going to talk about after you see what I have to show you."

The Commander walks over to the window, looks out, and sees the Earth." Interesting poster, though, now get out of my office before I have you arrested."

"Commander," Frank replies "You need to calm down and turn around. I am not in your office, and you would have a hard time putting me in a cell on that ship."

The Commander turns around to see that Frank is accurate, and he is not in the Commander's quarters. He looks once more out the window and notices that something is not right with that; he is looking at Earth. It appears that his ship is in a hanger.

"Young man," the Commander says, "you better tell me where in the hell we are at."

Frank reappears in the Commander's quarters, "Well, sir, I think I did that." Frank points to the window, "That's Earth, and you are not on it. So please take a seat and let me explain a bit more because time is not our friend. First, I have no time to lie to you, here is a data pad and I would like you to look at the information on it, and then we will talk." Frank returns to his seat and waits.

After about 15 minutes, the Commander looks up. "Let me see if I understand what I am reading is correct. The US Navy is at full steam toward Japan's west coast to evacuate as many people as we can. Does this thing say that it is a complete and useless task?"

Frank looks up, "Sir, it is not useless more like the noble pursuit of something that cannot be reached. In the end, it is not going to matter. Once those rods reach the water, they are going to do what that pad says. There will be no running from the storm that will be created. The storm will kill everything in its paths, and it will also be self-perpetuating destruction."

"So why are you showing me this information?" questions the Commander.

"Look, Commander, to be honest, you are one man. There is no way you can save the Earth or its people. But I can offer you an opportunity to save all of your men and women on your ship. I can also offer the chance for you to save your family and theirs. You see, once you choose to stay, I will give you the ability to save fifty people. I will do this for each of the crew on your ship. Both you and I know that unless you make this choice, you and your family are going to die. As well as all those who are on your ship."

The Commander returns to the data pad and rereads the information one more time. "Young man, it can't end like this; there are the smartest people on the Earth working towards a solution. Look how we stopped Chernobyl."

"Look, sir, you and I both know we did not stop that. We just slowed it down. There is no slowing this event down; it is already too late."

"Okay, what do I have to do?" replies the Commander

"Say yes, it is that simple than have a conversation with all of your crew. Give them the hope of saving their families as well. The ones who choose not to say will be sent down to Earth. With a different memory that fits the story.

Very well, just get my family up here and safe, and while I talk with my crew.

Frank radios to Mika and informs her that the Commander of the ship is on board. She needs to save his family. Just then, a small shuttle leaves the hanger heading towards Earth. Okay, sir, now you need to talk to your crew.

Soon ship by ship leaves the hanger and is speeding towards the Earth. All of the crew of the aircraft carrier have chosen to remain and to save their families. "Commander," Frank begins, "we need to head to the bridge, and you can meet the Commander of this vessel. I am sure he could use your valuable skills. We will also have your wife and children brought to your quarters once they arrive."

Okay, Frank, let us meet your Commander. Sir, you will not need your sidearm so you might want to leave it here.

Well, this is where it all begins; the end of the Earth is closer than many might even know or understand. Will the actions of two men save what could be the last vestiges of the human race? Did I make the right choice in Everett? Time will only be my judge. Now we must race to grab as many families as we can to exist. But a question must be asked of the future. When will the life of a God outweigh the need for greed? I have seen it twice with my own eyes; why did we not learn? I guess we better look at what is happening back on the ship.

CHAPTER 6

Chocolate Milk and Doughnuts

"Mika, I was looking at the Earth news feeds, and so far, it appears as nothing is going on in the world. Are you so sure something big is going to take place? I am starting to be a little worried," said Everett.

"Well, Everett, I am glad you asked. I was checking on Japan today. Saw these crazy images in the ocean and seas that surround and leading up to the islands, and I think you need to take a look." Mika replied

"Well, let's have a look at them on the main screen, put them up, please." Instructs Everett

Soon all those who are on the bridge can see streaks in the ocean. Much like a pinstripe suit, and the two of them stand on the command bridge with the others.

Mika begins to explain. "That is new, and I did not see those. The temperature must be rising. I think what might be taking place is that the rods have bored down to the water level, and we might start to see a geyser on the surface soon to the level no one has never seen before."

"A geyser? That seems a bit out of nowhere." Someone interrupts

"We could see a steam vent that is created from the rods heating the water to that level." Replied Mika

"That would be true if we did not have a feature to encase the plant and holes with heavy cement at the touch of a button to try to create a casement around the whole plant. I think if you zoom in, we might see that in action" states Neil

"Right now, all I know is what is on the screen and the data from Neil. So, let's zoom in and have a closer look at the plant," instructs Mika.

Soon the plant can be seen with a closeup, and just as Neil stated, cement trucks are pumping into the plant and the surrounding area.

"They do know that is not going to work that it might just cause a huge explos......" states Mika just as a significant explosion takes place and a geyser vents water into the air.

"Quick get me a side view of that geyser" orders Everett

"Neil is that thing bigger than the nuclear explosion at Hiroshima?" questions Everett

"From the naked eye I would say no, but it is pretty damn close though" comments Neil

"What the hell are those streaks in the ocean," someone questions?

"those are only going to be one thing, and that is ships." Neil instructs, "It was all part of the evacuation plan."

The camera moves to focus in, and everyone on the bridge can see hundreds of ships moving towards Japan's west coast. But that was not what they were seeing. The ocean appears to be boiling and churning up all ocean life in the lines. The room fills with gasps, and a sense of dread can be felt.

Everett, still in a bit of shock, clears his throat. "Find me some news from Japan and translate that to English I want to know what is going on."

Commander, "If I could, I would, but all I can find is the same thing on every mainstream tv station. It is a blue screen with instructions on evacuation centers."

"Okay, John, it is your job to find me what the hell is going on. This is bad, very bad. That means all the groundwater will be toxic within days. The Pacific Ocean will be dead inside a week or two." states Everett

Commander Everett, "I don't think you need to hunt too far; I know that Mika is correct about the ships. Those ships are evacuating all of Japan. It was part of the last resort solution put in place in case the containment failed. I am not sure as to what the data they might have, but I assure you none of them will make it. That water is extremely toxic as well as what goes up must come down. There are hundreds of ships private and what appears to be Naval. Look at all the air traffic as well; those dots are planes, and they are on their way to Japan." Neil points out

"Thanks, Neil, "I am just a bit despondent on all that is going on. Mika, is there no other way to save more lives?" Asked Everett

"I am sorry, Commander, there is not. We talked about this, and we knew it was going to happen. Now from this point on, all we can do is watch. So, I think we need to get busy and set up structure and jobs for everyone." suggests Mika

"Yes, but Mika, I see space everywhere on this ship. We could save more people." Begged Everett

"There is something you don't quite understand. When I located this ship…" Mika is interrupted

"Located?" questions Everett

"There is much of the history of the Earth that is entwined with Mars. Mars has a history that is linked to this ship, and where it came from, they didn't know. But we can talk about that information later right now we need to get all the ships back to us as fast as possible. So, I suggest we speed things up a bit. For now, let me say this when I found out that this ship was not finished. I have been learning for what seems like forever on how to finish it. There is a lot of space, and we could save more possibly a lot more. But what you don't see is the hard facts that I know all too well. We can't feed them, clothe them, and shelter them; there is not enough water for them, and last but not least, the ship physically is not finished. But then we have one other issue that the medical systems also could not cope with all the others. So, we would start to see lives lost until we could reduce to the amount we have now. So, in the end, we would not be saving lives; we would just be prolonging the inevitability of death." Mika answers

The room falls silent as the harsh reality that not even their rescue ship was ready for them.

"I know that was not what you were hoping to hear. I won't sugar-coat the darkness that surrounds us all right now. This ship is older than both of our civilizations. Technology that was withheld in an attempted to avoid what we see on Earth. We thought that Technology was the anchor that dragged us down. It might have been the one thing that could have saved us twice. But I am not a politician; I am an engineer who has been trying to fix a machine that is unfinished and being used." States Mika

"I am not fully convinced that we cannot save more lives. How close is this ship to being finished?" questioned Everett

"If I have to give you a number, I would say about 30% to 40%. But it works and can keep this population-level alive. That is the first goal we must focus on, and I will not jeopardize that for anything. Yes, it is devastating to see millions perish because you could not save all of them." Firmly states Mika

"But you do know that our population on this ship is going to grow, and I need to know if we can handle that? Because if we can't, we need to talk to everyone about not having sex. You put two people in a high-stress environment where they start thinking outside the norm. We are going to see babies." Everett replies

"I did consider that. But with a workforce in this population, we can prioritize what needs to be finished. We have plenty of time to do that before the want rises to a need." Mika says as she points to the main screen that now is showing the full outside of the ship that they are all in.

Gasps amazement fills the lack of sound in the room as the actual size of the ship is revealed. They are showing a cityscape in the center of the massive structure.

"Mika, this ship is huge millions could have been saved." A shocked Everett states

"I know, and I have done this twice. The first time was before my people worked on it before the death of our home. Then I worked on it for years before I noticed that I had to save all of you. I am one person who has skills, but I am only able to do so much. I had so much hope that this time would never come to pass." Mika softly replies

The room falls silent again.

Several hours have passed since the number of people on the ship has been filled. The leadership team has joined with Commander Everett and Mika. We now join the leadership on the bridge as choices are being made for roles and positions based on the talents of the people aboard.

"Do we have the data from our communications with everyone on board?" Asked Everett

"It is coming in slowly. I think we have enough for the engineering team as a lot of them came from the Aircraft carrier. We have a group of pilots who can be trained for flying the ship's support vehicles to Mother," replies John.

"Oh, I hate calling the ship that." Stated Everett

"Well Everett, take the time a change it" replies Mika

"Really?" Says Everett

"We never really named it; we did not see a point to it. The nicknames just stuck as we were building them. I would not be offended if you changed them." Replied Mika

"Well, we will put that on our list to do. Like near the bottom, I think we need to see that everyone's needs are taken care of first. Commented Everett

"John, we will need to create a chain of command to remove the confusion of who is in charge. We will also need to make sure that support for all the leadership is in place. I want to make sure that when a Captain arrives at the bridge, they are in charge, and I will be in charge of them. I will take some time to create a leadership team in the next few hours, but as I look around this room, I will be asking some of you to assist in that. Once I have done this, I would like it sent out to everyone to make sure everyone knows what is going on. But make it look nice to give an introduction and tell people who we are. This is not a democracy; there will be no voting on any decisions being made. We, the leaders, will make choices based on need before we want. Does everyone understand me on this?" Everette finishes

Just as Everett finishes talking to John, he is then approached by another person on the bridge. "Commander, some people in your office would like to meet with you."

"I am kind of busy right now, is it important enough to stop doing what we are doing? Replied Everett

"They seem to think it is, sir."

Everett deep down inside cringes at being called Sir

"Okay, John, please take the time and talk over all the positions with everyone. Give them a quick rundown of what has to be done and then let people volunteer for roles we need to fill. Mika, can you please work with John and the others to do this for me?" Everett says as he gets up from the Commanders chair

"Not a problem Commander. I will get it all done and brief you on the results as well."

"Thanks, John," says Everett

"Very well, we will have to chat about this interruption and when it is okay to do so in the future." States Everett

"I am sorry sir I am new to this kind of thing."

"It is okay, I think we all have a bit of learning time, and we will all need some breathing room in the learning process. We have to remember there is a lot to learn and understand as we move forward as a cohesive group. Let's hurry this up so I can get back to the Bridge as soon as I can. Let's go see what these people want." Replies Everett

Everett leaves the bridge and begins to walk down the hallways towards his office and quarters. As he is getting closer to his office, his children burst out of the quarters, screaming to scare him.

"Oh, you got me, good job, guys. Are you doing okay?" Everett says lovingly

The children explain everything they have seen in such great detail and with such speed. Everett listens with complete attention and to every one of their exciting day so far.

"Well, okay, guys, I will love to hear more about it when I get back, but I still need to do some work, and when I am done, I am all yours. I am so sorry for being so busy. Right now, some people are waiting for me in my office." Everett grabs them and hugs them making sure they know they are loved

"Ahh, dad, not so hard. We know about your meeting we had to leave your office so they could wait in there, replied Gabriel.

Gabriel is one of Everett's younger sons, blessed with very handsome features and confidence to match. Many say he is a very respectful teenager.

"We drew you some pictures in there because the room was boring," said Niamh.

Everett smiled and looked at their shining faces, kissed them on their heads once more, and said: "I will love all of them as much as I love you." Then they head back into their quarters. He sees his oldest daughter and gives her a nod of thanks. He continues his walk down the hall towards his office's entrance. As he enters, he is greeted by ten people.

"Hello all," Everett says

"Hello, Commander," they reply.

Everett says, "We need to make this short and sweet, and to the point, I have much to do to make sure we are all taken care of on this ship. So, what can I do for you?"

"One man speaks up and introduces himself. Commander, I am Chaplin Lieutenant Samuels, and I have been asked to be the spokesperson for the various religious groups on the ship, and we have a few things we would like to ask you."

Everett takes a deep breath and thinks to himself, *"Oh boy, here we go again."*

Everett keeping his composure, "Great, now let's get started, what do you need to ask of me."

"Well, sir, we would like permission to have services for those who have faith requirements."

Everett ponders for a second or two, not wanting to look too eager or restrained. "That will be fine, will you need needing a room for that?"

"Well, sir funny, you might ask that there are several leaders here would like their own spaces for their services."

"Well, Lieutenant, let me make this clear to everyone in the room. If I could give every one of you a room to use, I would never do it. Space is so minimal on this ship, and with that in mind, if I had a spare room, I would fill it with more people from the surface and try to save more lives. As you also know that even on your former ship, you know that space was a premium. So, what I will do is find you a place for your services

once a week. That is the best I can do for you at this time."
Replies Everett

Just then, one of the religious leaders' interrupts, "No, we want sperate spaces; it is wrong to make us share."

Everett looks at the man and says, "Shut up and sit down. You are in no positions to make demands on my ship. I think it is time for a little education. Mika chose me, and I chose Neil and 49 others. Indirectly I chose you, and I chose everyone upon this ship. I take my heavy burden very seriously. In no way are you going to dictate what I am going to do. You are going to get one space; it may not even be a room. In that space, you will be able to use it one day a week, nothing more, is that understood Lieutenant."

"Yes, sir, thank you, sir, we will make do."

In a calmer voice, "Good, what is the next item on your agenda?" replies Everett

In a less confident voice, the Lieutenant begins again, "Well, sir, many here would like to request that I have a seat on the leadership council that runs this ship." As he swallows hard

Everett places his hand on his forehead, gently rubbing the sides. He stops just before speaking and calms himself. "Let me tell you a joke, do you know why some people go bald? Well, there are two main types of baldness the managers and the thinkers. The managers are the ones who are losing their hair right here, and Everett points to where his hair loss is near his forehead. This is because they get a lot of headaches, and so they rub, thinking it will all get better. The thinkers are the ones who lose it at the top of their heads. This from scratching it too much while trying to keep their brains in. Everett points to his thinning hair."

The one woman in the group asks, "Well, what about people like you?"

Everett replies, "Well, it is effortless. I am part of a scarce group of people called leaders. We have the Managers' hair loss from understanding that stupid acts of smart people cause our headaches. Then we have the thinking hair loss from wondering how we can fix their errors. But to top it all off, we have the new location of hair loss. For your information, it is on the sides of my head. This hair loss is where we pull hair out, trying to think of ways not to killed stupid people for stupid choices or questions. Think about that, while I answer your request."

Everett pauses for a few to allow what he has said and to allow him to regain his composure.

"I understand the desire to have a voice on the council to assure that your needs are looked after. But I am going to reject your request and here is why. In less than a hundred days, we are going to find out if Mika was 100% correct, and from what I have seen and heard today, it has already begun. Since she is correct, we are going to see a large number of faith-based issues on the ship. So, I have a question for all of you, do you know how many people we have on this ship?"

A moment of silence begins. It fills the air of the room, making it feel like the dead of night. Everett continues, "I see none of you know, but you want without serving first. In less than five days, you have already failed your god." Everett could tell by the looks on their faces that they did not like what he had just said.

"I have read all of your religious books and know them well. I think you need to go back to the basics of them and follow what they did. Serve, and then when you have done all that, you can serve once more. If there is a need, there will be a structure in place to assist that need if it can be met. But at no time will there ever be a religious voice in the council that runs this ship, is that understood? For your information, there are 150,000 people I am in charge of all of them on this ship. If I could, I would find a way to bring aboard one more soul, and then I would find space for another and so on. But there is not, and I will carry with me the choice I made of fifty people for the rest of my life, and so should you. "Everett stands up, signifying that he is done with the meeting. As he moves his chair away from his desk to turn around, he stops.

Let me now ask you another question. "We are facing a change in our future as a people, so I want to know what are your views are on the LGBT+ communities? Because I assure you some people on this ship identify as such. Please tell me about your views. Allow me to be enlightened by you." Questions Everett

The woman speaks first, "God created every one of us, each with our own set of challenges and blessings. I believe that if God did not want us to be who we are, he would have never created us this way."

"Thank you for your answer," Everett replies.

The Lieutenant replies, "I am here to serve, and I have no right to judge others, that I will leave for God, in the end, that is his job, not mine."

"Thank you, and it is good to hear such wisdom." Replies Everett

An older gentleman stands up and begins to speak, clearing his throat. "Well, it is straightforward; it is a sin. In the bible, it is broken down as such, and therefore I have to treat it as such. Yes, I know that there are a lot of sins in the bible, but I cannot change what is written. What I can change is how I react to that sin. It is God's choice in what he does for that sin, not mine. I am not going to punish, because it is not my right to do so. I love and support that person no matter who they are or who they love. That is all I have to say about that."

"Thank you for your honesty," says Everett.

A few more say their views about the subject, with a few causing more concern about their answers. Everett listens thanking them for all of their input. He notices that two people did not answer his question, so he directly requests that they do so.

The first man stands up and simply says. "With the love that was shown for me, I will show for others. I will only give the service that is needed, and nothing will I ask in return. I believe in God, but not one who is filled with Hate, Anger, Vileness, and Vengeance. My God is filled with love, understanding, and compassion. He walks with all of us no matter who you are."

"Wow, thank you. I hope you have meant every word you just have said. You give me hope for the future. Replies Everett "You sir," Everett, motioning to the last Gentleman.

"What a load of rubbish," the man replies. "All this crap about acceptance. All of it is a sin and needs to be treated as such. God does not accept those who are like that in his presence, and they must be shunned and sent back to Earth to die in the flames that will come."

Just then, Everett raises his hand in a stopping motion. Please do not continue. This is my ship I am in charge of, and I have given every one of you a life jacket to save your lives. Therefore, this is not acceptable on my ship and will not be allowed on my watch.

The Man interrupts, "We must purge the wickedness from those who are on this ship. Let them burn for their sins. I accept only what the bible has written. If you believe otherwise, then you Commander deserves to perish as well."

A short pause of shock enters the room

Everett yells, "MIKA!"

Soon after, Mika walks into the room very calmly and replies, "Yes, Commander."

Mika, I would like this man's fifty brought to this office, and I would like Roe and Al in here as well.

Everett returns to his seat and sits in silence with a straight back. Then lowers his head to his raised hand and begins to rub the sides of his head.

The man continues to rant about the sin of others.

Everett's eyes are closed as he sits back up his hands slowly lowers to meet and cross over the other hand on the desk. Everett begins to speak calmly and softly. But the man's preaching is so loud and excited that it overpowers Everett's voice. Everett tries once more remaining calm. But the man continues to ignore Everett.

Everett finally gets to the point where he has lost his calmness with the man and yells in a booming voice. "Shut Up, sit down, and for once in your life remain this way until I give you the right to speak again; this is my ship. No one will tell me how to run it."

Everett pauses to regain composure

"Let start by saying this I am not perfect, nor will I ever claim to be. I will make mistakes, and I will pay for them in my own time. But at the same time, I hold every one of you to the same level of accountability. Right now, I am waiting for your fifty to arrive because I need to make a judgment, and I can only do it by meeting those who will be directly affected."

Upon saying that the door alert rings and Everett says, "Enter." In steps, his two closest friends. "Please, both of you please come grab a chair and sit near me."

Soon the door alert rings once more, and Mika enters and walks over to Everett and whispers in his ear, "Would you like those people in here?"

"No, thank you, there is not the room for that many in here."

Mika looks at Everett and says "Why don't you come out and meet them in the hall there is only a handful? Ten people at most."

"Mika where are the others?" questions Everett

"They are all he chose." Mika looks concerned after saying that to Everett

"What about the rest of the family's choices" replies Everett

"Well I think that answer is for another day" angrily replies Mika

"Take me to meet them. The rest of you stay in here," commands Everett

"They are his direct family," says showing Everett to the door

After a few minutes, Everett returns to his office with

Mika. He walks over to Roe and Al and stands between them both. It can be seen that both of Everett's friends do not know what is going on; it can be seen by the look of confusion upon their faces.

"Very well, let's get this underway. Right now, I need to make a choice. Sir, what you have said goes against everything I stand for and what I hope for the future of humanity. That type of hate is completely unacceptable for the future. Right now, do you have a defence for your statement? To the response to my question about the LGBT communities aboard this ship? I am giving you a chance to defend what you have said."

"I remain firm on what I have said. You should send those queers back to Earth and let them die with all the other sinners. God will purge the Earth with fire, making her anew." The man replies once more with the same bravado

Everett once again raises his hand once more in a request for the person to stop talking. The room is silent once more.

Everett begins to speak, "I need the following to stay, and the rest of you, please retire to the hallway until I call you back in. Lieutenant, you will be staying for the voice of the accused. My friends, you will be staying for the voice of people. Mika, you will stay as the voice of the mission of humanity, and I will stay as the voice of the accuser. Lieutenant, please go with and speak with the accused and come back to me when you feel you are comfortable with his defence."

The room empties quickly. As the man passes Everett, he states, "You will burn in the fires of hell."

"Okay, everyone, please go." Orders Everett

Soon there are only the four left in the room. Everett takes the time and explains the issue to the two friends. Soon the door alert rings and enters the Lieutenant. "Sir, he has no defence other than that is what God wants."

"Okay, let's make this short and sweet this man stands accused of the charges of not being acceptable to continue with the mission of saving Humanity all those in favour say I...."

"Bring them all back in please Mika," Everett instructs

"Thank you, please understand that upon the ruling of the three, a sentence will be handed down. Mika, how say we three."

Mika begins to speak, "As of the three, and we feel that it is not in the best interest of Humanity to allow you to continue with our mission."

Everett speaks once more. "Unless you have anything else to say in your defence, I will apply judgment."

The man speaks once more, "You will all burn in hell."

Everett stands to face the man and the others "I as a result of this make the following sentence on your choices, sir, will be returned to Earth effective immediately, and two children will replace you from an orphanage." Upon Everett saying that the man is gone. Everett looks to the ten, "Now you need to choose to stay or return."

A woman speaks up, "We are his family, and we will return as well." "No, Auntie, we will not. Auntie, I am gay, both you and Uncle have treated me with such hate and anger that I would rather stay."

The mother replies, "well, you will burn in hell then just like we told you would. You are no son of mine, says the woman."

"I will speak for my other siblings who are too young to

make this choice. You did not want us, but you saw slaves and took us because of that."

Soon, the other two other children agree and refuse as well in support of the Young man.

"Fine, you will all die just like your mother and father you ungrateful brats." Screams the woman

The other four chose to leave with their mother. Five more people disappear for the ship.

"Find me 12 more children, Mika," requests Everett.

Everett looks at the children and offers. "I am a very busy man, but I have space in my quarters for all of you. It is your choice if you wish to stay with my family."

The only woman in the group of ministers speaks up as well. "Children, I don't have any, and I would be honoured if you would like to live with me as well."

The first child who spoke up begins to speak. "I have taken care of all my brothers and sisters. Even when my Aunt and Uncle hated me and used me as an example to them, I am strong, and I can continue to take care of them. We are a family, and we will be strong. I could use a little help here and there, but that is about it."

Everett speaks once more, "Everyone, but Mika and the children are dismissed. Please understand this as you go. I do not want to have to do this ever again. All will be treated equally, or there will be problems with me, and I'll send you back to where you came from."

Everyone has left, and the children and Mika remain.

"Please, sit-down," Everett offers.

Look, you appear to be sixteen years old, is that correct? From your story, I can guess you were thrust into taking care of the children you have missed so much of growing up. I can't fix that, but what I can do is offer you a place in my family. I can't replace your mom and dad. But I can provide you with the freedom to make choices in our family."

The oldest of the three children laugh and say once again, and they are not our mother and father. The other children's heads begin to shake and say, "No way silly, we are all adopted" our mother and father died in a car crash, and they said they came to our rescue. But it has been a nightmare for months."

"Ahh, I can see now how it all fits together," said Everett. "We will talk about you three in a minute. Let me finish talking with your oldest brother and working out something for all of you. Okay, mate, what I want to offer you is just a room and place with people who care. You may have had a family who mistreated you, but my family will never do that. Would you like that?"

The young man begins to cry as tears are rolling down his face.

Everett continues, "Look, I can see that you have been very stressed for a long time. Mika, can you find Jas? Jas, my oldest daughter. When Jas comes, we will get all of our family together to make introductions?"

"Sure, thing Everett" replies Mika. As Mika leaves the room, she turns as she looks at the caring face of Everett as he begins to talk with the children. Mika thinks to herself, *"He looks like my father did when he used to look at me."* Her heart begins to fill with a warmth she has not felt in ages.

"Okay, you three one more thing before everything gets going, let's have another quick chat. Look, I can't replace your mom and dad, but I can offer a home with love and care. Plus, my kids are kind of cool and fun. They will not care, and they would love to have you around. But we need the rest of my family here if this is okay with you."

The oldest boy of the three speaks up, "will we be equals?"

Everett replies bluntly, "Look, and I just sent people back to Earth because of a fight over equality. I treat everyone equally, and I am not about to change my ways because you are coming into our family."

"Well, if that is what you say, then you now have three more kids," says the young man.

"Great," replies Everett.

Soon the door opens, and Jas steps in

"Hi, Jas, can you please get the family in here, and let's take care of introductions. All of the family, please."

The first of the family that runs it is Everett's three little children, followed by his oldest Daughter Jas and her Husband. Introductions are made, and soon more and more of the family begin to fill the room. The five youngest children are then scooped up in a wave of hugs, handshakes, and plans. Everett starts to smile as Jas looks at him with a nod of understanding.

Everett begins to speak, "It has been a tough day. Everyone my quarters for a family dinner tonight, Mika, you're coming as well. But right now, I have a few more things to do."

So, time for all of you to get out and go enjoy yourselves until say six pm tonight?" Everett looks at Jas questioning

Everyone agrees as they leaving the office Everett's youngest son Hezekiah rushes back in and tackles Everett with a big hug.

As the door shuts, Everett is left alone with his thoughts. Hit sits back in his leather chair and begins to cry. Anger begins to fill, and in a fit of Rage, he stands up, grabs his chair, and slams it down rapidity onto the desk. Screaming incoherently and breaking the chair and the desk into several pieces. But his anger is not quenched; a rage has surpassed it. The destruction does not end with the desk and chair. His eyes begin to search the room for more stuff to break. He grabs the next available chair screaming at the top of his lungs. He starts smashing it into the table that rests in the middle of the room. When the chair is unable to provide enough damage before it crumbles, he moves to the next chair. It has taken three chairs before the table gives way to the immense brutality. Other chairs that have not been damaged to this point now become his next targets. One by one, Everett begins to smash them into the walls of the office. The last two chairs remaining are used to destroy each other. Within a few short moments, the office is destroyed, and Everett lays in the aftermath of his rage-filled destruction, sobbing. Soon the door alert rings and in walks his father.

"Wow, son, are you done yet?"

Everett begins to explain his anger over everything that just took place. "Here we are on the verge of the world being destroyed, and yet we have people like that family who can only see their hate for those that are different. This is the reason I feel no pain for some of those who will be left to perish. But then there are the children who have been corrupted by their parents hate that they are not able to speak for themselves."

Everett picks up a chair piece and throws it against a wall.

His father walks over to the food dispenser and orders

Chocolate milk and some doughnuts. "You know I am getting a bit old to sit on the floor, but it looks like I don't have much of a choice move over, so your old man can sit down, and we can talk this out. You did what had to be done," said his dad as they stop to have a drink.

"Oh my, that is just not right; something is just wrong with the flavour of this milk."

Both men try to be as polite as possible as they spit the milk back into their cups.

"I could not even swallow that it was so bad." Both of them shaking their heads as they laugh in disbelief.

"Well son so much for technology" they laugh

"Hope the doughnuts are better," says Everett. He takes the first bite of a doughnut. With a mouth full of what should have been a doughnut, the two men look for something to spit into. With no other choice, resign to the cups of milk. "Nope bad; I wish for toothpaste just to get rid of that taste."

"Dad, I need a hug. This is so much, and it is almost too much."

Everett's dad reaches over his son's shoulder. "Son, through adversity, leaders are made. Heroes are shown for who they are. My son, you are going to face challenges that no one else could ever have faced before. You will be tested, and you will always have my shoulder and my time to talk it out as always. But we need to get the chocolate milk and doughnuts fixed asap."

Then men stop talking, and soon Everett relaxes.

"Who do I talk to about getting this fixed? Stated Everett.

"Leave it to me my son, that will be my goal for tomorrow." They move the Milk and doughnuts to the side. His dad begins to speak once more. "Listen, son; you cannot force people to think the way you do. The pathway to true justice is never an easy one. A man who thinks it is, he is not even close to knowing what it is himself. I have always taught you to mean what you say and say what you mean. By this, men shall know that you are a fair and just person. You are a good man bringing those children into your home and our family. That shows you accept responsibility for your actions. Some men would have just dumped them on someone else to take responsibility. Others will see this and respect you for it. I say to you a good job, and I am proud of you. Now get cleaned up and get out to that bridge make it look like you are hard as nails."

"Dad, that is not me, I would rather lead with my heart than by the iron fist."

"Son, you don't have to be the iron fist; you just have to know when to use it. I will talk to Mika, and we will get this cleaned back up." replies to his dad.

"I don't, but think duct tape will fix it this time." laughs Everett.

His dad replies, "You never know I am pretty good at that."

Just then, Mika walks in, "Oh no, I am in trouble now."

His dad laughs, "I am leaving you to explain this now, good luck son....." Everett's dad leaves the room.

Just as the door shuts, Mika begins to speak. "Wow, I did not think you had this in you. What was your anger about?"

"I am not too sure if you would understand," replied Everett.

"Oh, why is that" asked Mika.

"These feelings, stuff can be a bit complicated. I am sure you have other things you would rather be doing than to try to figure out human emotions."

"Everett! did I ever give you the impression that I was not a living being with those very same emotions." Mika replied?

"Well, to be honest, yes. When we first met, all you did was hide, shock me, and talk to me like I was a child explaining everything. We never saw you, and then when you did expose yourself, and it still was a bit odd that we had never met. There was no real personal touch. So yes, once again, I was and am understandably confused about who you are. Then we have the issue that from your story, you have been on this ship for as long as humans have been upright." replied Everett.

"Oh, so you like a little background on me? It is so it is simple. I had a father and a mother. I even went to an advanced school. We had a house that was a bit bigger than most as my mother was part of the government, and my dad was a builder working for the government as well. I don't want to spend too much time talking about it all. But maybe at another time when it is right."

"Okay, I am sorry, Mika. I did not know, nor did I take the time to ask. I hope you can forgive me."

"Everett, I already have," replied Mika.

"Mika, I am so sorry for what I did to this office. I'll get to cleaning it up right now."

"If you look, everything is already starting to be repaired. It will take a few hours, but I will have it fixed. If you think you are the first to destroy this office in a rage, you are so wrong. Everett, I never told you once this was going to be an easy role. But I will tell you right now. I am very proud of you. Not many would have taken the stand you just made in such a dramatic way. But it was very effective, and the way you chose to take charge and care for the children did not fall short with those who were here. The compassion you have shown with love and understanding. It is for that very reason I chose you for this role. Now we need to go out to the bridge; there have been some changes, and by the time you come back in here, all will be fixed."

They begin stepping over the rubble and head down the hallway. Everett notices that all of his family is on the wall, including the three new members.

"Thank you, Mika, for listening to me. Sometimes I am not sure what I am doing is the right thing to do."

"Everett, you see right there is the sign of a great leader. If you never question your actions, then you cannot grow from them."

"Thank you again. But we are going to have to talk about chocolate milk and doughnuts. Something is wrong with those...."

CHAPTER 7

The Button Pushed

In a small country in a grand office, a short fat man sits in his highbacked leather chair looking at a computer screen as twenty of his Generals try to explain the image he is looking at on the computer. Even though they think they are getting through to him, he recoils back and starts screaming.

"They are coming for me, and they plan to invade my country. I will show them all I will kill them first before they can even reach our shores".

"No, sir, there is something else that is going on we have some reports that something bad is about to happen in Japan."

"You're lying to me," he pulls out a handgun and shoots two of the Generals in the head before they can react.

"HA! I always was a good shot."

He reaches into his top desk drawer and presses a button, despite the objections of the 18 other Generals. But it is to late he has given the order to launch all nuclear missiles.

Back in the United States, the President has locked himself in a room with the Nuclear football.

I am not going without a fight. He opens the briefcase and

then turns the key enters his code and presses the button to launch all nuclear missiles. Screams are heard all over as people in the Whitehouse begin to scramble for shelters.

Without word without warning, generations of fear come to reality. From behind a desk, a small man with a low vision launches headlong into a nuclear war with several countries, and a fat man hiding in a closet presses a button. No questions are asked; others react in kind launching their missiles. The prediction of MAD has begun.

As the person who is walking down the street, the trails from missiles can be seen in the daylight. In other parts of the world, the night is filled with white streaks of light extending upward. In some ways, it can be seen as apocalyptic art with the white stripes contrasting against the skies.

Soon the internet is ablaze; radios are dusted off; people desperate to rush home are stopped by hundreds doing the very same thing. Freeways and highways are filled to the max. Bumper to bumper traffic, there will be no relaxing the chaos has only begun. Missile warnings sound through archaic alert systems, but most know it is entirely in vain. Thirty minutes at most is all they have left if they are lucky. Not even enough time to make it home, and maybe a call if you can get through. The reality of that two-hour commute begins to sink in. Schools close their doors and rush children to safe zones. There will be no safe zones in this madness. Phones no longer able to get through as they are busy with people calling loved ones.

Within 5 minutes, small-minded fools begin looting. But they are not taking things that would make sense like food or water. It is TV's and computers, whatever else they can grab as well: the world leaders and the rich rush to their perspective bunkers. But every scientist knows they are more like coffins with friends. This time a bell line to the surface will not save them once they are buried. They are only prolonging their death.

Planes that are in the air begin to search for airports, fields, highways, and safe places to land. The ones that have not been hit by the launching of missiles. Common sense tells the pilots to get out of the sky. As once the missiles reach land, planes will begin to fall. Parents weep because they cannot make it to their children on time. Churches begin to fill up as prayers are being said to a God who has not answered in a very long time.

Within ten minutes, People start to abandon their cars in hopes of finding safe shelters. It is not time to think of the future, and it is time to think of the here and now. There is no fight reflex, and the only flight reflex is what that counts at the moment. The bomb shelters are all gone from years past now they search for subway tunnels. But they forget if a firestorm is above ground, will suck out all the oxygen from the tunnels. They are all dead; they just don't know it yet.

Fifteen minutes have passed as some missiles have already begun to reach land. The Earth starts to shudder. Blow by blow mother Earth is being attacked. It finally starts to sink in that this is the end of their lives. It wasn't by some mugger, some home invader, some drive-by shooting, or even some crazed person in a mall, or even in a church, and it does not matter who you are, you are going to die. People begin to fall to their knees in a last-ditch attempt to draw upon a God that has not saved them in the past. Most likely will not save them this time. For the lucky few, as those missiles reach their city, they are dead, quickly. But then the firestorm rages as people begin to run from the initial impact. As the firestorm reaches them running, they start to notice their skin is burned off. They cry out in absolute pain as the oxygen is stolen from their lungs as they are engulfed in fire. Soon the firestorm ends, and the radiation begins that combined with the heat. People start to see their skin boil until it falls off of them. Then the muscles, tendons, and cartilage melt away next if they are lucky, they will die before their bones fall to the ground.

Within 20 minutes, in some places, the horizon is dotted with mushroom clouds. Others begin to see the sky is filled with only a blood-red hue. In the night they see only fire in the heavens, the warm glow of impending doom now replaces the darkness. Sea to shining sea begins to boil fish float to the surface and are burned up in the fires.

Within 30 minutes, all missiles have reached landfall. Firestorms and mushroom clouds are now commonplace. Wildfires eat up all vegetation, Polar caps melt, and glaciers no longer fill the mountains. Lakes boil dry. The blue sky begins to fill with the thick black clouds. The breath of humanity starts to fade. The Earth starts to crack open like a swollen fruit. Volcano's that once were dormant burst to life as the dying breath of the Mother Earth screams in pain. Molten lava pours forth from every crack, every volcano and every fissure in the sea. This is the blood of Gaia being spilled. Her blood will stain the hands of Humanity that might survive.

Yet all that remains of Humanity on Earth are the voices on the winds of time.

"Hey, so why don't you and I sit on the couch and read

your favourite book, okay daddy." In the end, the firestorm wipes them from the face of the Earth.

"Hey guys, can I have a hug asks a mother to her children just before they die to the explosion."

"Dear God, I am so sorry for all the wrongs I have ever done in my life," as the flesh of his face begins to fall away as he prays.

"Please, Guard, don't let me die in this cage," "I am sorry, my friend, we are both in this cage together as we die."

"Is this how I am going to die stuck on I-90 in traffic", in his eyes the flash of light is the last thing he sees.

"Where is my God, he was supposed to save me."

Soon the voices stop, and there is nothing left, but the complete and utter destruction of all that humanity has built and was.

We return to Everett's home in that small town. As the backdoor to the house opens and Crystal exits on to the decking. She looks towards the sky, looking at it with a confused look upon her face. Then like a memory of an event has been made clear to her. The memories of the nights before, return like the tide rushing in. Soon she is overcome with the understanding of what she has done and lost. In a fit of rage and anger, she yells at the sky, "Everett, you bastard, I fucking hate you. Give me back my children!" Just as the sky fills with a red hue as the flames of destruction engulf their home. Crystal is now just like so many others, only a memory.

[Dust in the Wind – Kansas]

Humankind is not only dead; so is their god that asked for nothing but gave everything. She is killed by those she gave everything for, her children.

CHAPTER 8

Aftermath

I am sorry, but you needed to see and hear the final moments of Earth. You needed to know why I had to save as many as I could. I did not think it was going to be like that, though. What I saw was the loss of viable ecosystems in the oceans. Then the failure of all the food systems that come from the sea. But at the same time, all water on Earth, both Salt and fresh are linked. It was going to take a few months before all the water was poisoned. I saw the rods opening up a fissure that would create geysers spraying superheated poisoned water into the atmosphere. To say I was shocked that it would be a Nuclear war that would be the end of everything is an understatement. I would have thought leaders were just using them as measuring sticks.

Well, we better return to the ship and see how they are doing. Something tells me they are going to be in for a shock as the reality of their situation takes hold of them. Then they will know that I was sadly correct that it was going to happen.

Everett and Mika walk on to the bridge in smiles and laughter. The faces of horror and shock greet them. It is easy to see the tears as they roll down the faces of those who are watching something. Both Everett and Mika turn around to see the streaks of thousands of missiles that fill the blue skies of Earth.

"Shoot some of them down!" Everett screams.

Mika turns to face Everett and replies, "It is already too late, and we are too far away to do that."

"What about that family we sent down, can we recall that ship."

"I am sorry, Everett it just landed it won't make it back in time."

"Okay, please tell me, did we get some children to replace them?" In a panicked voice, Everett asks.

"The ships won't make it in time."

"Give it a GO!! Cries Everett, please! I beg of you!

"Everett, this is the reality of the pain we all must carry."

In a disheartened voice "Everyone, please go to your families now that is where we all need to be at," says Everett

People start to rush out the doors to their families. Everett walks out of the Bridge to his office and then to his family. He arrives as they are all starring out the windows at the Earth.

Everett stands at a window gathered are his friends and family. They begin to watch the once beautiful blue marble slowly and steadily turn in to a cloud-filled sphere. All the beauty that once was is no longer to be seen. Below the clouds, millions begin to perish. Everett turns to his family. Then opens a communications link to all on the ship.

"Don't turn away; let this burn into your minds. Never forget we allowed all of this at one point in time. We voted in the fools. We agreed to the missiles, the bombs, the wars, and the senseless killings. We agreed to the pollution, the greed, and the want for more never thinking there would be a cost. Below we see the destruction of once was our home. We never thought that it would end up like this, but yet here we are looking at it. So, don't you dare turn away, let your children see it too. Answer their questions with brutal honesty. Where we will go, I do not know. That is something to be talked about later. Our time here is done, we have killed something beautiful."

Everett's words, while stark and cold, serve as a reminder to all who hear his voice. Even I did not know it would end like this. I had thought it might take several times over the years, but there was always someone who backed off. It seems like millions of years have not separated us from the past. We keep making the same mistake over and over. When are we going to learn?

Everett stands next to his children, tears rolling down his face. His three children are locked together with him in a solemn embrace. He reaches out for the three other children to join them. Soon other family members participate in the hug as well. Nothing is said but the sound of tears as they fall to the floor. Soon the embrace ends, and the hour's pass by the room starts to empty. Nothing is said as people leave, there is nothing to say. The stress and soberness of what they have all seen have taken its toll on all of them. Children have fallen asleep in chairs, as of the children hugging their favourite toy bears or one another. One by one, Everett begins to take the children to their rooms. He notices all the tears stained shirts they have on. As he lays the last child down, the oldest sits up and asks why? Why did they do it? He looks at the young man and says, listen, I have no answer why, but maybe a bit of wisdom. He says, listening carefully when good people lead Humanity; Humanity will prosper. When evil men are placed in positions of power, only evil and destruction will follow. Get some rest mate soon; the hard work will begin. Everett pats the young man on his shoulder, then turns and starts to walk out of the room. As he reaches the door, the young man says, thank you for taking care of us. I wish I could do more, says Everett as he walks out of the room.

[Goodbye My Lover – James Blunt]

Everett returns to his office, making sure to leave the door open in case someone cries out. He walks up to the window and places his hand on it. Falls to his knees and cries out. Crystal, why, why did you have to return? You did not have to die, and you could be here with us. There are no more tears to fall, but yet he cries out. Yeah, I knew things were not great, I knew about that guy, and I knew about your plans, but watching you make poor choices that impact the lives of our children broke my heart. Hearing you say that you would rather die, and now you are dead. I feel so empty inside. I would have done anything for you. As he closes his eyes, he falls asleep in the pain of his lost love.

Time marches onward Everett wakes up to feel a small child's head resting upon his lap. There was the youngest of all the children. I don't even know who this child is, much less her personality. Hmm, who placed this blanket on us? I wonder how long I have been sitting here. Okay, let's see if I can remember how to scoot out from under a child's head. I have to start to remember these new kiddos' names. Phew, there we go, she seems to be okay. Everett looks at the Earth to see if it has cleared up. All he can see is clouds. Every so often, he can see flashes of light that highlight an area of the clouds. Well, shit looks like they are still fighting down there.

"I am sorry to tell you, Everett, that is not what is going on. I came to see how you were as I saw you resting with your hand on the window. I went and got you a blanket, but when I returned, the little one was resting with you. I think you have someone who is very thankful to you. She also appears to need loving people around her that are willing to show that love and compassion." replies Mika.

Everett begins to become more alert and looks at his hands as they are strangely sore. He notices that they are stained red up the forearms to his elbows. "Mika, what is on my hands and arms?"

Mika turns and looks at him sadly, takes a deep breath. "what did you think that Humanity could kill a God and escape punishment? Everyone on this ship has or will ask the same question. I hear it time and time again. This is the mark of a god slayer. All of you will have it until the last one dies. As she finishes, she begins to take off her gloves and reveals the same has happened to her. I have worn mine longer than yours. Many in time might see it as a strength, but those of us who were branded will know it by a different name, Shame. Now you shall know it as well."

Everett gets up and runs to the sink and begins to scrub in disbelief to no avail.

"Everett," Mika calls out, "Everett, this time she begs, Everett she cries, listen to me I know you on this ship you are just like us. You thought about how this can be?"

"I worked hard not to do the wrong things.", Everett interrupted

"But you forgot about this or that. You poured out something on the ground that you should not have. Maybe a time here or there drove your vehicle when you could have walked. We all did the same thing. But what is worse is that while yours might just be on your hands and arms, mine has grown because I did not teach you to do better. By saying that, Mika takes off her top, and she is covered halfway down her torso. She dresses quickly to avoid unnecessary stares. You thought I was not flesh and blood, didn't you? Here is your proof now, I am the same as all of you." Replies Mika

"How are you alive?" Everett looks at her confused

"You and I are connected to this universe in ways that you cannot understand. Your people were supposed to do better. Those that once stepped foot on the Earth were to teach you." Mika tries to explain but once again interrupted once more.

"Teach us what!" Yelled Everett.

In doing so, the child on the floor woke up. Seeing her hands began to scream and scream. Soon Everett could hear his other children screaming. He begins to calm the youngest child. He throws the blanket over her arms, so she is unable to see them. Just them from down the hall, his oldest Jas begins to scream, "DAD!!". He scoops up the child and begins to rush down the hall. At the same time, Mika calmly follows him with a look of understanding upon her face.

"The Children are all covered in red on their arms.", Jas states

"What is going on, Dad." Asks his oldest Son

All the children hold up their arms. Everett gently sets the child down and shows his. Mika calmly walks into the room and reveals her arms as well. The little girl removes the blanket. Just then, Everett's father rushes in his arms bare, and he sees the children and his son. More and more of Everett's family rushes in, followed by others.

Mika turns on the com systems and a camera. All the monitors on the ship turn on, and she readies to speak. Mika, in a soft tone, begins to explain. "Gather around please, listen to me, and I will explain why your arms are red." She shows her arms, to show that she is the same as them. "Now listen and listen carefully, you and I are tied to the universe in ways that you cannot easily understand. But I will try to explain some parts and why your hands and arms are now red. Hear me, oh humanity, hear me, oh the children of my people. You are the children of those who are now long dead and gone. We, the elders, were to teach every one of you. But it appears that we have failed you, our children.

Understand this now, where you are walking, I and others have walked before you. So far, since those before you have failed, I shall teach all of you. So, sit and be calm, listen, and learn the truth of who you are from one of the last elders. Every one of you is connected to the other. In ways that genuinely make you responsible for the other person sitting next to you. Each life, each life means more than just humans; it is all living things. Yes, we eat Animals, but we do it in a way that is respectful of the gift that they are to us. The question you keep asking is, why are your arms red? Well, I can only put this blunt. You have now been branded with the red mark of a god killer. You are the same as I, to a point. As she says this, she lifts the bottom of her top to show the midriff of her torso, and it too is now stained. She lowers her top, and I am branded twice. Every planet houses a God."

Just then, a child speaks up and asks, "The moons too?"

Mika bends down to be on the same level as the child. "No little one, they are just big rocks that protect the planet. Sometimes they miss things, and the planet gets hurt, but it heals."

One of the older young men speaks up and asks. "Wait, what about black holes and stars that explode."

Mika stands and faces him to answer. "Everything has a life cycle Birth, Death, and then Renew. It is not easy to be alone; the gods wait their turn to host people like us. Some will host us for what seems like forever, others only a short time. But they know we will be back and they wait for their turn. From what I have learned, we are not the first who have been branded, but we are the first of our kind that I know of who have not learned. That is not your fault; that was my people's fault. So, it appears that I am branded for their error.

A young girl speaks up and asks, "What happens if you turn all red?"

Mika looks at her with a face of fear and dread. "Listen to me, child; I did not feel the pain of the first branding; all I knew was the fear of the color of my skin. Now I understand the pain that is burning into my skin. It is like a raging fire that has yet to stop. But I am still able to walk and talk amid the pain that lies upon my skin. I would fear to feel if it were to happen again."

Mika turns to face the camera to address everyone once more. "I have talked enough about this. The libraries are fully opened now. Heed my warning! Learn the history of your people first before going into mine. You need to teach your children. I will help your teachers to understand my history and they will teach you. It will take time, and right now, all you have is time."

Everett's father speaks up and asks, "Where shall we go? Where is another Earth-like planet?"

Mika replies, "In one of your books, it was said that a man leads his people to walk 40 years in the desert to learn and be forgiven. I do not know how long we will be in the darkness before we learn and are forgiven. Remember this well, the God you killed had a name, and it was Gaia. Never forget what we have done."

Mika then turns and walks out of the room down the hall. The monitors are still on.

Everett stands and begins. "Listen to me, oh remnants of Humanity. We have all learned a horrific lesson today. One we will carry on our skin for all to see. So, let's take a day and dwell upon what was done below and then plan for the future of our people. Parents let your children play. They will learn in time as we learn. But never forget those who died and never forget the name of Gaia."

"Monitor off" Everett commands.

Everett looks at his family "please go eat and rest. Let's keep it simple today. I have a few things that need to be done so I am going to go to my office. Jas and dad, can you take charge for a little bit."

"Yes," they say as they look at each other.

"But don't work too hard son there will be time for that soon enough." Everett's father says

Dad, I wish I could agree with you on that, but I am not sure right now. Everett turns and begins to head towards the office. Questions race through his mind, "*Is this what we have to expect of our future? Are we destined to travel space until our hands are clean? What hope will we have if we do not find dirt below our feet in the future? What will we have left if we can't hear the rush of water or feel the wind on our face? What a loss will we know if we never again see the beauty of flowers bloom or smell their sweet perfume.*" With that thought, he turns and walks into his office. The door shuts his attention is turned to notice Mika lying on the floor.

Everett rushes to her side, she whispers to him, lock and secure the doors. Everett rushes and secures the office, then rushes back to her on the floor. "I'll call medical."

"No," she whispers, "take me to my room."

Just then, a doorway opens one that Everett had not seen before. He then gently scoops up, Mika in his arms, and begins to take her to her room.

She breathes out, saying, "no one must know about this but you."

Everett does not see a bed, but the room does have a strange pod on the side of the room. He walks over to it, and it slides open. As he lowers her into the pod, he notices his shirt. It is covered in the blood that has seeped through hers. The pod shuts and goes dark. Everett looks around and sees that the room is filled with many personal items. He does not linger, and he feels it would not be right to probe. As he begins to walk out, a droid comes to him with a com device.

Commander, "Mika asked me to give this to you," a droid begins to interrupt the chaos, "she needs rest and will be with you later. The pod will take time, but it will save her life."

He looks in the mirror and notices the shirt. "*I need to get this shirt off and get into a new one.*" He messages his father in the other room. "Dad, I need a new shirt, can you please bring me one I have spilled a drink all over me."

"No problem son, I will be there in a sec." his dad replies in a questioning tone

Everett sits at his office desk, trying to understand all that he has seen and trying to figure out what to do next. Just then, beep at the door. "Shit, I forgot it was locked."

He gets up and opens the door forgetting about the floor and his shirt. His dad steps in and quickly turns and locks the door behind him.

"Son here is your shirt, what the hell is going on where is Mika." His dad demands

"She is in a medical pod in the other room." Everett points towards the doorway

"You did not do something stupid, did you?"

What? Everett replies, "what are you talking about, dad? I came in here, and she was lying on the floor hence the blood on the floor."

"Son, please don't play stupid with me; it never worked even when you were a kid, and it will not work now. I know what a person looks like when they are wounded."

"I did not do anything. But I am going to watch the security footage in this room to see what took place."

Soon the both of them are watching Mika walking into the room and collapses as blood starts to show on the floor.

"Dad, I am sorry for being angry, I think she is in bad shape she had a medical pod in her room, and that is what I put her in." She asked us not to talk to anyone about this.

"Son, you are the Commander of this ship and 150,000 people. We don't need to know everything that is going on, but we need a purpose and an understanding. Talk to your leaders and only tell them the basics. Sometimes too much information is just too much. Well, at least you don't need to worry about the floor. The little machines seem to be cleaning that as we speak. I am going to let you get back to work. Don't worry, and I have everything under control out here with the family. I think we need to go for a walk and meet new people today. Plus, checking on how people are doing might help comfort others."

"Okay, dad, thank you for everything and the advice. I will talk to Frank and let him know that I am going to do that."

"Frank to the Commander's office immediately," Everett speaks over the intercom. Frank enters the room and notices the stain on the floor. "Well, back to the bottle, Uncle?"

"Ha, you are funny. Grandpa has suggested that I go for a walk and meet some of the people on this ship."

"Well, Uncle, that sounds like a wonderful idea, and I would like to join you on your walk if you don't mind." Replies Frank

"Great, it is a deal after breakfast."

"Uncle, I think it will give hope and let others know you care about them. There are a lot of people, and I don't think we will get to meet everyone."

"Yeah, I know, but at least they will know who I am. It's that putting a face to the name."

"How is Mika doing?"

"What do you mean, Frank?"

"Mika put me in charge of security as you know, and there is a system that tells me when someone gets hurt. You took care of Mika before I could make it back here in time. I watched you put her in the pod."

"Okay I will call you when I am ready to go for that walk, I am going to take a bit longer of a breakfast with the family. Would you and the family like to join us?"

"Thanks, Uncle but mom, has asked all of us to come for a family breakfast at her and dad's place."

"Well, tell her I said hello."

"You know she does not bite, and it might be good for the two of you to talk over the problems."

"Yeah, you are right, but I am not ready for having to deal with her at this time. Just say I said Hi. It is a good first step towards an olive branch."

"Alright, I will look forward to your call, Uncle."

Days pass as Everett focuses on his children and the family as a whole. Though every night, he sleeps in his office, waiting on news that Mika is better.

CHAPTER 9

Hope

Weeks later, Everett walks into his office. As the door shuts, he rests his back against the wall. "What am I going to do? I feel like I am flying by the seat of my pants. I am sometimes trying to figure out things from what does this button do? This is not always the best way to find something out. At least we can enjoy milk, cookies, and doughnuts. As you know, that is important, ugh."

"People have jobs, and I have met a lot of families and had lunch with people I have never known before. But I am not sure where we are going or what we can do about our future. Then there is that mess of a planet below that we keep looking at in hopes that it will magically fix itself."

"Okay, I have done enough today, and the shifts are changing for the bridge. Nothing has blown up or been reduced to ash. So, I am going to call it a day."

He then turns off the computer he left on. Still noticing the staffing model, he was working at and walked over the where the door was. Surprisingly, sure enough, it opens without having to tell it to open.

"Well, that was a shock I thought I was going for a long shot with that," Everett says out loud.

Everett walks into Mika's room and finds a chair to sit beside Mika's medical pod. He then reaches forward and places his hand upon the top of the pod and begins to speak to her.

"Mika, I am not sure if you can hear me, but I think I speak for all those who have survived. We owe you our lives, and we are so very thankful for the opportunity of your efforts. We will not let you down. We will teach our youth until our dying breaths not to do what we have done. We will guide them to a better future.

Though I think it goes without saying, I need your guidance now more than ever. We are orbiting our dead planet, and we need to find a source of hope and direction. Please come back to me, and I feel so lost without you. If I could take your place, I would. Everett rests his head upon the pod. Why did you choose me, you could pick her over me? Granted, she would not have invited me to this point, and I would be dead instead of her. So many others would have been a better choice than I as well."

"You know I can hear you" Mika's raspy voice can be heard over Everett's commlink.

"Mika!" Everett replies joyfully, then quickly changing it to a more professional manner.

"How are you doing?"

"Well, the bleeding has stopped, and I am healing to the point where it is looking like a tattoo more than a branded mark. I was lucky that you got me to the chamber when you did, I think I would have bled out if it was not for the uniform. Though I am very sore, breathing is painful as my chest expands. Moving my arms, wow feels like a bad sunburn. But all in all, I will survive."

"We just finished a meeting about what we are going to do for the next week or until we have heard from you," Everett replies

"Everett, I know you have been sleeping in the other room."

"What? How could you."

"While this is a medical pod, I still got up and went to the bathroom and got cleaned up. Come on weeks without a shower, yuck! But if you get out of my room, I will get up and come say hi to the kids and your dad."

"My dad? Yeah, what you did not know is that you two are so much alike he came in one time when the door was still opened and read me a chapter of a book. He told me he would be back the next day, and like clockwork, he came in and read another chapter. Though he kept calling me Kiddo."

Everett laughs "I will let you in on a secret about my dad. When you get called Kiddo, you have been put in the good books of people. He respected you even that you are younger than him. Then once you are at that stage of receiving the name Kiddo, he will go out of his way to make sure you knew there is someone who cares about you and your future."

"Okay, thanks for that insight into your father. Now, will you leave my room so I can get dressed."

"What if I don't want to leave?" Joked Everett

"Well, you are going to be sitting there for a while, and I will be in here, hungry!"

"Okay, I'll go make dinner, and you can join us. Sound like a good deal?"

"Yeah, it is a good deal."

Time is magical only to those who can wait for it. Mika sometime later walks out of the office and into Everett's home.

"Knock, knock, can I come in," announcing herself to everyone.

Soon it can be heard all over the house, "Mika!"

All the young girls are commenting on how pretty she looks as she turns the corner into the lounge room where the adults are waiting.

"Well, don't you make an entrance. Look at you making the room that much brighter" states Everett

"It has been a while since I was dressed up. I figured that I should stop hiding behind everything and be honest as everyone else is. We are now all the same for the most part. Plus, it is nice to dress up after all this time." states Mika

Just then, Jas enters the room.

"Wow, Mika, you look amazing I never thought of you this way. Your hair is so beautiful, and I love the dress."

"Oh, thank you, Jas. That means so much coming from you and everyone else."

"So, there is something that you need to know about the men in my family. While they can be charmers, but they are the worst at keeping secrets. They don't even have to say anything. I hope you are feeling better. I watched my Grandfather seeking in every night to read to you. Then I would watch Dad seek into sleep in the office to be by your side. Then Cousin Frank was also keeping an eye on you when no one was looking." Replies Jas

"I did tell your dad to say nothing."

"Oh, he said nothing, but his body language says so much more all the time."

The two women laugh

"Hey, give me a break. I did do as you asked. But it is good to see you up and about. Are you feeling well enough to enjoy a good meal?" asks Everett

"Everett, it will take me time to heal fully. But the way I see it is right now people are still grieving the losses. That means we need to give them time to be ready to move on. Plus, we need to train those that are working on the bridge. But that is work stuff I want to know how you guys are all doing." Replied Mika

"That's right; this is time to enjoy being friends and loved ones. Will one of you kids get your cousin and his family. I am about to put the food on the table." Orders Everett

Soon the foot race begins the boys of the house all rushing out the door and down the hall. Roe and his family enter, followed by Al and his partner. The house begins to fill up with a family of friends. The food is being placed on the table. Enough to fill everyone to the point where some are close to falling asleep while others are close to vomiting.

"Everyone, can I have your attention, please. Here we are a Sunday night dinner friends and family to sit down and welcome Mika back to health. So please everyone, raise your glasses and join with me in a moment of remembrance for those who cannot be here with us. You are not forgotten, and once again we leave this glass for you as we remember you fondly" Everett says kindly

"Is that seat empty for those who cannot join us?" questions Mika

"Yes, it was started by a few people on the ship who asked others to remember those who are gone with an empty seat on special occasions. I refuse to let it be a sad moment where we remember those who have passed. There are good memories, and we must remember them fondly." replies Everett

"I like this have you been doing this every Sunday night?" questions Mika

"Not this many people, but you are healthy, and you mean a lot to everyone here. So, we gather to show you we care about your return to health." continues Everett

The dinner continues with several conversations going on. Children are sharing the magic of the new life in the family with their cousin Frank's new family addition. With the return of Mika, something starts to return to what can be called the new normal. As the night rolls on, people filtering out and children shuffle off to bed. Everett is left with just the core family.

"Everett," his dad speaks up.

"Yes, dad."

"Why don't you and Mika go for a walk, and I will clean this mess up."

"Are you sure, dad? I mean, I am okay with cleaning. You cooked; you know the rule if you cook, you don't have to clean."

"Okay, dad, thanks."

"Mika, would you like to go for a walk to the observation deck?" asks Everett

"That would be lovely."

"Dad, we'll be back later."

"No worries, son, take your time, you two."

"Everett, you know your dad is a wonderful person."

"It took some time for me to see him as an adult and not just my dad. It always seemed like when the chips were down, and he was there for each of us kids. He never asked for anything in return. Sometimes I am not sure why he does it. But I am very thankful for him."

As the two of them continue their walk, they pass other couples in the halls of the ship who are also going for walks. Smiles fill the passers-by. Without a word, the two move closer and continue their conversations about anything but the ship. Soon they reach the observation deck where other couples are as well.

"Would you like to sit over there?" asks Everett

"That would be a great view" replies Mika

The two of them sit down, and just like magnets, they attract each other. Within time an arm is resting on the shoulders of the other as a head rests softly on a shoulder. For what seems a lifetime, they are enjoying the company of each other without words. They are looking into the beauty of space.

"I never knew it looked so beautiful" states Everett

"Nor did I, but the present company might also have something o do with it" Mika replies

The two of them smile at each other they return, looking into space.

"I think we should look at getting you home so you can rest a bit more."

"I think you are correct, Everett it has been a very long day. But it has also been very magical."

The two of them get up from their seat. Mika reaches out

and takes Everett's hand. Nothing is said as they walk back to the quarters. Soon they stop at her door.

"You know I never noticed this door before," states Everett

"Well, it has been here the whole time,"

"Mika, thank you for tonight. I have not enjoyed myself in such a long time. Can we do something else soon?"

"I would like that Everett," says Mika as she leans in to kiss him on his cheek. "Good night."

"Good Night Mika"

Everett stands at her door until it closes.

He returns to his quarters

As he enters his quarters, his dad is waiting

"Hello, son, did you guys enjoy your walk?"

"Yeah, dad, it was so beautiful, almost magical."

"Yeah, I have also sat there for hours enjoying the beauty that I have never seen before."

"I am going to head to bed dad thank you for cleaning up."

"Son before you go. Tonight was good; it was nice to see so many smiles and to feel a sense of hope return. We will need this in the days to come. Do it again with others on the ship. Give others the same hope. They all need it right now."

"Thanks, I will do my best, good night, dad."

Everett heads to bed

As the next morning comes about, Everett is greeted by all his children sitting at the foot of his bed.

"You went for a late-night walk with Mika..."

"Listen up, guys' I never hide anything from you. But this is not right. If Mika comes in for breakfast, do not make a big point of it. I do like her, and I would like just to take my time and see where it goes. As you know, I am still a bit heartbroken with what happened the last time I gave my heart to someone we all got hurt. I cannot have that happen again to any of us. I love all of you, and seeing any of you hurt would break me."

Gabriel interrupts, "Dad, we know what mum was like towards you. You tell me all the time don't judge everyone by one person's actions. Is that what you are doing?"

"Yeah, in a way, I am. I want to protect my heart, and I want to protect all of you. If that means I take this very slow, then that is what I am going to do. Okay, enough about this. How about I make French toast for breakfast?"

"YEAH," kids are all screaming as they rush down the hall.

"*Oh, it is too early for the screams*" "I should have thought that out better," Everett says as he rolls slowly out of bed. "*Is it too early to invite her for breakfast? Okay, keep it slow and let it happen naturally.*"

Everett is cooking for the children with he hears "Knock, Knock, is it safe to come in?" Mika calls out

"You are already in so, yes. You are always welcome to come in. Don't mind the kids running around this is normal chaos in any household." replies Everett

"Okay, well, today we" Mika starts to speak when Everett interrupts

"No, no, no, no, and no at any time when we are sitting down for something to eat, work is always left at the door. We have to have a separation of work and home life. This is part of what we have to do to keep hope alive. So, sit down. I am cooking, and everyone needs a good start to the day. Kids get to the table."

Just then, the door opens, and it is Jas. "Hey guys, nice PJ's dad. Don't you think you should be dressed when you have company?'

"Thanks, kiddo, just for that I am going to retire and get dressed, and you can finish this breakfast."

"Damn I should have kept my mouth shut" replies Jas

"Ha-ha," her husband starts laughing out loud. But his chorus of laughter is met with an apron in his face.

"You have just been assigned dish duty" replies Jas

Mika smiles

"Don't think you can get away easily, as well. Here is your plate eat up." smiles Jas as she hands Mika her plate.

"Okay, kiddo, do I look okay to eat at this table?" Everett asks as he steps into the room.

"Yeah, dad, sit down."

"Thanks, kiddo," as Everett roughs up one of the kid's hair.

After a time sitting with the family at breakfast, "Okay guy's, Jas is now in charge you know the rules" Everett orders

"Dad, I am going to take the kids for a walk to the park today" states Jas

"We have a park on the ship? I think I need to learn more about this ship. I feel a little bit left out."

"How about after work you and I join the kids there, and you can see that side of the ship," Mika says

"Deal sounds like a good plan" replies Everett

Time moves on, and we join the leadership team in Everett's office.

"Team, we need to get underway with the learning on all levels of education. We need to know this ship inside and out.

We need to also bring back a sense of normality with kids going to school." Everett starts off the meeting.

Then we need to make sure all essential staff is trained for actions on the bridge and engineering as I am learning that these are the core areas of this ship. We also need to find all those who know about construction and get those areas of the ship that are not finished underway. From what I have been told is that we have all the supplies we need to do that we just need a workforce." Everett begins the meeting

"Everett, I think those are some fine ideas to start. I think all of you need to know the basics where you came from before Earth. Then we need to find a new planet to call home. Living in space is a temporary solution. I think it took me many years to come to that reality. It was only reinforced last night." Mika states

"Well, I have an idea, plus I am the one who knows the most about what is out there for us. How about we go to Mars? Mika, you said that is where we came from, and maybe we can return and resettle it." comments Neil

Mika stands up, "That is not going to happen. Mars is dead; what lies there is a shell of a planet. No life will survive there, not my people and not your people."

Neil interjects, "Mika, and we have the technology and the ability to bring it back to life."

Mika slams her hand on the table, "Listen to me! There is more than just what the eye can see on that planet. My people killed it, and I watched it die as well as what happened to my people. Going back is a very foolish idea."

The room falls silent at the show of force by Mika

Everett takes back control of the meeting. "Mika, please sit down I can see that going back is stressing to you. We are just looking at our future. We need to see what we can do for our people on this ship. We need to give them hope for a bright future."

"I am sorry, but I know what took place there. I just know it is not safe." Replies Mika

"Mika, it has been a long time, and we sent robots to the planet to test the soils levels came back fine. There was nothing unexpected. Don't you think time could have fixed the planet?" asks John

"John, robots are not alive. Ask yourself this why have all your efforts failed to show life on Mars? I can answer that. The God of Mars is dead, and my people killed him. Look at my hands and look at yours. The curse is real, and with the death of Mars came death to my people." Replied Mika

"Okay, how about this, Mika? You said your people our ancestors came to Mars from somewhere else. Were your people cursed when they founded Mars?" asked Roe

"Not that I have found in any book or was taught in school. But there is a lot of historical information that we saved from my planet" replied Mika

"That is okay, I have an idea" speaks up Graham

"Okay, Graham, well, what is it. Don't keep us waiting." Replies Everett

"Well, uhm, if you would allow me, I know a few of my close friends who know how to dig for information. There are about 20-30 of them, and they would enjoy looking for that information or something that could help us."

"Well, Graham, there is a small problem with that idea Graham. Mika has said that there is a language issue. She had to learn English. So it is safe to say those books are written in her native tongue and not ours." replies Roe

"That is not that big of a problem as one might think Roe. I have a device that will teach them how to speak read and write all the languages of my people" replies Mika

"Okay, here is what I am going to do. Graham, this is your project. But I want weekly reports on how things are going with the research. Mika, I would like you to make that device available for everyone to use so they can learn if they would like to know more about your histories.

Now I am not going to spend the rest of my day talking over stuff. You all have your assignments, and we will gather back here in one week to find out the progress of them. Mika as we discussed can this ship be moved to another location to where the Earth is not the main focal point?" states Everett

"Yes, I can turn the ship, but I am not a pilot, so flying this is not my talent." Replies Mika

"Okay well I want you to teach the bridge how to turn the ship" instructs Everett

Later that day, Everett and Mika are walking around the ship heading towards the Park. As they arrive at the door to the park, Mika takes control of the conversation

"Okay I want you to close your eyes, I am going to blindfold you. I want this to be a surprise for you." Others in the hallway are watching Mika place the blindfold on Everett. "Okay, are you ready?" Mika asks

"Do I get a choice on the matter?" jokingly replies Everett

"No, you don't" Mika giggles

"Mika, people are watching us."

"I am glad they are I am spending time with you, and I want everyone to know."

"Okay?"

"Let's do this" as the door opens

"Oh, wow, where are we?" as Everett removes the blindfold, and seeing the park for the first is shocked to view it.

"You are in the central part of the ship where a park was built. From what I can find out has been this was the main focal point of the ship, and everything you know about this ship was built around this park. I am going to take you to see the lady in the park. I was in complete shock once I found this part of the ship. Something is significant about this part of the park."

"Mika, is all of this real? The Birds, Bees, and flowers?"

"From what I have discovered about this ship is that everything you see here is authentic. Wait until you see the fish in the lake."

Soon the two of them walk over a small hill to see a lake with a giant statue of a woman standing in the center of it pouring water into the lake from a vase.

"Who is that?" asks Everett

"I don't know. I only found this park about ten years ago."

"Okay, Mika, let us sit down here. I have to say a few things, and some of them might be hard to hear and might be even harder to answer. You keep talking in years and timelines. That makes you sound very old, but you don't look a day over 20. Why?"

"Everett, I don't know why I have not aged. It has been something I have been trying to find out. I am hoping that

the people that Graham is putting together can find out why."
Mika says seriously

"It is okay, Mika, you are a wonderful person. Over that
short time, we have known each other you and I would like to
keep getting to know each other outside of the command of
this ship if that is okay with you?"

"That would be wonderful, but I don't know much about
dating. I have never done that. All I have ever done is pour myself into this ship and trying to save lives." Replied Mika

"Well, it has been over 20 years since I dated anyone as well.
How about we continue to take our time as we have been."

"That sounds wonderful."

"Hey Mika, is that my dad and all those kids swimming in
the lake?"

"Yeah, I think it is. It is Bill, look at all your kids having so
much fun." Replies Mika

"My dad hates swimming even more than he does being in
the water."

"Should we head down and say hi to them," asks Mika

"No, they will be fine plus I think they know we are watching them," replied Everett

"Isn't that the running towards us now?" Mika points out.

"Yup, there goes the peace," laughs Everett

"Hush Everett, they are so wonderful, you are horrible,"
Mika says, giggling "We will have time for us later; let's just let
them enjoy life. While we watch, it is just so wonderful."

Everett just sits in silence, looking at Mika and the kids.
Everett thinks to himself, *"Am I taking this to fast? It has been
so long since I have felt like this towards anyone. There is just
something so wonderful going on between the two of us."*

Weeks move on, and so do the lives of those on the ship. We join Mika and Everett sitting after dinner alone, looking out into space.

"Mika, I am going to break my number one rule, and that is no work at home. But I need to talk with you about a choice I have to make. I need to know how you feel about what I have to say."

"My past lies in Mars and its sands. I have been hoping we can gather some information from the library and avoid going back there. But it appears Graham and his team have found that there is some information that was purposely left behind that belongs to our ancestors. But I know the dangers that lie there, and I am not so sure it is the wisest of choices." Mika replies as tears roll down her face.

"I am sorry for asking. It just seems like we are running out of answers. If we look at it, we are left with so many questions that only going back might be the only way we can find the truth."

"This ship left before the full destruction of all living life. They were trying to build more ships to join us and to leave. But from my records, I cannot see if they were successful. In some ways, I would like to know why."

"Well, reluctantly, I think you are going to get your chance to find out why," replies Everett. They move closer, just enjoying the time together.

As another month passes by, we join Everett and the family at dinner once again.

As the dinner is laid out on the table, Everett takes a deep smell, looks at his family, and says, "this is nice."

He looks down the table to see the whole family. "Pardon me as I stand to talk for a second,"

Clearing his throat, "Listen, I know we have all looked at what went on down below, and some of us might be going through a moment of faith issues. But I want you to know that if a planet is a God. Someone is still looking after us. I don't know who and don't know what they want or what is going to happen to us. But I do know this much. We need to take the time and give thanks that we are alive and that we are safe. Let's enjoy this wonderful meal that Jas and others have created.

He sits back down and starts to dish up the food to the children before himself. He turns to the youngest, facing her, and begins to talk to her. Jokingly "Now I know you're new to our family and I don't even know your name and I am so very sorry. But I won't forget it from this point on."

She looks right at him with a beautiful little smile and replies back, "You silly, I am Connie, and I am 4 and 2 months, and I am not an accident."

"No one is ever an accident, surprises yes but wonderful ones at that," Everett replies.

Once again, a soft smile appears on his youngest daughter's face.

"So, can I call you dad?" the child asks

Everett looks at Connie and says, "you know what, little one. You can call me anything you feel comfortable with is that okay with you?

She looks up at him and says, "I know you are not my dad, but I want to call you dad is that okay?"

"Yes, little one, it is okay. I will do my best to be here for you when you need me. I hope your mum and dad will rest well, knowing you are loved and cared for as part of our family."

The little girl leans in and whispers, "does that include Mika as well?"

Everett leans over and says, "That is for Mika to choose, but between you and me, I think she enjoys being part of our family."

"I think so too" replies Connie

Next, Everett turns to Samara, who is looking shyly down. "Samara, you know I don't even know how old you are or even your birthday. Could you please tell me how old you are?"

"Well, I am ten," she replies softly.

"Well, ten is a very special age," replies Everett.

Samara lifts her head and looks at Everett and begins to speak. "I don't think I have had the chance to say Thank you for having us join your family" Samara starts to cry.

Everett sets his fork down and walks over to her and hugs her. "Well, you are more than welcome. If you ever need to talk just remember this much, I always have time for you just like everyone else."

Jas speaks up, "Even when he is busy, he'll make time for you. He always did for me."

"I promise," says Everett. When he is sure she has regained some composure, he returns to his seat and dinner.

He looks at Christopher, "so how are things going in your training with the engineering department?"

"Yes, Sir, I am enjoying it."

"Okay, kiddos, we are at the dinner table, and I am not a commanding officer. Please drop the sir line," asks Everett

"So everyone knows Christopher wants to be part of the Engineering team. I received good news today that he has been promoted to his level two apprenticeship."

The family as a whole begins to congratulate him on his promotion. A smile starts to erase the look of uncertainty that rested upon his face ever since the moment he spoke up for himself and his younger sisters.

"Christopher, I like your smile you need to do it more often, ok?" requests Mika

"I am sorry it has been a long time since the three of us have had anything real to smile about," replied Christopher.

"Well, being a part of a family has its ups and downs. But we try hard to make more ups than downs," stated Everett.

As the dinner progressed, he made sure to talk to each child and adult at the table to see how they were doing. He was surprised to see his son-in-law's family joining them he included them in the questions as well. After dinner, someone broke out a guitar, and they all sat around singing songs most of them knew. Soon the music is being turned on in the house. People are relaxing and enjoying each other's company. Soon a favourite song of Everett begins to play.

Just like that, he jumps to his feet. Grabbing one of his daughter Niamh and they begin to dance around being silly.

[Rock Lobster – The B52's]

A few songs later, everyone is enjoying dancing around the lounge. Though as it gets late, children start heading to bed, and before too long, Everett is alone with his thoughts.

The next day after lunch, he waits for Mika and makes sure

all the children are ready to go for a walk. Soon Mika joins them, and they start to head out of their quarters. But just as the door opens, he is greeted by a mountain of a man.

"Hello, Commander," in a deep Russian voice.

Everett begins to start to look up and up, before being greeted by a smiling face. "Do you always smile when people realize how tall you are?" asks Everett?

"Yes, sir, I find it funny."

"Okay, first things first, who are you, and how can I help you?"

"Well, Commander, I have been assigned to be your family's bodyguard by the master at arms."

"More changes that I did not authorize," Everett says in frustration

"Do you wish me to stop, sir?"

"No, he does not" Mika speaks up 'Everett I put Frank in charge of security on this ship, and with 150,000 people, not everyone is going to always like the choices you are going to make. So, if Frank says you get a bodyguard, then you can deal with it."

"Okay, guess I have been told. But let us get some ground rules out, and you will follow them. I will accept you are walking with us but not in front of or behind me with me. When dinner is served, you will join us as part of the family. I like to go for another walk after dinner to meet new people and see more of the ship. This is the weekend, and the children wanted to show me a new section that found and was finished."

"Now, my big friend, I did not get your name."

"How about you just call me Yuri that is short for my real

name and I don't mind it instead of people beating the hell out of my birth name."

"Great, Yuri, it is." Yuri stands at 7' 1" with a broad physique. A very chiselled chin with short tight brown hair and light blue eyes that pierce into you as he looks at you.

"Well, my friend, we are going to spend some time getting to know each other at some point. One day I would love to know your full name and if you take the time to teach me how to say it correctly. I will respect you by saying it from that day forward correctly."

Yuri just looks at him and smiles.

Later that same day, just as Everett tucks all the children into their beds. He walks back into the lounge room to relax.

"Son, would you like a drink to help you take the weight off your feet?"

"Oh, high dad, yes, please a lemon and lime soda in a full glass of ice; it has been a very long day."

"Well, I'll see what I can do, Jas taught me a few tricks here and there with the food machine."

After a few minutes, "Hey Dad, how are you going?" asks Everett.

"Oh, don't you worry, I have this all under control."

A few more minutes pass, and his dad walks up to him, "Here, you go, son. Uhm, dad Sprite is not brown."

"Yeah, I know I messed it up a few times and I just gave up. Then resigned to just making you a Coke. I have that down pat."

"Well, a Coke is just as good" he takes a drink and spits it back in the glass. "Dad, this is not Coke. I am not sure what it is, but it is not Coke. But thank you for trying I am going back to the water."

"Thanks, I needed a lab rat to see if I was on the right trail of it."

"Funny dad, that was a good one. Though please, next time, give me a heads up on your testing. I might be able to sip it and give you some insight into a few changes. But now my taste buds are in shock."

"Okay, I will take that on board."

"Thank you, dad, for trying, though."

"Hey, what did you want to talk about earlier?"

"Well, son, I was listening to you talk to Mika, and I heard the tone in your voice, and it reminded me of the way you used to talk to the children's mum. I know it has been a long time since you and their mum had that connection of caring. Just take it slow, you lost their mum, and I know that has to be hard. Just be smart; there are more hearts than yours this time."

"I know dad, and some things have a way of working themselves out in some way in the future. Well, I did make my first mistake with her." Replied Everett

"Oh yeah, what did you do," asked his father?

"I fell head over heels for her to the point that it is almost painful to take it slow. I just want to be around her and talk with her. Do you know we have not even kissed?"

"Well, son, it is a strange feeling when you come to terms with your attraction to someone. Though between you and me, I have enjoyed seeing the two of you care for the children the way you do. In ways, it warms my heart to know that they are cared for."

"But dad, I am not sure about what I am doing. The way things ended with the kid's mum has left some scars on me."

"Well, son, I might be old, but I do have a lot of wisdom from a lot of living. I watched her too, and she cares for you in a way that is very different from the kid's mum did."

"I don't know why dad, I am no one special. Hey Son, when are you going to get it through your thick head. You are special, you're my kid, and I know your heart sometimes better than you do. I see you with all your children, and I know all I need to know about you. How many parents would invite others into their family and treat them the same as everyone else? Not many can do that, but those three kids feel loved and cared for because of you. That is my son, the true meaning of being a great parent. That makes you special, and that is what Mika sees as well."

"I, I, just don't know some times dad, I want all the best for all of us. I am just not sure how I am going to do it."

Soon a silence falls, and the two men just stare into space."

"Son, listen to your heart this time. Don't waste time second-guessing when you know that she wants to be with you. It has been near six months if the time is right, and the person is right, don't let the time fly by."

The men return to looking into space

"Hey, dad."

"Yes, son. Has it crossed your mind about what we could have done better down there? Well, son, I'll be honest. There were times when we were on the farm, and I sent you to pour out the oil on the gravel. That was wrong; I knew it was, but I knew it would help the gravel bond. Remember when we had that old trash barrel, well, we burned everything and anything. We did not think it was causing harm. Then I did not know every time I sprayed the round away, and I was killing the planet. I was not the only farmer doing it, so you stack all that poison, and it might have been more than a scratch to Gaia. When I was in Vietnam, we sprayed agent orange to kill off the undergrowth. Looking back now, I can see what we have done and the damage we did without thinking. So, in a simple review of your question, I have looked at it. I know the shame that this brand on my body. The meaning of it weighs on my heart to see, and I could have stopped my actions so many times over the years."

The two men return to looking at the planets and the moon below. Soon Everett's dad stands up, gives a big stretch, and says, "Well, I am going to head off to bed. You look like you need to try and get some sleep as well." Okay, I will do, dad. I think I just need some me-time. Buy just sitting here looking."

"Okay, goodnight, son."

"Goodnight, dad."

"Oh, I could use some music to enjoy and relax. I'll head down to the office and just play some music as Everett walks into the office and lays down on the couch. Everett calls out to ships AI can you play some music for me. What would you like, Commander? How about some old Motown music?

[Uptight – Stevie Wonder]

Soon Everett is up dancing with his eyes are closed. He did not notice that he was being watched from Mika's open office door. The music then turns to,

[Sexual Healing – Marvin Gaye]

Still, with his eyes closed, he begins to start singing and

dancing to the music. Still enjoying the view, Mika continues to watch this incredible show.

[Let's get it on – Marvin Gaye]

As Everett is dancing slowly with his hands holding someone who is not there. Mika matches his steps and joins him dancing as he opens his eye, feeling the warmth of her body next to his.

She whispers, "Don't stop; this is wonderful."

[Something's got a hold on me – Etta James]

Soon the two of them fall to the floor in a heap of laughter and smiles.

"Okay, how long were you watching me?"

"Just long enough to join in" Mika replies

"Mika, I…"

"Stop, don't say anything. I don't need you to I have been feeling the same about you. Every time we are even in the same room, I know that I have fallen in love with you. I want to be with you all the time. Sharing your life with the children. I want…"

Everett leans in, and they kiss for the first time.

"Promise me Everett, promise me that you will never stop dancing with me and singing to me."

"Okay, deal"

The two of them lean up against the couch as Everett continues to sing to Mika.

"Shall we get up and dance some more?" asks Mika

With no more words, they are back to dancing

[You really got a hold on me – Smokie Robbinson & The Miracles]

Somewhere in the night, he is awakened to the heavy feeling on his chest. He opens his eyes slowly to see the little Connie has joined him, once again and someone placed a blanket on them. He closes his eyes and drifts back to sleep. He is woken up by the smell of Bacon and Eggs. As he opens his eye, the little person has left, and he can hear giggle coming from the hallway. He slowly peaks out to see all of the kids cooking breakfast and setting the table. *"There is only one word for that, Beautiful."*

He starts the shower and gets cleaned up. As he begins to enjoy the shower, he thinks to himself, *"I must be one of the luckiest people. Despite all that has happened, my children are adjusting. Those sounds of the children's laughter are the best medicine."* As he finishes the shower and gets dressed, *"I guess I better get the day started."*

As he walks out into the dining room, he can see all the kids waiting.

"Wow, guys, look amazing who taught you how to make this? Then on top of it, you are all dressed."

"Mika did dad duh...." Hezekiah replied

Just then, Mika walked out of the kitchen with some toast and set it on the table. "Someone better go get grandpa and Jas, Lane, and the others suggested Mika."

"You know I would like it just to be us. Is that okay with you?" kindly asks Everett as he smiles at Mika

"That is a wonderful idea" Mika smiles as she replies to Everett

CHAPTER 10

Lessons Learned

"Well, kids' time to get off to school would you like me to walk you to it?" asks Everett giving a cheesy smile

"Dad, I am 4, and I can do it on my own," orders Connie

"Dad," Gabriel speaks up, "We will be fine getting there, plus the young ones are going to take Yuri with then today as it is showing and tell."

Yuri looks at Everett with a look of Help. But Everett, with his wisdom and skills in leadership, just smiles back. Then gives Gabriel gives a sly little wink to let him know he has it in control.

"Okay, wow, you guys are so smart, I'll leave it in your hands. Gabriel and Christopher, you're headed to training today?"

"Yes, we are kind of excited there were only so many chosen from each class," Christopher replies

"Yeah, dad, it is going to be great. But I am a little nervous about it all," replies Gabriel

Everett stands up and walks around the table, kissing the younger ones on the head, with a pat on the back for Christopher and Gabriel.

Talking to the two young men, "You both know nerves are a good thing; it just reminds you to do your best, and all things will work themselves out. You guys have a great day, and I will see you around dinner time, or if I can break away sooner."

Just then, Jas peeks her head around the corner and says, okay, you guys ready for school?

"Jassy" yells Niamh as she rushes over to her sister, followed by Connie, and Samara also gets up and rushes over to her for a hug.

"Yuri, I take it that you will be joining me when you are done with the show and tell?" Everett smiles again, knowing he has just gotten out of the "Hey look this is my dad the Commander" bit.

"Jas why are you dressed like a teacher?" asks Everett

"Well, it might come as a bit of a surprise, but I am now one of the Math teachers. I think you played a part in getting me that role."

"Who me, I had nothing to do with it. But wow, I am very proud of you, but I am not surprised. You have always been a smart cookie." "Thanks, dad."

"Okay," Everett looks at his dad, "You're not getting off the hook."

"See ya kids," says Everett's dad as the kids are leaving.

"Well, dad?" Asks Everett.

"What I don't know what you are talking about."

"Sure you don't," Everett says to the Photo of the kids and Mika

"Okay, I might have helped the kids with that one" his dad smiles sheepishly

"So, what are you going to be doing today?"

"If you must poke your nose in. I am going to be working on the Eco deck."

"Eco deck?"

"Yes, son, that is where we are making a stage in the park for people to enjoy Music."

"Okay, I will make my way down there when I have a chance."

"Well, I am done and heading off to my office. See you later, dad."

"Son, not everyone eats like you."

"Okay, your right. We will talk later."

Everett heads down to the office. Sitting down and is about to think about what do I need to do first when he notices his calendar is open, and his first meeting is with the leadership team. After about three hours of working, Everett thinks to himself, *"Time for a break"* Oh well, that team meeting is in 25 minutes. Soon Yuri walks in. *"There goes, Lunch."*

"Commander, you wanted to see me."

"Okay, this is my schedule for the upcoming week, and since you have to be with me. I am going to put you to work because I don't buy into this whole line of crap that I need a bodyguard."

"Well, sir, that is where I know you are incorrect. I have worked for people just like you in positions just like yours. You see, I am more than just the hired muscle. I am an extra set of ears and eyes. I see things that most people don't pay attention to around them. I am always listening to everyone around me because people forget I am around. That is the privilege of being me. They slip up from time to time, and I hear them, and then I act upon the information I get." Replied Yuri

"So, what you are saying is that you work as a sort of spy for me?"

"No, sir, I am not a spy. I am, however, an agent of opportunity. If I know or hear something that is not being told to you, I am going to inform you so that you can make the best choice possible. That has added benefit is what having me your back all the time."

"But who told you to do this?"

"Well, sir, since you are Commander, you cannot do everything. From what I know, Mika was looking at all the files of people on the ship and what our skills were, and she found me. When I was asked what I did, I felt it was better, to be honest, and say what I used to work."

"Well, I do like blunt honesty when I am talking with people," replied Everett

"Sir, as I am sure you are more than well aware of people that were in power on Earth needed people like me who were there for them and not anyone else. The way I see it, sir, is I owe my life to you and Mika, saving my family. As a result, I will make sure you are always protected and helped out where I can."

Mika walks into the office in mid-conversation

"look, I am going to be honest with you. I don't want hired muscle around my kids. Mika is that is what you were thinking is a good idea. We have to talk before we do things like this.

"Sir, once again, I am not hired muscle. I will not fight your fights for you, but I will protect you from those who might not see eye to eye with you and wish you or your family harm. The Captain on the bridge has his man at arms. You have me.

Mika interrupts, "Everett, I love you and the children. We are about to go on a journey that many might not agree with your choices. We must always be alert to the reality of that. As you and I are getting closer, we need to look out for the others, and that is why I asked Frank to suggest someone. He came up with Yuri, and I am putting my foot down if that is okay with you."

"Shit," Everett gets up and walks into his quarters, not saying anything else.

"Uhm what just happened there?" asks Yuri

"Don't worry about it, Yuri," replies Mika. "Just continue doing what we talked about when it comes to him and the children."

"Yes, Ma'am I will do as instructed," Yuri replies and leaves the office

After some time, Mika goes to find Everett. Soon finds him in his quarters listening to music.

"Everett?" Mika touches him on his shoulder

"Mika, I am so stressed that I don't know what I am doing and all this just seems so much" replied Everett

"Everett, you have a great team of people by your side, so let us just take it one day at a time. I chose you because of who you are. I allowed myself to fall in love with you for the same reasons. We can do it together as a team."

Soon another leadership meeting,

"Commander, sir."

"Yes Graham"

"I think my team has found proof we need to head back to Mars. In several texts, there are clues to a vault of information that we have not found in anything we have from Mars."

"Okay so do we have the ability to fly this ship now?" asks Everett

"Yes, sir we are completely ready and flying towards Mars will take about six months and give us plenty of time to know more about handling the ship instead of simulators" replied Liam

"So, let us get that underway at the end of the meeting. Who is the Captain on shift at the end of this meeting?" asked Everett

"I am" replied Roe

As the meeting drags on, Mika begins to drift away in memory of the past.

"Mika, honey you should go home and get some sleep you have been here three days solid working on the design of the ship."

"I can't rest until I solve the problem of how to finish more of the structures to house more people. How am I going to save more? Dad, if we cannot get the supplies up there in time and work going? But the government is not helping me."

"The weight of those supplies is too heavy for the size of the ships we have down here, Mika."

"Dad, the design is solid as far as the technology they had back then. We need to follow what they started and finish it before it is too late."

"Mika, you are just going to have to build them up there. We will keep sending you supplies."

"Dad, I need more workers, but the government is not clear-

ing any more workers for this project. I have a bunch of children who are not skilled enough to do what needs to be done and a handful of adults who are taking care of those kids.

"The droids can only do so much, and I am only one engineer for this ship, whereas it should be about fifty or more. I don't know what I am going to do, but the time is running out."

"Mika, I will get into trouble for telling you this. But the Government has been building a ship down here to get people up to you. But even then, that ship will not save everyone. You are going to have to come to terms that you will not be able to save everyone."

"Let me guess it is for the government to save their asses from dying."

"Now, Mika, you know that is not true. Those who are not infected are going to be sent up to your ship when this one is ready. But until then, we will use the cargo ships to send you all of the supplies we can."

"What am I going to do, dad? I can't let countless people die. I just can't."

"Listen, my love, and there is never going to be a way to save everyone the longer we stay down here trying to solve this problem, the better the chance is for you and the others. So, get some sleep, and we will look at it in the morning."

"Okay, I guess you're right, dad."

"I love you, my girl, with all my heart."

"I love you too, dad."

"Mika, Mika, are you there?" Everett waves his hand in front of her face. "Mika, hello!!!"

Soon Mika snaps out of her daydream and is sitting in the

room with all the leaders looking at her. Mika smiles at all of them.

"I am so sorry I was lost in a memory of the past. Okay, I heard that we need to head back to Mars to search for some vault. Then I got lost in a memory."

"It is okay, Mika; we have closed the meeting, and I will fill you in. Are you feeling okay, it must be a bit of stress hearing us talking about going back to Mars," replied Everett?

"Thank you for asking I have never felt so scared about what we might find," replied Mika

Soon the two of them are alone in the office

"Wow, Mika, that must have been some memory. I had a hard time trying to snap you out of it" commented Everett

Mika begins to fill him on it

"Well, what happened were more saved? Were your parents able to join you?" Everett asks, hoping that more were saved.

Mika begins to recount her memories of what happened after she finished the call with her dad.

"I did as my dad instructed, I headed off for bed after turning everything off. Then I woke up and there was no one on the ship. I walked around and around, trying to find someone. But I was alone, and the portal rooms were already on the surface. So I wanted to see where they were, and one was in a storage area with armed guards as far as I could see. Then I saw the land covered the one your home would later be built upon; you know the one you sort of found. But it was underground, and I knew it was better to leave it alone. So I sat here over the years watching the Earth change. I saw your world wars and all of the changes some were good and some bad. I spent a few years feeling sorry for myself. But I chose to keep working on the ship in case someday someone might find me. I have never really worried about being alone on this ship. It sometimes talks to me with its noises. I read a lot and sent down a few probes to scan books I wanted to read. I also had to learn how to understand major languages."

"You were alone up here all this time? Did I hear you right?" asked Everett

"Yes, and when you built your home on top of the portal, I just watched your family. I know it sounds weird, and it was like watching a story unfold. In a way, it was uniquely magical as I got to know everyone."

"Mika, it is a bit creepy, but hey, who am I to judge you have been stuck up here alone. So, watching my family might have been interesting."

"I can see your point" replied Mika

"Seriously, did you watch everything?" Everett asked with a serious look on his face

"No eighteen years of just watching your family would be over the top. I would check in from time to time," replied Mika

"Oh thank goodness" commented Everett

Mika laughs

"So why don't you know what happened to you? Why did they not take you to Earth with the others?" Asked Everett

"I don't know what I do know is someone messed with my sleeping-pod, and I just kept sleeping."

"Kind of like sleeping beauty," replied Everett as he smiled "So how did you wake up then?"

"I am not sure, but I think the sleeping pod had an error, and it woke me up. It seems it was that simple" replied Mika

"Okay, let me catch you up to speed on the meeting. We have set in a course for Mars we think it will take us about six months to get there as we are taking our time and learning how to fly this ship as we go."

"Please tell me we know how to stop?" asked Mika

"Ah yeah, I made sure of that as well. I am also placing a lot of trust in my Captains. I am sure we are safe as we are taking it very slowly." replied Everett

"Since this was first brought up between the two of us. I have thought that if we head back to Mars. We should land and make our way to my home city. Then to the governmental vaults. There is a command center, as well. That command center should have some more information about where the backup ship left to go. If we go to those locations, I think it will be our best bet to look at our next course of action." Mika comments

"Mika, one of the Captains, questioned. You told us that Mars was not our first planet, what was the reason we left the other one?"

"Everett, I started hearing rumours about the home we had before. My dad would talk about this ship. But they could never find it. So I started looking for it. I watched the heavens for years, making countless notes. Then I found it, the government was quick to act, and they launched a ship into space to see if I was right. Next thing I know, our family was part of the government, and I was placed in an advanced schooling system. I heard once we may have outgrown where we were living, so this ship left to find a new home. That group colonized Mars. But there is a problem with that idea. This ship was never finished, and it was designed to hold ten times more than what we have on it now. So, the stories just don't add up."

"Okay, is there anything else you can remember?"

"Well, the more I thought about it all, the more I kept coming up with the same question. Why hide? Why would the government lock away all the history of this ship if we had flown to Mars to expand? When I first walked into the Library, there was nothing, not one single book. It does not make sense. But the more and more I had searched for the information on those early star travellers. I was blocked at every attempt but the government. At one time, it took my parents' influence to keep me out of jail. I was never allowed back on the surface of Mars. They said I was too valuable to send back down. I was only able to find the blueprints and what was still needing to be finished. There were many places I was not allowed to go even on this ship." Mika replied

"Okay so do you know where this vault might be in the government area that is holding all the information we are lacking?" ask Everett

"It might be the government building at the city center; it is only the most logical place I can think of."

"Thank you, my love" Everett replies

"Everett did you just slip up and call me your love?" asked Mika

"Yeah, I noticed I did just as it came out. I hope you don't mind it was just so natural" Everett's face fills with a blush as he replies

Mika leans in and kisses Everett

CHAPTER 11

The Walk

It is an early Saturday morning. We join Mika in her room.

Well, I wonder if it is too early to go and wake up Everett. I think this is a day where uniforms can be forgotten about, and I can dress up. She searches and searches for just the right outfit. She stands next to a mirror and smiles what am I doing. Am I taking this too far too fast, I must be crazy? No, this is not the time for self-doubting I will take the risk. She looks once more in the mirror. Yeah, this is just right a lovely yet simple floral summer dress, and some simple heals.

She walks out of her room and into the office. Talking to herself, "Can I do this? Can I take charge of this relationship?" She does not notice that she is not alone in the office.

Bill looks at her and surprises her. "Yes, you can do it, kiddo."

"Oh, crap, Bill, I did not know you were in here."

"I wanted a place to read without the kids running in and demanding my time. I must say you are very stunning today, Mika."

"Thank you, Bill, I just don't want to wait anymore."

"He is not up yet, so you have a few choices. You could

wake him up, and he might be floored. You could wait with all the kids telling you how wonderful you look. Or you could do something magical and unusual and get a few flowers and wake him up."

"Flowers?" asked Mika.

"Yes, it is a bit different, but I know my son, and I know how he will react. You might get him to blush. He is cute a cute kid when he does."

"Right flowers, okay, then what kinds of flowers?"

"Just get him some and keep it simple."

Mika turns and starts to walk out of the office.

Bill speaks up once more, "You do look very lovely."

She stops for a second, "Thank you." She continues to walk out into the hallway.

As the door shuts, Bill says to himself. "*I know, honey, I am playing cupid. But Everett and these kids need a complete family, and the two of them will do a great job. I know it has only been a few months since he lost Crystal, but that does not matter anymore. You cannot stop what the heart wants.*"

Mika starts to walk down the hall. Her heels can be heard, and heads pop out of rooms to see what is going on. Mika puts her finger over her lips to have people keep quiet. As she enters the kitchen, Jas turns and sees her.

"Oh my gosh, don't you look stunning?" Jas says

"He is still asleep?" asks Mika

"I know my dad can sleep through a war. I love that dress on you and those heals. All I have to say is wow. If he is not stunned by the way you look my dad is a fool." gushes Jas

"Jas, Bill suggested I get some flowers and wake him up. Where can I get the right flowers?"

"My Grandfather has no clue sometimes, don't get him flowers. My dad does not do flowers; they are not his thing." Jas says, shaking her head in disbelief. "Can we have a small talk?"

"What can I do for you?" Mika looked concerned at Jas

"I know you might hear my brothers and sister saying you remind them of our mum. When I was young, our mum was so caring, kind, and compassionate. I guess these are qualities everyone should have; you only notice them when they have left a person. Even more so when they have left a person you love. I watched that happen to my mum. It ripped my dad apart to see the person he loved was gone.

You entered into my father's life, and I saw something starting to return to him. The magic that made him such a special and wonderful father. I guess what I am trying to say is thank you for being you."

Mika walks to Jas to comfort her with a hug.

Little Connie walks into the kitchen. "Mika, you look lovely; you remind me of my mother."

"Thank you, Connie," Mika says as she brushes the hair out of the child's face

"I miss seeing her sometimes, and.... "Soon the child is crying

Both Jas and Mika race to her, placing their arms around her in a loving hug of compassion. Soon they are joined by Samara and Niamh, who then asks, "Why are we having in the kitchen a group hug."

That ends the moment, and a few giggles are let out.

"I am going to go wake him up; Jas, thank you for your

kindness. I will always do my best to take good care of your father," states Mika

As she passes Niamh, Niamh looks at her and says, "You look wonderful," then hugs her.

Hezekiah pokes his head out of his room, then puts his hand up for a high five.

Gabriel and Christopher just look out and tell her how nice she looks.

Mika arrives at Everett's Bedroom door she knocks on the door and hears nothing. She repeats once more just as she looks like she is going to give up.

Gabriel says, "Will you just go in wake him up."

She opens the door and is greeted by a table with a bunch of flowers and a note with her name on it. As she opens it all it says is,

I saw you in the kitchen; you look beautiful. I will be out soon. P.S. the flowers are for you.

Mika steps out of his room, holding the flowers.

Jas notices and says, "He called me at 3 am not knowing what to do. We talked for 2 hours about you. I want my dad to be happy. I want to see the man I have always known him to be. He deserves to be loved. He loves with all that he is, and seeing him in this light was poetic. He watched over me a few times in my life, and now here I am, giving him advice. I hope that the two of you have a wonderful day."

"Sounds like everyone saw this before I did," Mika replied.

"Well yeah, we did," laughed Jas.

After a few minutes, Everett walked out softly. "I think we better put those in some water."

Jas spoke up, "I'll do that."

"Jas, can I have one back?" Mika asked.

"Sure, which one do you want?"

"I'll take the daisy; it matches my dress."

"Well, have you had breakfast," asked Everett.

"Oh, I am not hungry,"

"Okay, that makes two of us then."

"Maybe we can grab a snack at the park."

"Everett, I have told Yuri that he will not be needed today."

"Though you know Yuri, he takes this role very seriously. He told me he is coming with his wife, and he promised to be like a shadow."

As they start to close out the day, the two of them just lay on the grass in a park. As the time moves onward, Everett slowly slides his hand towards Mika's, and that moment of human spark happens, and they touch. Soon both giggle and begin holding hands.

As the two of them sit on the grass in the park, Everett breaks the silence. "This moment in time is perfect."

"What do you mean" asked Mika?

"Look around us, see the children playing, families having a picnic, see the wind blow soft through the trees, and the grass is soft and green. What more could we want in life? Families are starting to be families once more. Do we need a new planet," states Everett?

"Okay," replies Mika, "Let go of my hand and just lay there with both palms down on the grass. Listen to my voice and say nothing." For a short time, the two of them just lay there. Mika asks, "what do you feel?"

"I feel the sun on my face, the warmth of it, I feel the

grass under my body and every so often a cool breeze," replies Everett.

"Now Everett, I want you to listen to the sounds that are not the kids playing and, at the same time, feel deeper."

"Deeper?" questioned Everett.

"Just listen and focus; you are needing to hear and feel for what you are missing," replied Mika.

Everett once again began to lay on the grass still without making a sound. He began to tune out the sounds of the children playing, the sound of Mika's breathing, and the people having picnics. Soon he was left with the sounds. But then it dawned on him, and it is not real, there is no underlying life to it all.

"I understand what you were telling me." Say Everett

"There is a rhythm to the wind, the sun is made by a light source, I can hear a hum that is coming from the ground, I can hear the birds, and the sounds of the bugs but they are lackluster. Last, there is something not right; there is not a sense of life to the ground at all. While the grass is real, it feels devoid of a sense of feeling."

Everett sat back up, resting on his elbow, leaning and looking at Mika.

"Mika, I think I get it now. I am not sure what is missing, but over it all, I can tell you parts that are missing. I could hear the sounds of the ship. But there is something else, deeper that connected us on Earth. Though I am not able to say what it is and why it is not complete."

Mika continued to lay on her back, and she turned her head towards Everett. "It is so very simple Everett, but most never take the time to hear it. On Earth, Gaia was so alive. She was a part of you. Some of your early cultures knew this and worked with her, but in time, humanity lost their connection to her. Now you know it is missing; you will long for what you don't have."

"People used to talk about what I just felt is missing. Stories were written about her; you are right; they could feel her heartbeat. But here we are in a space ship that is disconnected from any God. I now know we can't feel that connection because it is not there. The dirt that is below the grass is only deep enough for root systems on the trees. But there is no place for a living God to stay. We have to find a new home, or we will slowly lose what made humanity so very special, and that was a connection with God. Once humankind forgot who she was and started to replace her with other gods we were doomed." replied Everett

The two of them lay silently, holding each other's hand. Everett rises to his elbow and leans over to face towards Mika. Then he bends over and kisses Mika.

"It is still stunning in here. Mika, I have enjoyed being with you these past few months. I long to hear your voice every day. It feels so empty without having you around. Would it be too much to ask for us to share my quarters and you to stop going away every night?"

"Everett, are you asking me to move in with you and the kids?"

"Well, mainly me, the kids don't need you to sleep in their rooms. But I would like it if you slept in mine." Shyly replies Everett

Mika pauses, "I would also like that, but there is something you have to know."

"Okay, I am listening to you have my full attention."

"Everett, I cannot have children. You see, part of the curse from Mars was some women were born without the ability to have children. I am so sorry. If this changes your view of me, I can understand"

"Mika! have you seen how many kids are running around the house at all times? We do not need any more than what we have. Plus, just because you cannot bear children does not mean I would love you any less." Everett says lovingly to Mika

Soon they stand up and start to head back home for dinner with the family. The night rolls on, and kids are put to bed, then it is just the two of them resting on the couch. One thing leads to another, and Mika asks Everett.

"Will you put some music on and sing to me again?"

Soon they are dancing and holding each other tight.

[You are so Beautiful – Joe Cocker]

"I think we better head to bed," Everett says as he takes her by the hand, and they retire to his room.

"Everett, I told you I could not have babies" Mika reminds him

"Mika, there are more reasons for spending time together than to make babies. Can you trust me a little?" asks Everett

The lights turn down, and the music starts

The next morning Jas enters the house; everything is quiet. Gabriel is the first to greet her.

"Hey, Jas, got news for you."

"Oh yeah, what?"

"I think Mika spent the night here last night" replied Gabriel

"Listen, Gabriel; I think it is a bit more than that. I think dad has asked her to move in."

"Do I start calling her mum?" asked Gabriel

"What did dad say to the new family members?"

"Whatever makes you feel comfortable, he will adjust. Do you think Mika is much like dad is?" replies Gabriel

"That is correct, and do you think dad would be with someone who was not like that as well?" asks Jas

"No, I don't. I know mum, in the end, was not very nice, but I loved her, and I sometimes wish she was here with us," Gabriel says as a tear rolls down his face.

Jas walks over and takes her brother in her arms.

"Thank you, Jas. I needed that from the moment mum refused to stay. But I had to stay strong for the others."

"Gabriel, Mika knows she cannot replace mum. She is not even trying to. She is in love with dad, and he is in love with her. So, let's enjoy it with them and watch how they grow together as a couple. I have a feeling it is going to be very magical and special." Jas says as she hugs Gabriel.

"Thank you. Jas" Gabriel replies as he hugs his sister once more

"I've got you, bro. Now I need to talk to the others before the whole house makes a big deal about it all. Please, if Grandpa walks in to keep him busy and away from dad's door. We don't want him walking in on anything." Jas winks at Gabriel as she walks down the hall.

An hour later, Everett softly walks out of his room and down to the lounge where the kids are resting and reading books.

"Hi guy's uhm can we talk" asked Everett

The children move closer to Everett as he sits on the couch.

"Uhm... Last night I chose to ask Mika to move in with us. I know that this might be hard on a few of you. But there is not going to be many changes in the house. Though I would say, just running in and jumping on our bed might need to be adjusted. Of course, if you are feeling yucky, that is fine. But knock any other time, please.

Now I have already been told by Mika that she does not want to make this hard on you guys. She has told me to tell you that you can keep calling her Mika if you would like. She has also said she is not here to replace your mum's who are not with us.

Please understand I am in love with her, and that does not change how I feel about anyone else."

Gabriel interrupts, "Dad, Jas was here this morning, and we had a chance to talk it out with her. She listened to our concerns, and we worked through them. We will continue to treat Mika with the same kindness we always have. We know you love all of us, and that will never change. So, can you please stop making this awkward and let us enjoy our Sunday lazy day?"

"Right, on that note I am going back to bed then" replies Everett

He can hear the kids giggling as he walks into his room and closes the door.

CHAPTER 12

Preparation

Hours before the Monday team meeting Mika approaches Everett

"Everett, we need to have a private talk. I need to tell you more about Mars before we go there. I need to explain a few things about my first home."

"What?" Replied Everett.

"As you know, Mars is a dead planet as I have said, but there is something else that I have not talked about."

"Great, what haven't you told me about Mars?"

"Everett, please remain calm; it is worse than just being a dead planet."

"Worse?" Everett's tone in his voice changes as he sits back in his office chair.

"There is a lot you need to know about before we return to Mars. The God of Mars is dead, which is easy to understand. He was our first great sin. As you know, Mars is why my hands are stained red. Mars was always an angry God; in his dying throws, he cursed us over and over again. He also did not go out quietly, he made it known that what we did was on our heads, and we were going to pay for it."

"So, is that why you cannot have children because of one of the curses?" questioned Everett

"Yeah, when I was born, all the girls and boys were born infertile. Our parents could have children but not us. It all started so very simple. First, our foods started to go off faster than they had ever done so before. It got so bad that at one point the apple you just pulled off the tree you thought you were going to eat later would rot in your hand within hours. Water became harder to get for the crops. In the beginning, we just thought it was normal for the water to freeze in unusual locations, not at the poles. We began fighting back with factories that would melt the ice into water and send it to the farms. But then some of the crops would no longer grow correctly. We were an advanced civilization; no mythological God was going to tell us what we can and cannot do. So, we started to "fix" those."

"What do you mean by "Fix" them with the hand gestures?" Asked Everett.

"We started to genetically modify them to the point that they would grow faster and use less water. Mars was so brilliant, and he saw that they, we were trying to play God, as we were killing him. So, in revenge, he changed the weather patterns. Okay, we adapted to that with ease; we moved crop planting seasons and the locations. We started using energy that came from this chaos. We were not going to be defeated. But then Mars took another trick out of his book, and animals began to die ones that we thought would not have that great of an impact on us, so we ignored that. This angered him with a rage that shocked us. It started so very fast we woke up one day to find thousands of our herds were dead. There was nothing wrong with them; they were just dead. So the meat was harvested as not to waste it. Then we started to "Fix" the animals as well. We were going to protect our food sources.

But Mars saw through that. Looking back now, I see that was a temper tantrum he threw. Then he became upset when he did not get the response he wanted. We did not listen. What followed was a yell, then a scream, then anger, then rage and, in the end, became Hate. He saw us for what we were. We were spoilt children playing God. Mars, in his Hate and Anger, breathed out in his death in the last days a curse the final curse upon us. No one could have been prepared for what was to come.

He released a sickness that covered everything and touched everyone in some shape or fashion. It was like nothing we had seen before; it started with a simple cough. Nothing too big, not even shocking. Then came a sore throat, from what I was told it began about mid-chest almost like heartburn. But then the people said every day it just grew and grew until the top of their throat was like breathing fire. In a close examination, the oesophagus was severely irritated to the point some were bleeding. But we could treat that. Then lesions, bruises, and painful bumps started to appear on their skin. The lesions could be addressed, and the bruises would fade in a couple of days. But the bumps, that was bad. See, the bumps were pockets of air. When they burst open, it left a dent in the person's skin. There was no blood or infected puss, or any leakage what so ever. More to the point, it looked like the blood that should have been there dried up. All that was left was a dent about the size of your pinkie nail. The Skin under this bump was delicate. Something was strange, and we could not put our finger on it. So before one burst, we isolated the person and tested one of the bumps; it was a spore that had grown under the skin, and when it burst, it released its poison in the air. It was so bad on one person; there were hundreds of bumps. When they burst, you could not see by the naked eye the "spores" for lack of a better description. Now times that by the millions of people who were sick. It was commonplace.

But that was not the end of it. The next stage was Rot. It sounds so simple, but once that started on a person, it was hard to look at them. You see, it started with a little piece of dry, dead skin. White in color, but easy to scrape off and see the new skin below. But the Rot was not so kind. This was happening all over their bodies. The skin would fall off if you sat in a chair for some time. People stopped wearing dark clothing because it showed the skin flakes. That was manageable to a point we were advanced enough in our medical technology that we could help in the early stages. But we were so foolish whatever we did the curse would get stronger the skin could not heal as fast as it was dying. It got to the point where their skin started falling off their bodies, and that would die pain-filled last hours.

Oh, we thought we were so smart. We developed a spray-on the skin that coated the whole body. It acted just like our normal skin. The sickness could not beat it. But then the illness changed once more. The final stage took months to complete. We could not see what it was doing until it was too late. The sickness was attaching itself to all the calcium in your body. But it never did anything until it was attached to every bit of Calcium. You know the bones in your body are so amazing. Without them in your body you are dead,"

Mika snapped her fingers and said, "Just like that, a person would be walking down the street looking fine, nothing wrong that anyone could see. Then all of a sudden, they would fall over dead. People would rush to try to help them, but all they would feel when they touched them, they were nothing but a bag of goo. There were no bones in their bodies. There was no calcium at all; it was just gone.

I don't think that it was the issue of dying. I believe that it was a time frame if you got the cough. You knew you were going to die within six months to a year.

We did not know how to stop this curse, and it had no pattern to it as well. No one ever made a year. It drove people crazy if you had a sore throat, you knew you were dead. Our civilization had mass suicides on a scale never seen before we lost close to 1/3 of our population in that first year.

The sickness made no sense, we could not find a cure, and it kept changing day by day. In some cases, it changed right before our eyes. Under the microscopes, we watched it mutate. We might cure a person, but then the next day they were infected once again this time it was different, yet the same. Some were lucky, like me. We were immune, but yet there was nothing we could find in our blood that could fight it off. Once the blood was taken and tested from our bodies, it would become infected. If you put that blood back in for some reason, it would be fine."

Everett could see the tears streaming down Mika's face as she recounted the horrors of her past.

Mika took a drink of water and began again

"I designed and created an invention called a Bio-suit. The suit would allow a user to interact with daily activities. Then when they got to a clean and safe environment, they could remove the Bio-suit and walk around as usual. I first designed this suit in a way to protect children over the age of twelve. You see, some children were safe from the sickness, some not all. What I mean by children if they were under the age of twelve, the disease never attacked them but here and the children above twelve could become ill at any moment. Thanks to my invention, parents were placing their children in the Bio-suits to save them. But there was no pattern. Then the government decided to take all the children from under the age of eighteen down to newborns away from their parents to try to save them. They placed them in sealed environments, and it did nothing. The mortality rates stayed the same. Even with the Bio-suits were not always protective. I could not figure out why. I would redesign the suits so many times each one was better in testing. But for some reason that I could not figure the curse out when it came to children. The God of Mars was winning.

It was also at this time the government finally agreed that the planet was dying and we needed to find a new home. Stupid fools it was not dying; it was dead. We saw Earth we knew she was very young and our seers told us her name was Gaia. We hoped that due to her age, she might overlook our mistake and or not notice it. As I said, I found this ship and was an engineering student.

While I was off-world fixing this ship, I saw that everyone who was off-planet never became ill, and those who were possibly got better. But if they went down to the surface and they were in the age groups, they would soon become sick. Some would become ill in hours; others became ill within days. The remaining children were all sent to this ship even though it was not fully ready for them. Anyone who was not sick and could work was off-world was never be allowed to return to the surface as the ship was being worked on with high hopes to finish it. Soon we started to see that the focusing supplies were speeding up the though I noticed that they were not the supplies we needed. They were rations and shelters. I started to ask questions, but they kept playing games with the shipments some building supplies would come but not enough to finish the ship so I would complain. My dad told me that they were building a ship to bring a large number of people up.

I felt I was kept out of the building design of that ship as it was chosen to be done on the planet. That I also have enough of a job already going. Why cut me out of the design process. It made no sense to keep people on the surface to build the ship when we had ways to get them up to this ship, and we could finish it sooner, saving more lives. All I was told is that it was underway and would soon be done. I watched the population of the world becomes smaller and smaller. I watch my parents hope for the ship to be built on the surface to speed up the completion date. My dad told me that the leaders all thought that a wise move. I was not convinced I tried to say to them there would not be enough fuel to leave the planets gravity well due to the massive size. I was told that the ship was different, and it could make it off.

When I asked for the information, I was told more than a couple of times, "That it was a need to know basis." I was not in need to know, even though I was the lead engineer of this ship. But what made this one was so different? I could see the news reports, and we knew the timeline to its lift-off.

I need to know why it did not make it off, or if it went to the second option planet in case, the Earth was not a viable planet. I have no idea about any more information, as I said I went to bed that night and woke up thousands of years later. I had hope that we could have finished this ship to save as many as we could; the curse did not exist on this ship. Meaning, once they were off-world, they could be saved.

I know the Commander, and I did not always see eye to eye. I asked for permission to return to Mars and see if we could save others. After being refused several times, I gave up and started to think of another way to do it. So, I tried to take over a cargo ship once with only the crew, yeah that was an issue of poor planning. I wanted to go back to the surface and check to see if we could gather the others. I was placed under arrest and sent to serve out my sentence in the office. I think the cryo-chamber is part of the medical systems in the pod. I guess I ruffled my Commander's feathers to the point that he messed up the date or something. All I wanted to do was save more lives, and when they would not listen to me, I was punished. So that is the story of the final days of Mars as I know it." Mika wipes away the tears that run down her face.

Everett stand up and holds her close for some time

"Wow, Mika, that is a lot to take in. Even more to hold in for so long. I am glad that you trusted me enough to share it with me. Can you give me some time to think about all that you have said?" Everett kindly asks

Soon he walks to the food dispenser and ordered a tall glass of Chocolate Milk and some doughnuts;

"Would you like some?" he asked.

"No thank you, Everett I am just going to sit here."

Everett returned to his desk and sat in his chair as Mika rested on the couch. As minutes became hours, the look of concern was more than evident on Mika's face. As she looked at Everett, all she could see was his blank stare at the data pad.

Everett, still looking down, began to speak. "Mika, what I am going to tell you to do," he paused, then said, "needs to be done and never think otherwise. You know what your world was like from when you were on Mars, and you have a small glimpse of what our humanity was like we are not that different. So, what I am about to tell you to do it for your own best interests and the best of everyone onboard." Everett paused again; after a few deep breaths, he began to speak again. "From this point forward, you will never talk about, tell anyone else, or even write it down. The part of that story regarding disobeying and trying to go back, just leave that part out of your story. Let it go; let it die. Mika, do you understand me?" stated Everett

"No, I don't Everett I don't think I do." Replied Mika

"There are a lot of former military on this ship, and if you cannot obey orders, they won't trust you no matter who you are. Now, do you understand why?" Everett asks again

"I understand now."

Everett stands up straitens his uniform. Strolls over to Mika and bends down to be eye to eye reaches out, and takes her hands he looks her in the eyes.

"Mika, you know that I love you and that we can figure this out, but we need to be smart about everything we do when it comes to Mars. I know it has been a very stressful few weeks with moving in with the kids and me. We have seen so many challenges together. I want you to know I am so very thankful for you being in my life, and I do care for you. Would you mind if I ask you a few more questions? As he sat on the coffee table in front of her.

"I can do my best to answer what I can for you, Everett." Mika looks at his as she replies

"Thank you, Mika, do we need to go back to Mars, is it worth the risk? What will we gain from that risk? I need to know the facts before I remake a choice to go back to that dead planet. What about the sickness, can it lie dormmate? For all this time, because that is a major risk to all of us. Would it be better to send down a probe and test the soil first? I need to know these answers. I will not risk one single soul on this ship if it can be prevented."

"Everett, I don't know if the sickness can lie dormmate, it is a huge risk I understand that. But I have hundreds of years to work on the Bio-suits; they are nothing like what I designed in the past. Plus, as I spent time working on this ship, I found their spacesuits and used some of their technology to enhance what I built. I feel healthy people can go down to the surface and return without problems. This was tested time and time again as supplies were being brought from the surface to build this ship. Yes, we can send a probe down first to test the soil. But I don't think it is going to tell us much we are talking about thousands of years."

"Thank you, Mika."

"I have a personal question for you."

"Yes, Everett?"

"Why did you keep putting a blanket on me, and I wake up and find a little girl has stuck to my chest or on my lap?" Everett, I was not the one placing the blanket on you. That little girl was so scared and alone. She would wake up looking for someone to cuddle. She would go looking for you since she trusts you. If you were not in your room and she logically searched out where you were. Find you somewhere, place the blanket on the two of you, and drift off to sleep. I caught her once she has told me that you must be cold, so she brings a comforter with her but then is too tired to go back to her bed, so she sleeps on your lap."

"Okay, I'll have a chat with Jas and get this sorted."

"Everett, don't you dare!" Orders Mika as she looks him straight in the eyes. "Now it is time for you to listen to me. I see everything on this ship, I know it from top to bottom. I know a lot more than you think.

She talks to me, and I listen to her. The first time she called my name, I was a little scared to answer, but she needed someone. So, I sat with her in her room. She told me that she is so very thankful she was for you. She says she loves you for all that you have done for her. She told me of her nightmares of when she was with the mean people. So here is what you are going to do. You are a good man and a beautiful soul. You need just to let her be a little soul who cares for you. She will heal in time, and the nightmares will go away. Now, if I have to do what you say, then now you need to do what I say this time I know better than you do.

Since you and I are sharing a bed, we need to be mindful of her needs. After we have our time, we need to get back to being dressed just in case."

"Yeah, I was thinking about that. I know kids enough that the 3 am vomit cart happens from time to time."

"Vomit cart?"

"Oh my gosh, there is no alarm clock like that of a child getting sick near or on your bed. You wake up with eyes wide open. Mind you, the rest of the day will be shot to shit after it." Everett laughs

"Everett, I can't fix that."

"You're right; no one can; it is not possible to be fixed."

"You see, these are things I did not know about being a parent."

"Mika, that is okay. You will learn them in time. Just remember if, in the dead of night, you are woken up by a kid saying I don't feel well, get a bucket and fast."

Just then, the door com rings.

"Yes, come in," answers Everett.

"Commander, can we talk. "

"Sure, Gordon, come on in the door is open. The door opens, and the Captain walks in. Hello, you two you have been in here for some time. I cancelled today's team meeting, as I felt you guys might be going over some important things about Mars. You do know we are one month away from it."

"Yeah, I do thank for the reminder, though," Everett calmly replies.

"Well, sir, I think it is about time we start looking at how and what we need to get there and get the job done right. I have some questions that I need to have answered. Before we head to the surface, I need to know everything about your homeworld, Mika. I will not risk one single life without knowing what we are facing down there."

Mika looks at Everett. "Do you want me to tell him?"

"Go ahead," replies Everett.

"Captain, you may want to sit down for all of this," Everett suggests pointing to a chair.

After about an hour, Mika has recounted once again the final days of Mars though this time avoiding personal details. Everett gets up and walks calmly over to the food dispenser and orders a double Scotch. He walks over to the Captain, who is sitting opposite Mika with a blank look in his eyes. Everett places the drink in front of Gordon

"Here is a drink," says Everett

The captain takes the glass and drinks it in one solid gulp.

The Captain looks at both of them and says, "I hate to say it, but I need more information. Look, my men are all good men and will risk their lives for the greater good. But I will not send them down there blind and unprotected. Hell, none of us has ever thought that we would be walking on a different planet. Let alone one that might want to kill us. We don't even know how to fly the damn ships that can take us to the surface. We cannot even find the engines start buttons.

Mika starts to laugh, then pauses. "Well, I think it is time I show you another discovery that I found on this ship, this one will change so much of what we need to know and how we are going to learn it. Shall we go for a walk to the library, Gentlemen?"

The Captain just looks at Everett and nods his head.

"Okay, Mika, lets head down there and see what you have for us."

The Captain hits his commlink, "Number two, you are in charge; yes sir, is heard in reply."

"Mika, you do know they are using the library for the kid's schooling," Everett reminds Mika.

"Oh yes, I do; it was the best suggestion for it. You'll see when we get there."

After a short lift ride, they arrive at the door to the Library.

"Come, Gentlemen, you have some learning to do, and this is the perfect place." States Mika

As they open the door to the Library, they are greeted by the shining faces of all the young children listening to Story-time.

"Mika!" Yells Connie from halfway across the class. She gets up and runs towards her for a tackling Hug. Connie then looks up and Everett and just smiles and say, "Oh hi, dad."

"Connie," Mika says in a motherly tone

"yes Mika" replies Connie

"you need to return to your seat and listen to your teacher. We are here to do some work. We can talk later today, is that okay?" Mika lovingly instructs

Connie begins to giggle and runs back.

As the three leaders continue their walk, they hear Connie say, "I told you my dad was the Commander and Mika is my mum, she's is so, So there!"

"Okay, let us make a detour first." Everett takes charge and begins to walk over to the class as soon as the three leaders reach the children. Everett motions the teacher to see if he can interrupt.

"Hi everyone," Everett says as he pulls up a chair and sits down on their level

"I can see you are doing reading time. Can I take over and read one of my favourite books. I promise you will like it as much as I do." Everett says with a huge smile

Yuri sits down with a thud, and the children giggle

Form out of nowhere, Everett produces a small Golden Book that is titled "There is a monster at the end of this book" Soon, the other leaders are also both sitting down and other adults in the library are finding seats as Everett reads on with his unique animations and voices. It is clear to see that he has everyone's attention that is within earshot. Soon the children are on the edge of their seats as Everett reaches the end of the book to the laughter of children that fills the air of the library.

"Okay, kids, I heard Connie say that I was her dad. So, I dragged her Mum, Yuri the Giant, and the Soldier over with me to meet you all. Thank you for letting me read you a book I hoped you enjoyed it." Excitingly Everett says

The teacher stands up and takes over the class as the children are all saying, "Thank you."

When Yuri stands up, the children are a bit in shock at having a Giant in the classroom. The leaders return to their walk to where Mika was leading them to what she wanted to show.

"Everett," Mika says his name to get his attention.

"Yes, my love" he replies

"I don't think everyone knew about us" she replies

"Mika, we are on a ship of 150,000 people. One pebble tossed into this pond creates a ripple that all the shores will feel. People were talking when we were on the observation deck; they saw us at the park with the kids and even watched us as we interacted. I know some of the crew had bets on if it was going to happen. Plus, then we have my dad, who has never been able to keep his excitement under control." Laughingly said Everett

As they continue their walk, Niamh, Everett's Daughter, runs up behind them and screams, "BOO!" Both the Captain and Everett are entirely caught off guard. Niamh begins to laugh at her ability to scare them both.

Mika turns around and says, "But you missed me. You are too hard to get Mika, but I will get you."

"Hello, Niamh,"

"Hello, dad," she replies, and she begins to hug him. "I want a real bear hug!"

Okay, Everett replies as he picks her up and gives her a good squeeze. "Listen to me kiddo we need to get back to work, and you need to get back to class."

"It is break time, plus I just heard you read your favourite book" she smiles

"Busted, I admit it. But we still have work to do. Can we play some games tonight when we get home?"

"Yeah, Dad, that sounds like fun. I call out the first game, Uno, because we need to teach Mika."

"Deal," Everett sticks out his hand for a handshake, and the deal is set.

Yuri looks at Mika and says in a deep Russian voice, "You're in for it now. In for a penny in for a pound." Then laughs

Soon Everett's youngest son Hezekiah runs up and Salutes the Captain and gives Everett a high five. "Can't talk its lunchtime bye dad and then runs off screaming, oh, and Hi Mika and Yuri."

Everett turns to the Captain and asks, "How long has he been saluting you?"

"A couple of days now," replies the Captain. "I get more Salutes from all the kids than I get from the crew."

"Ahh, the price of fame," Captain, says Everett and laughs.

Mika stops just after entering the Library and says, "We will have to wait here until their class is done; they are using the room we need to be in."

The doors open in a few minutes and out walks Gabriel.

"Hey, dad," giving a hug to Everett, "what are you doing here?"

"Well, I am here to learn. Mika needs to teach us something and what a better place than your school."

"Hey dad, when you get home tonight, can we just have some time just the two of us?"

"Yeah, you bet, but it will need to be a bit later as Niamh just asked for a game night."

"Oh yeah! Are we playing Uno?"

"You bet, mate!"

Gabriel points at Mika and says with a smile, "Fresh Blood," then laughs and walks off.

"Everett, is there something I need to know?"

"Relax it is only a card game, honey" Everett smiles

"They are going to eat you alive. Glad it is not me this time," laughs Yuri. "He lies they are ruthless at the game."

"Hey, Gabriel," yells out Everett

"Yeah, dad."

"Alright son, you stay with us, and I'll give you a break from school, and we can sneak away from Mika, and the Captain at some point does that sound okay."

"Yeah, dad, I would like that." Replies Gabriel

Everett looks at the Captain. The Captain just nods and smiles with complete understanding.

"Alright," says Mika as they walk into the classroom

"This is an advanced learning room. It is time for my turn

to have a show and tell. Gabriel, please close the doors. Gentlemen see the six circles on the floor, please help me move the chairs away from them. This room is designed to teach anything and everything about this ship." Mika instructs

Just as the floor is cleared, the six circles rise out of the floor, exposing six high back chairs with helmets and armrests. They looked like something out of a steampunk movie. The windows are frosted over so that people are not able to see that inside.

"Gentlemen, everything is not quite what you think it is. The brain is an amazing organ. Our ancestors found a way to teach higher learning faster than what both of our civilizations have been doing. The former captain of this ship refused to allow people into this room. He had guards posted outside of it at all times. When the ship was empty, there was no one to stop me from learning, so I learned how to use it."

"Pardon me, Mika," the Captain speaks up, "So you know everything about this ship?"

"No, there is so much to learn. I also found out that for about a week after using these devices, you just want to rest. You are overloaded with information, and it comes so naturally that you are also trying to comprehend that you know it." Replies Mika

"So Mika, what you are saying is that you end up knowing something, and then you have to come to terms with knowing it?" Asked Gabriel

"Yeah Gabriel good job understanding that" praised Mika

"Then why are we learning the slow way about subjects like engineering" questioned Gabriel

"Because I am concerned about the impacts on young

adults. If it takes an adult a week to come to terms with the new knowledge, I am not sure if a younger mind could handle that stress." Replied Mika

"So Mika can my pilots use this to teach them more about flying that the slow simulators have been doing?" asked the Captain

"I don't this that this is a be-all solution. I think it was meant to be used in conjunction with those." Mika replied

"Great, this is a bit of good news, Commander. I will get the teams that I have assembled to go to the surface in here asap. We will be ready when you give us the green light." Informs the Captain

"Everett, you and Gabriel get out of here and spend some time together," Mika says smiling at Gabriel

"Thank you, honey, let us get out of here kiddo," says Everett

"Thank you, Mika" as Gabriel hugs her

"We will see you, boys, before dinner time, okay" instructs Mika

"Yes, my love," replies Everett, then turns his attention towards Gabriel as he wraps his arm around him and roughs up his hair.

"Captain, get this underway now" Mika instructs

"Yes Ma'am" he replies

After all the events from a very busy the family settles in for some games of Uno. Popcorn and snacks the children devour as they fill the home with smiles and laughter. Soon the game night draws to a close, as Mika has been given a rude awakening to the family's Uno house rules.

"Everett and children, thank you so much for tonight. I

really enjoyed all of us spending time together. Can we do it again in the future?" asked Mika

"Oh yeah, we can any time you want, Mika. There are other fun games, as well." Replies Gabriel

"Okay, you monsters go brush your teeth. Then we will get you all tucked in bed," said Everett.

CHAPTER 13

The Missing

"Hey, dad,"

"Yeah, son."

"What do you miss the most about the Earth?" asks Gabriel.

Everett reclines back in on the grass as his son rests back as well.

"Well, that is a deep question. So let me think for a minute as we rest here because I have a lot of them." Everett replies

The father and son lay there deep in thought. Everett began to reply to his son's comment. "It was a wonderful summer day, and it was a Saturday. I woke up and had a bit of a stretch. I looked over and saw that my wife, your mum, was lying in the glow of a warm sunny morning. There was just enough heat coming through the window to make you want to stay in bed a little bit longer. The light was coming through the window just at the right angle to rest gently on the bed. I never saw her so beautiful than a moment in time." Everett recalls his memory of Gabriel's mum

"Oh, dad, please don't tell me about a sex story with mum."

"Shut up," they both had a chuckle, "Just listen, I am sure you will enjoy. So, where was I? Oh yeah. The sun was resting upon our bed. You could see a few little dust particles in the air. They added this sense of a magical feeling to what I was seeing. I was in so much love with your mum, and that was just one of those days that I was thankful to have her in my life. I softly walked down the stairs to the kitchen and began to cook breakfast for the family. I can still feel the cold eggs in my hand as I cracked them open and placed them sunny side up. The smell of the grinders as I put salt and pepper on the eggs. I soft sound of the eggs as they began to cook. It was like a bubbling creek, not too sharp but just at the right sound. The bacon that was cooking began to fill the air with a smoky smell. That combined with the eggs. I knew it would not be long before everyone woke up. Just at the time that I was about to get carried away with the smell of my youth. The toaster popped up the bread, and I began to butter it.

First, one child, two children, then the rest of you rushed down the hall, and the silence was broken. I dished them up each a plate and sat them in the warm sun-filled the dining room. It was silent once more. I returned to the kitchen to cook for your mum and I. While at the stove, two hands began to slowly encompass my sides as they move forward to complete a hug around my waist. I could feel her breath on the side of my neck as she whispered in my ear, now this is sexy. I could not help but smile. I plated our breakfast up and suggested that she quickly return to our bed. I grabbed a serving table and a flower that I saw outside. I placed the plate and a coffee and began my walk down the hall, making sure to avoid the Lego's with each step.

I returned to see her once more laying in our bed with the warm summer sun resting upon her. She had drifted back to sleep. I carried the tray over to her side of the bed. Softly speaking, love, love, hey love, I have breakfast for you, and the kids are taken care of watching cartoons. Slowly she opened her eyes as a soft, gentle look of love and compassion filled her face. I knew then; I have to remember that moment in time."

"Gosh dad that was beautiful, why could she not stay like that?" asked Gabriel

"I don't know why, sometimes people change when life is not going the way they want." Calmly Everett replied

"Did she love us?"

"Listen, mate, while things were not good at the end, there was a time that all of us mattered to your mum more than life itself. I don't know why she changed the way she did. So, I am trying to just focus on the good times. When we were happy and a family."

"But now you have Mika in your life. How do you juggle that?"

"Mate, as I said, you take the good moments, and you hold tight to them, and you throw out all the bad ones. Then you start something magical and make new memories."

"I like having Mika in the house she is something that was missing for all of us," Gabriel says as he sits up. "is there any-thing else you miss?"

"Oh yeah, a tall glass of ice-filled to the top and a Coke in the hot summer sun. But I was not finished with that memory would you like me to finish?"

"Yeah, that would be great to hear dad."

"Okay, son."

"I grabbed the book she was reading as well. We sat and talked over enjoying our breakfast. Then I told her I am going to leave you to enjoy some reading time. I'll take care of the kids as I walked out the door, softly closing it behind me. Bit by bit, I started to pick up the hallway of Legos. I went to go placing the toys away correctly.

I went back down to the kitchen and made myself another cup of coffee and began to clean the kitchen."

"Dad, I don't remember that about my mum and you. Are you sure you are talking about my mum?"

"I know who I am talking about, but please let me finish. You were very young." Everett continued.

"After cleaning the kitchen, I cleaned up the messy table. The dishes were cleaned off and washed as the warm soapy water filled the sink. I can still smell the lemon soap that I used. It always made me think of cleanliness. As I dried the dishes and put them away as one of your sisters came in and asked the ever-famous line, what are we going to do today. Shh, I said, now brush your teeth and get dressed I have a surprise.

I recall the look of happiness that was upon her little face as she ran off to do what I said. Soon your brother came in and asked the very same thing. I was feeling like a robot with the same answer. Then off he waddled to the bathroom. I love the way diapers used to make you guys waddle. I returned to my coffee as I enjoyed knowing this was going to be a beautiful day. Soon all of you guys came back, but it was not time to go, and their mum was still enjoying the morning break. Of course, as children do, they had to ask when we were leaving. Soon, so I suggested that they go and enjoy a bit of cartoon on the TV until it was time to go.

Soon I could hear the steps as she moved closer and closer. Her hair was all a mess, and still looking like an angel. She smiled and placed the tray on the counter. I know you, she said softly, what are you planning. I looked at her and smiled as I returned to my coffee and just enjoyed the thought that I surprised her. It is going to drive her crazy in more than one way. As I finished the last drop, I cleaned up the rest of the dishes. I waited for her shower to end.

I walked down the hall to see her step out of the shower. There she was looking lovely as the first day I saw her. I walked up behind her and placing my arms around her waist and whisper in her ear, get dressed, and we will begin our day out. I slowly kissed the side of her neck as I drew in the smell of her hair.

When I finished my shower and was dressed, it was time to pack everyone up in the car. Autumn was on its way; as I drove, we could see the colors of the leaves were beginning to change. One by one, they filled the sides of the backroads we were on with colors of green, red, yellow, and orange. It was the end of summer, and I was ready for a change. We stopped in the little town on the way to the lake. I ordered some fried chicken and other fixings. Then we returned to our drive.

Unknown to all the people in the car, I had picked out this picnic spot days prior. As we drove, you could see the beautiful colors that filled the view now included a stunning blue lake, a blue that seemed to be the same shade as a young child's eyes. The green grass that invited you to relax and enjoy a wonderful meal in its comfort. This was mother nature at her best and artwork that could never be correctly depicted again. As I parked the car and stepped out, I grabbed the children and their blankets as we set them out for the start of a wonderful meal. I grabbed the first basket, took it out to where she and the children were seated. I said to myself I will never forget this day and I haven't.

I sat the plates out with something to drink, wine for us, and juice for the children, next to the cheese and crackers and snacks for the kids. Soon we were laughing and enjoying our time. I returned to the car for the second basket. We sat and served up the fried chicken, and smiles filled the air, and soon we were all full. But seeing this magic of a happy family, we knew the time was moving quickly. Kids were starting to get tired, so I got the dessert out. Watermelon was on the menu for the kids and cheesecake with fruit for the adults. Smiles and full droopy eyes, energy low it was time to pack up and go. The children quickly asleep before we even got 10 minutes into the drive, she leaned over and kissed my cheek. I can still feel her soft lips as they press upon my skin. Her words echo in my heart even to this day. Thank you for today.

I remember our drive home. I cracked the window to capture the smell of the evergreens and cedars. That surrounded the journey, our day is almost done, and we would soon be home. As I pull into the drive, the children still asleep; we had to carry them in the house. Laid them in their beds as it was time just to enjoy being the two of us. Turn off the lights as I kissed their heads good night. I went to clean out the car, and there she was just a little faster than I. She looked at me with eyes so full of love, and it's my turn go inside, she told me.

I thought I would just sit for a moment. I closed my eyes as the sound of the leaves blowing in the gentle breeze outside. I could still hear the water that bubbles in the stream that helped fill the lake. My eyes began to feel heavy, and I drifted off only to be woken up by her soft voice, love, love it's time for bed. Nothing more was said that night; it was a perfect day."

Everett looked at his son, and he had drifted off to sleep on the grass. I guess I still have it.

[Dream Weaver – Gary Write]

"Sir, it is time to go," Yuri tells Everett

"I think we will sit here for a few more minutes" replied Everett

"Mind if I sit down?" Asked Yuri

"Sure" smiled Everett

"Sir, I wanted to say thank you to you. I have learned so much about being a good parent from watching some of the things you do for your children."

"I am nothing special, Yuri. I look at them and think about what I would want if I was at that age, and then I act upon it. I am not perfect, and I make mistakes just like everyone else. But I try to show more love." Replied Everett

Soon the silence is broken by Everett's commlink

"Hello"

"Hi Honey, are you coming home soon. Yeah, let me wake Gabriel up, and we will leave the park."

"He is asleep?"

"Mika, he is a teenager he can fall asleep anywhere and any-time for no reason but to sleep. Sometimes I am surprised he has not fallen asleep at the dinner table," Laughs Everett

"Was this time what he needed from you?" Mika asks

"I think so, a lot of changes have been going on in his life, and it might have been a bit much for him, and he just needed time with me to feel cared about." Replied Everett

"I love you, Everett."

"I love you too. Oh, I can see Yuri just picked him up. It looks like we are on our way." Everett tells Mika

"Yuri, you can wake him up, you know he is 14 and…"

Yuri interrupts, "Let him sleep just a few minutes more."

"Oh, okay if he wakes up in your arms your dealing with his shock" laughs Everett

Soon the three guys are home with Everett laughing as they enter the house. With Gabriel wiping the dust out of his eyes.

"I am going to head home you guys have a good night," Yuri says as he leaves.

Later that night, when Niamh has noticed that her father is relaxing listening to music. "Dad, can we talk?"

"Sure thing, what can I do for you?"

"I miss my mum. I wish I could see her face again. I am not able to remember how she looked. When I think of her, I see Mika, and Mika is not my mum."

"There is a lot to unpack with what you have said. Let me take my time, and I will work on an answer for every point you have raised. You are correct Mika is not your mum, and she does not want to take over her place. If Mika were here with us, she would tell you the same thing I am. We are going to put a photo of your mum in your room next to your bed. Does that sound like a plan to help you in your sense of missing feelings of her? Next, you can look at your data pad, and I will put every photo I can find of her on it for you. Will that help you remember her?"

With a deep sigh, "Yes, but I am still missing her."

"Oh, my sweet, I wish things were different for you though I am very proud of you for taking the time and coming to talk to me about this. I wish your mother would have made a better choice. But I would not be with her had she because I needed it to be over." Replied Everett

"So, dad, do you love Mika?"

"Well, Niamh, as I told you, good things take time to build. Then we started to do things away from work. We were spending time just getting to know each other. Then we started wanting to be around each other more and more. Then we knew we were falling in love with each other. So yes, I am in love with her." Replied Everett

"It is nice not to hear mum yelling at you anymore. How do you feel about that?"

"There are some memories of your mum that are very special to me. Then there are some that I don't want to remember. One thing that is nice to have with Mika is we talk and do things with each other. I love our walks in the park and meeting new people." Replies Everett

"Well, what do you think of Mika?"

"I liked having Mika around to talk with about girly things. Well, thank you for taking the time and talking to me. I am starting to get tired, so I am going to go to bed."

"Give me a hug before you go," requests Everett

Everett is once again alone in the lounge room. Mika sneaks up behind him placing her arms over him in a loving embrace. Then softly, she whispers in his ear, "Is it our time to go to bed now as well?"

CHAPTER 14

The Descent

On the Bridge, Commander Everett and Mika meet with the Captains and the landing crews' leaders.

Commander Everett begins to address everyone. "After months of planning, we have chosen to descend to the surface of Mars. You have all been briefed on the condition of Mars and the viruses that are possibly both airborne and soil-based. The Pilots have been instructed not to open your shuttles doors until the dust settles and pilots are in their sealed environments. If there are any mechanical issues with the shuttles, you will return to this ship.

At no time does the shuttle return to your loading dock. Until the Docks are clear of all personnel and will sit in space will then open all doors and evac all air in the said ship into space. Once that is done, they will land in the docking bay. Data from the recon will be uploaded, and then we will teleport teams into the quarantine bays in the medical departments. The Teleport teams will send them to quarantine as naked as they came out of their mothers. Then we will begin the cleaning of the docking bay and the shuttle inside and out. Those teams will stay there until we are sure that there is no possibility of contamination on the shuttle or in the docking bays. We will then review the data and decide if other missions are warranted. Live streams will be kept on at all times.

Pilots, you will need to make a couple of passes to make sure that you can find a safe landing spot. Thousands of years of dust cover the cites, so we will try to guide you from here. Does everyone understand what is at risk here? If you are not sure, now is the time to make sure you do have all the information that is needed to make this mission successful. I want you all to return home to us in the same shape you left us. If you find cryo-chambers, you leave them alone; this is not the time to worry about those.

Spend today and review your suits and what are the mission parameters. In 24 hours report to the cargo bays. Any question right now?"

After a short pause, Everett begins once more. "From this point forward, all questions will be passed up the chains of command. All are dismissed and get to your duties of preparation. Bridge and Captain, you have time to review once again all of the mission guidelines with the crew of the Bridge."

"Mission leaders to my office now." Order Everett

As the door to the office shuts, and all are attending Everett begins.

"Listen to me, I will make this clear, and this is for our ears only. If someone's suit is compromised, they will not be brought back to this ship. We cannot risk Mars, releasing his curse upon all of us. Even if in the past, this has not been the case. If that means shutting the doors of the shuttle leaving that person, it is a price then we will have to live with for the rest of our lives.

Gentlemen, I don't think I need to stress that the greater good outweighs the life of one or two. You do what is required to be done to make sure none of the lives that are on this ship are put at risk. I also have a sinking feeling that Mika does not know everything that took place down on the surface since the day she left. I am sorry, Mika, but I cannot ignore this feeling.

"That is okay Everett, better to be on the safe side" Mika replies

"Okay, let us continue, give crew on those shuttles updated weapons in case they need to protect themselves. Remember, the vault is this main point of this mission, with the secondary being information from the command center. Which can tell us more about the other possible ship? Though I cannot stress this enough, I have a gut feeling that something is not right.

"Commander, all forces will be completely ready for anything, and we will switch over to a yellow alert as soon as those shuttles leave. Mika also made sure to set up the shielding on the shuttles to protect them from all sorts of attacks, including Biological. This will burn off any possibilities of contamination making it near impossible for those to enter the shuttles." Informed the Captain

"But that does that mean when the shuttle lands it will still be at risk due to touching the ground?" questioned Everett

"No, sir, you are incorrect on that, the system was designed to remove all foreign bodies that might come close to the shuttle. There will be a scorched ground effect below the shuttle as there a bubble around the shuttle. Upon returning there will be a secondary cleaning of sorts as it enters the docking bay with the shielding that Mika has said is around this ship" replied the Captain

"Look until the all-clear is given from medical staff we are not going to risk it, period. Then until the cleaners in the docking bay give the all-clear, that area will also be off-limits. Therefore, not risking anything is that understood? I cannot shake this feeling."

"Well, sir. If there is anything my years in the service has taught me is to listen to our gut instincts. Most of the time, nothing happens that shocks us, or we are not ready to handle it. Why? That is very simple we always over-prepare. You see, the moment we don't pay attention to the gut feeling is the moment we take situations for granted, and that is when people die. We will do our best to return what all those who go down. I hope that helps you" informs the Captain

"It does thank you for understanding my concerns. Mika can you excuse the Captain and me for a minute?" asks Everett

"Sure, I needed to use the restroom anyhow too much coffee" replies Mika

"Gordon, we are sending the two shuttles with extra drones and probes. But I want you to launch the drones and probes once you are in the city. I want to know the value of everything. I want to know what we can and cannot take. I hope you understand. This is for your ears only!" orders Everett

"I understand sir" replies the Captain

"24 hours until mission launch, dismissed," says Everett

In the hanger, a group of chairs is filled with the first soldiers ready to leave for the first mission to Mars. They sit in front of a whiteboard with a man doing his best to set out the mission parameters. Mika's high heels can be heard clicking on the hanger floor, and both Everett and Mika approach the group of soldiers. As the leader who is giving the instructions is about to draw attention to the two guests.

Everett holds his hand up to have him continue without interruption. After about 15 minutes more as the meeting is drawing to a close.

Mika quickly interrupts, asking if she may address them with information about the city to where they are headed. After about 20 minutes, the meeting concludes.

A pilot approaches Everett "hello, Sir. I am Domino, and I will be the lead shuttle pilot today. Would you like to come over to see the bird?"

"Yes, that sounds like a great idea then to meet everyone who is taking the huge risk for unknown gains," replies Everett.

As the leadership team walks with the pilot, Everett begins, "I am also still trying to get this all out in my head. Here we were for the last 20 years as humans trying to figure out how to get to Mars. Then in Less than in 6 months, we are planning on performing a mission to the surface of it."

"Oh, I know, sir, I think it is so wild that I am one of the first two pilots flying down to the surface. I am just so amazed that I am doing it. Yet I have been rejected every time I have applied for NASA, and now I am going to do something they said I could not do. I am so thankful for the trust you have in me."

Everett puts up both hands, "wait, wait, wait you owe that to your Captain, he spoke very highly of your skills. You were his first choice when I asked him about who could be trusted to do it right."

"Wow, I thought that old man hated me," Domino chuckled.

"Well, why don't you show Mika and I the shuttle you will be taking. I have heard that you have done a few changes to it."

"That is the beauty of being an engineer and a pilot, sir. I know what I like in a control setup, and so I adjusted a few of the controls." Replied Domino

"Oh, did you" Mika interrupts. "I would love to see what you have done."

"Well, great, let's go take a look at her if you follow me," Domino suggests as he leads the way. After a short walk, they are greeted with the sight of the gleaming ship with diagonal black stripes on the side of the body and a figure of a Knight attacking with his sword.

"Pardon me, Domino, what is it with the paint job on the shuttle?" asks Mika.

"Well, Ma'am, we are a proud group of soldiers. We were the Black Knights when we were on Earth. Flew our colours proudly, and people knew who we were from the moment they saw those colors. We will never let them run. Since we are the first squadron on this ship, we are going to keep our colours. If anyone messes with this ship, they mess with all of the Black Knights."

"Okay, I see I have a lot to learn. Thank you for taking the time to tell me that. I can see that you are proud of them." Replied Mika

"From all the information I have gleaned from the leaning

systems that all these ships are equipped with some light-based weapon systems. As well as high mirrored surface should be able to reflect some similar type light-based weapons as well. But at the same time, it looks amazing," replies Domino.

"Okay, so I understand the stripes and the Black Knight. But why do you have a name on the front of the ship that says Black Betty, asked Mika.

"All of a sudden, Domino begins to cough. "Sorry, Ma'am, there is a story behind the name of every plane. I dated a woman whose name was Betty, and well, she was darker-skinned. I was in love with her if you don't mind; I would like to leave the rest of the story there. She has been my guardian angel ever since, and this is how I respect her memory," replied Domino.

"Okay, thank you for explaining that to me" replied Mika

"Why don't you show us what improvements you have done inside," Everett tries to change the subject

"Great, I can't wait, let's go," excitingly replies Domino.

"After about 20 minutes of explaining all the changes which all seem to soar right over Everett's understanding of mechanical engineering.

Mika points at a small datapad on the dashboard of the controls, "What's this?"

"Ahh that's my iPad, I know it is old, but it works, and it has my music on it. Please don't tell the old man he hates when I play music while flying" replies Domino

"The old man?" Mika looks confused

Everett interrupts, "Mika, and he means the Captain."

"Isn't that a bit disrespectful? Oh no, Ma'am, I have known the Captain for years away from the service as well. I asked to be under his leadership when I joined. Because I have always respected him as I was growing up, he was the father that I did not have. That is another story that needs to be left alone as well if you don't mind." Replies Domino

"Okay, Domino, I respect that answer," replies Mika.

"So what kind of music are you playing? Asks Everett

"Well, sir, I tend to change it based on the mood of the mission. Others might not agree with my choices in music, and I don't care because I am the one in charge the moment my plane is in the air. Once I am underway, it is my job to get those who are trusting me to where they need to go safely. I will take these men down to Mars and return them home. Sorry Ma'am I take my job very seriously, and I am good at what I do." Replies Domino

"Okay, Domino, one last question if you don't mind asking."

"Sure, fire away I'll do my best to answer it."

"Why the name, Domino?"

"Hahaha," Domino begins to laugh, "Well, when I joined up, I was fortunate, and then when I joined flight school, I got in just barely. Everything just seemed to fall into place. While in flight school, one of the guys was reading a comic called X-Force, and there was this character named Domino. One of them saw it and started calling me that. It stuck, so instead of being angry about it, I chose to own it. I knew that they were having a bit of a go at me because that character was a woman who was just like me very lucky. At least that was what I thought it was, but it was more about Betty; that we were a mixed-race couple. But I have always had Betty looking after me, and I kept up with that callsign as yeah if the shoe fits wear it. I am lucky, very lucky, but I have the skills to back up that luck. Betty is my wife; she knows that my planes are named after her. Because she always keeps me safe and out of trouble."

"Domino, when this is all done, I would love to meet your wife."

"Ma'am, I think she would love to be introduced to you as well. But I lost her while she was in childbirth. We also lost our daughter at the same time. I hope you don't mind if I stop talking about her right now." replied Domino

After a short pause that allowed Domino to regain his composure, he continued with his original thoughts.

"Though if you ask the Captain, he might say I have a mouth that draws away from my skills and luck. But I try to be level headed, but I am a pilot. I am cocky, and I am good at what I do, so Domino it is and has always been, my call sign. Now no one makes fun of Betty or me" replies Domino

"Thank you, Domino, for taking the time and talking with us." Says Everett

"Captain, can you introduce us to the other members of the mission. I will know everyone before I ask them to risk their lives," asked Everett

"Yes sir, let me introduce you to the ground-pounders. I think it is best if you take the incentive and introduce yourself to them. I also need to get to the bridge to be ready for lift-off."

"Very well Captain, we will join you once we are done here" replies Everett

"I'll take you to meet them." States Domino

"Once again, thank you, Domino." Replies Everett

"Mika, would you mind if I do the talking this time?"

"Sure thing."

"Right now, their minds are very focused, and they might not want to answer a lot of questions. Walking towards the other men, one soldier jumps to his feet and shouts Attention! The Commander on deck."

"At ease men, Gunny, I assume?"

"Yes, Commander, what can I do for you?"

"Well, I just wanted to make sure I meet the men before you all went on your mission."

"Men give the Commander your attention, please."

"Thanks, Gunny, I wish you all the best and look forward to talking with each of you when you return. The command team will have your backs all the way, and you will have our full support in all your choices on the dirt."

"Thank you, sir, very kind of you to check on us, and we will return home with our mission completed."

"We'll leave you up to you and your team then, Gunny."

"Very well, sir."

As both Everett and Mika are walking away, Mika turns to Everett.

"Everett, you did not ask them anything."

"Mika, there are two mindsets with those types of soldiers. One when they are away from missions and one while they are on a mission. While they are in the mission mode that is extremely focused on mindfulness of getting the job done and returning home in the same shape, they left it in. But it does not always work that way, and most of them just want to focus on what they have to do.

Men like Gunny have seen hell walked into it, kicked the Devils ass, and walked out. Any distraction from that mindset is not helpful to them. We should let them know we are here, and we have their backs and give them the ability to make the choices they see best at any given time on the ground." Replies Everett

"That is very intense Everett, do they always think like that. Sadly, Mika Earth was a lot rougher place than most know or even understand, and men like that were needed from time to time. They are the best of the best for a reason. They will get the job done come hell or high water. I trust them completely, and we will support them the best this ship can."

"Commander, Domino told us we could find you over here. I am Hitcher, and the gentleman to my right is Reaper, then Bishop, we will be providing the escort to the shuttles on this mission."

"Wow, great to meet the both of you. Why do you show us your ships" replied Everett

"Sir, you want to see what we are flying?" Questioned the pilot named Reaper.

"Yes, I would love to see what you will be flying," replied Everett.

"Right, this way, then, sir."

Mika leans over and whispers into the ear of Everett. "I know what these ships are for and how they look. If you wanted to know, I would have shown you in your office."

Everett whispers back, "Mika, we provide emotional support at all costs. Let them feel like they are important and cared for. This will show them that all of them are valued, trust me."

"Well, here they are, sir," says Hitcher pointing to completely different looking ships compared to the Transport.

"Wow, those are amazing, and I can see you stripped the paint as well," Everett points out.

"Well, sir, we are talking about an idea from Domino, who is the luckiest Pilot I know. If he says we should strip the paint and put the Black Knight on it, I am going to take his suggestion." Replies Hitcher.

Plus, sir, they look so damn wicked with all that shine to them and the Black Knight logo." Reaper yells out from his ship

"Oh, I get it now," says Mika "The ships are part of the same group of people the Black Knights." Wow, I don't know why I was drawing a blank on why you guys did it.

"Yes, Ma'am, on this ship, we are the Black Knights," smiled Hitcher.

"Okay, I like that, thank you, Gentlemen, for explaining that."

"Not a problem Ma'am we all have that blonde moment from time to time," says Reaper.

"So, do you mind if I ask why you have the call signs that you have?" asked Mika

"Well, Ma'am, most call signs are given due to something we are like as with Domino. Some of us have names like mine for our actions, I have an extremely high kill count, and you only see me when you are about to be dead, so I got renamed Reaper."

"They gave me the callsign Hitcher after the old movie The Hitcher because the people he does not like never expect how ruthless he is."

"Ruthless?" questioned Mika.

"Yes, Ma'am, I saw him once toy, and I do mean toy with an enemy pilot for what seemed like 5 minutes."

"Right, toy?"

"What do you mean by that" asked Mika?

"You see, our old planes used to have guns on them as well as missiles. He toyed with the other pilot by chasing him, and pot shot him every so often. He could have finished him off several times, but like a cat with a mouse, he wanted the game. Then when he was tired of the game, he ended it. It was ruthless to the core. So, we called him Hitcher, and it stuck."

"Well, Sir, Ma'am, it was a real pleasure meeting you and the Commander. But we can see the mission clock, and I need to get suited up."

"Well, Reaper, we will see you all when you return and share a drink or two." Replied Everett

"I'll look forward to it, sir." Said Reaper

Soon the shuttles begin to be loaded with the supplies and vehicles. One by one, the men load up, sit down and strap in. Soon Domino and the co-pilot enter the shuttle. Domino stands outside of the cockpit and begins to talk to all the men as the shuttle doors begin close, and the engines start to warm up.

"Alrighty then time to buckle up boys and girls today I am your pilot, and Domino is the name. To the sides are turrets, and I would like to have a killer on each one. When we land, you will be exiting at the rear of the shuttle. In case of emergency, we will all grab our ass at the same time because I could not find any parachutes on this baby. Gunny, are you ready?"

"Ready Domino, we are a go."

Domino slowly sits into his pilot seat and buckles in here we go. "Bridge, Domino, and shuttle one is a go."

After confirmation of all the ships, the Bridge clears for disembarking.

"Time to put on some tunes, and let's get the party started.... Here is a little Hells Bells.

[Hells Bells – AC/DC]

The rear door shuts,

Domino starts, "Shuttle one locked stocked and ready to roll requesting permission to disembark."

Shuttle one permission granted the Bridge replies.

"Lt. Domino, this is your Captain speaking, next time will you please turn down your music before opening the channel the bridge."

"Yes, sir, sorry about that."

"Very well, Lt. Domino safe travels."

"Alrighty, then let's do this.... slow and steady, just like the book said."

"BOOK, someone yells from the back."

A shocking laugh can be heard from the cockpit

"Muhahaha" as the shuttle leaves the ship for the first time.

"Told you, boys, there is nothing to worry about ol' Domino is at the stick."

"One of the ground pounders asks why do they call him Domino?"

Another one answers, "Simple until he is turned over, you never know what you are going to get."

"Hey," Domino yells back "But it is always an adventure. Look, I promise to get you back in one piece unless you do something stupid."

The shuttle leaves the hanger the first time with Domino flying. "Wow, now that is a smooth ride so far. I did not think space was going to be this way. I like this shuttle. I like it a lot. The simulator does not do it justice."

"Simulator! another voice of concern in the back."

"Relax mates, I have not lost a soul yet, and I am not about to start now."

"Shuttle to Bridge, I am going to see what this baby can do. Give her a little test run before we hit the atmosphere of Mars."

Domino yells to the back of the shuttle "Alrighty then grab your hats boys and girls we are going to give this bird a bit of a test." as he hits the full throttle and precedes to do a corkscrew, then straitens the shuttle out and does a 180 flip while reversing the thrusters to keep the ship going in the same direction.

"Woo" does another 180 with throttle change to correct the flight path. Then he punches the throttle to full with afterburners.

"Shuttle to Bridge, wow, if this is what this bird can do, I can't wait to see the fighters. Oh yeah!"

"This baby is a rocking kid's let's get it on." Says Hitcher over the mic

Soon the shuttle starts to enter the limited atmosphere of Mars pulling back on the throttle he can hear someone in the back losing their lunch.

"Whoa,! We have a winner! Clean your mess up when we land as I can't open the doors until it is all clean. Ha-ha......"

Just then narrowly missing the shuttle three unknown objects streak by the Port side of the ship.

"Bridge, Shuttle, we just had three unknown object streaks by us. They might be headed your way; we are switching to combat mode."

"Confirmed shuttle one, we have the unknown inbound for us. Continue with assigned mission parameters. Confirmed."

"Guys get to battle stations, I need a forward gunner up here now," orders Domino.

A soldier enters the cockpit, "Listen, kid, once I close the door, you are in here for good understood."

"Yes, sir" replies the soldier

"Now, get in that nose gun and protect us as much as you can."

"Shutting and sealing the cockpit door. Computer lock door" orders Domino.

"Domino inbound objects they are headed for us what do you want me to do," questions gunner.

"Take them out; what else would you want me to tell you to do with them. It is a fucking gun, not a pancake turner?" barks Domino.

"Time to change the music to some battle hymns" as Reaper turns on some music this time. They are cutting in front of the shuttles to wipe out the incoming objects.

[Got your six - Five Finger Death Punch]

Domino screams over the mic, "Hold on tight boys; we are going to start having some fun." Then over open mic "Shuttle two, this is one, break to staggered port wing position."

"Hey, the kid keeps track of your kills got it. I want nose-paint for each one."

"Woo! One, Two, and Three

"Shuttle one; if you can target paint the ground locations where they are coming from, we will be able to assist you. We will rock those locations with a bombardment from the main ship.

"Shuttle to Bridge, one confirmed we are primed and ready when you are to light them up."

All of a sudden, the music ends with a distorted crackle and on every channel.

"Attention inbound ships turn back now or risk being shot down. This planet is quarantined and not fit for exploration."

Then due to age, the rest of the message is unable to be understood. It is repeated over and over again.

"Bridge, can you hear me?"

"Shit, there is no reply to our coms; they seem to be jammed. Can we locate that number 2, asks Domino to his co-pilot?

"On it, I believe that it is that dish-shaped object we can see."

"Okay, number 2 since we are not able to use radios gunner light that piece of shit up."

"Yes, sir, I have paint on her. Just then, like fire from the heavens, blasts hit the ground on and around the target. Just in time as the music changes to play loudly over the speakers.

[Mr. Scary – Dokken]

"Bridge, confirmation to continue," requests Domino.

"Shuttle one proceed with orders unless you are not able to comply."

"Bridge received and will continue at this time."

"9,10, 11 shit 12 just missed us."

"Doing a great job, gunner, keeping us safe."

"Shuttle two, let's take them down to the landing point A1."

"Confirmed orders, Shuttle one."

"Troops hold on; this might get a little fun." Orders Domino as he dodges two objects.

"Got a paint, sir."

"Bridge could use a bit more of that muscle here," requests Domino

As he finishes, a beam of light rushes between both ships and strikes the painted target. With a great explosion, a vast dust cloud obscures land-bound position.

"Well, Bridge, that is one way to clear the dust."

Soon two other shots from the main ship fly by both shuttles as the computer picked up other targets.

"Woo, that's the way I like these flights, nothing simple eh gunner?"

"Done and dusted, sir."

In about three minutes, the inbound missiles stop.

"Phew! Okay, keep your eyes open and your guns warm we are headed down to ground level."

"Bridge, we are changing landing point to A2 point to wait for the dust to settle."

"All crew, we are going to hugging the terrain and staying low keep your eyes open for threats. After about an hour, both ships have reached the secondary waypoints and found safe landing points. Mika, we have touched down, we will be awaiting further instructions. Confirmed shuttle one, we will be in touch soon as the dust clears. "

"Confirmed shuttles are at the primary waypoint. Do not

exit ship until primary locations have been cleared of the dust cloud."

"Confirmed Bridge will stay in a sealed environment."

"Shuttle two; see if you can make it to your waypoint."

"Shuttle two, we are landing now. Waiting for orders to unload."

"Bridge to shuttles, you may begin unloading of troops and supplies."

Before doors, open Domino warns that if anyone removes suit or suit is compromised, they will be left behind. Understanding the risk, the soldiers agree, ready to disembark the shuttles. Everyone is warned one more time about Mars and the sickness that is in the soil and within the air. The rear door opens onto a dead city on a dead world.

"Shuttle two, let us lose the dogs of war, and open the cages."

"Bridge ground pounders are underway switching com control to Gunny."

"Bridge, this is Gunny I am taking command of the mission."

"Bridge to Gunny confirmed"

Back at the shuttle, "Side gunners get into position."

The flight into Mars has been met with some shocking revelation that they were not very welcome. After about 5 hours, the dust has cleared, Bridge can zoom in on the landing sites.

"Shuttles one and two, escorts are returning home we will be ready to assist in your evac."

"Thank you; escort looking forward to returning home with you."

"Shuttle one to bridge" in a shocked voice Domino radios

"Go ahead, shuttle one."

"Do you see what I see? This city we are looking at is about five times bigger than New York City. It must have been amazing in its hay day. I've never seen a city this size before."

"We are unable to see what you see, shuttle one."

"Well, it might be that there is a huge dome over it."

"We have been informed that the city has an active camo going at all times."

"Well patching through video feed then because you have to see this place. Though I can see nothing is alive, but wow, look at the size of these buildings. Look at the size of those dead trees. Can you now see what I am looking at?"

"We can confirm the video feed is up, but it is inconsistent, thank you shuttle one."

"Bridge this is shuttle one we can also confirm that the shielding is working there is a burned ground effect. The shuttles shield creates a bubble effect in the dust, pushing it out and away from the ship when it landed."

"Shuttle one, just keep your suit on and the internal cockpit shield up as well."

It was the first line of defence to the motherships. Received bridge and understood.

CHAPTER 15

A False Hope

"Alright, you men, let's do this, mind your Bio-suit you have been warned. I have never lost a man to stupidity, and I am not about to start today, weapons off stun we aim to kill, Oorah!"

"Start this thing up and back out of the shuttle" Daniels

"Michaels, you have rear gunner duty."

"Johnson, you're the heavy gunner."

"Gunny shields are on and fully functional."

"Thank you, Simons."

"Wow, Gunny looks at all that dust outside the shield; it moves and acts like it is alive."

"Well, I bet it is only static electricity that is making it cling to the shields and dance around like that. So, don't worry about it and keep your head focused on the parameters of our mission, understood."

"Yes, Gunny," the men shout.

Domino turns to his co-pilot, "You see, and that is why I was never a ground pounder."

"Shuttles, we are underway."

"Thank you, Gunny, seal the shuttle up; they are all clear."

"Alright, men, it looks like we have only a short distance to our first point of interest, and that would be the dome area about one click to the south of here. The Gunny orders group one onward to waypoint alpha."

"Group two, you have your orders make way to your first objective."

"Gunny, we have departed and underway. Group two head west to waypoint beta and report on arrival."

"Confirmed, Gunny out"

"Gunny, this is Ghost I will have your six all the way."

"Confirmed Ghost good to have ya."

Group one continues for another half hour and reaches the first point of interest, the Dome.

"Bridge, group one we have arrived at the Dome, and we have been barred entry by a biometric scanner, please advise steps to proceed."

"Group one advised placing your data pad upside down and on top of the scanner and pressed the blue button on the back. Please confirm the directions received as we are still receiving some interference..."

"Directions received and actioned, and we have access to airlock proceeding forward. Confirming noise interference."

"Gunny, do not, repeat, do not remove helmets or any part of the Bio-suits. No matter the quality of the air inside of the dome."

"Confirmed reminder and will reinstruct team."

After about a half-hour of cautious driving through the dust that is up to the belly of the transport, they receive word that group two has arrived at its second-way point.

"Hey Gunny, do you feel that everything is a bit off here? It is almost like a sense of death hangs over this place."

"Well, what did you think this is, a walk on the beach? It is, after all, a dead planet." Gunny replies

"Bridge something is very wrong here" radios in Gunny

"Please explain, Gunny."

"The streets are littered with Bio-suits. They are hard to see as this dust covers them. We only find them when we drive over them. Almost too many to avoid hitting. Some of their vehicles we can see also seem to have Bio-suits in them as well. There is a clearing up ahead, and we are somewhat near the second point of interest this looks the best place for us to launch"

"Dust Gunny?" asks Mika

"Yes, Ma'am, but it is not like household dust or desert sand type of dust. It moves and licks at our shields as we move through it. Do you have any input about it?"

"Sorry, Gunny, there is no information about the Dust you are talking about in our research. The main shielding of the city should prevent any of the dust storms from swamping it. So, I do not know why you have dust in there." Replies Mika

"Gunny don't stay too long in one position" Bridge out

"Group one this group two we have arrived at the third point of interest and followed the same instructions for bio scanner, we have entry will advise as to progress."

"Group two, once through the airlock, do not remove Bio-suits repeat do not remove Bio-suits, over."

"Confirming none removal of Bio-suits, Gunny."

"Gunny, this is group two; we have released scanning

drones. It does appear the hanger is fully intact. We are in a safe environment, and this is one big ship repeat this thing is huge."

"Hold position relaying information to bridge."

"Bridge group two has made contact with hanger, and there is a large ship inside, please advise?"

Mika looks shocked at the discovery of the ship.

"They were to launch it to bring people up to this one. Something must have gone wrong. Inform them to investigate the ship."

"Gunny updated orders to collect as much information as you can about this ship."

"Confirmed new orders are to investigate the ship and collect data, correct."

"Confirmed"

"Team two is to proceed to the ship and collect as much information as you can as to why it did not leave hanger."

"Confirmed we are moving towards the gangplank to enter ship should take us about an hour to reach it."

"Bridge group one underway again towards third waypoint. It should take us one hour. Advising that the Bio-suits that we can see are still viable and are holding what appears to be a liquid."

"Gunny, whatever you do, do not break their seals. Those are the liquidated bodies of my people. They could be highly infectious and possibly corrosive. Avoid contact as much as possible."

"Avoidance is impossible; we have driven over a number of them. The sound of the Bio-suit giving way under the pressure of the weight of the transport was how we found out the information we relayed."

It can be seen on Mika's face that this information is disconcerting to her.

"Mika why don't you take a couple of minutes in the office for a break" Suggests Everett

"No, I am going to stay here until our people make it back safe and sound," Mika replies

"Gunny, your video uplinks appear to be jammed. Though do continue to record" instructs the Bridge

After about an hour, team two has reached the gangplank.

"Gunny to Bridge, team two at what appears to be a gangplank entrance to the large ship."

"Confirmed team two make an entrance and collect data."

"Gunny negative this is not a ship, repeat this is not a ship; it is a large husk of what appears to be a ship but is only empty and devoid of real structural integrity. There is no way this thing could be a ship, let alone a child's playhouse."

"Team two gather scans of the husk and move on to finding any sorts of blueprints of the structure."

"Negative Gunny, there is nothing in this hanger, but the scaffolding for this empty husk. It appears to be all for a show there is no way that this could have ever been a ship or even could be made into a ship."

"Confirmed team two, move on to the fourth objective."

"Bridge team two's third Objective was a no-go more information upon return."

"Confirmed gunny bridge out."

"What does that mean?" demands Mika of the Captain

"Mika, Ma'am, that means the information has been collected, but there is something wrong with what they found. That also means they have collected sufficient data to returns to us and explain why he made that call. We need to trust Gunny and his call." Replies the Captain

"Sorry I lost my cool I want to know why that ship did not leave" replied Mika

"Mika, I have known Gunny for years, and he has a reputation that excels where others would give up. If he says they are moving on, there is a damn good reason for it."

"Thank you, Captain."

"Gunny team two onward to fourth way-point, ETA one hour."

"Confirmed team two."

"Bridge team one has arrived at second objective; we are making an entrance."

"Confirmed Gunny"

"Bridge main entrance is free of dust, though it contains several Bio-suits. It can be assumed that they did not bother collecting the dead. We are launching drones to scan the building."

"Gunny make your way to the lift systems use them to go down to what might be the fourth sub-floor is what we have been informed that an entrance to a vault might lie. As per information from the research team."

"Negative Bridge, the lift system is non-operational as there is no power to it at this time. Requesting another means if known."

"Gunny, there is no other access point to that floor."

"Thank you, bridge; we will then improvise."

"Gunny, this lift is a magnet lift type of a system with electromagnets on both sides of the lift. That can be changed to move the lift up and down. It appears that without the power, the system locks into place. We have located the locks. We can release them, but them gravity will take over and BOOM."

"I do not see any other way to proceed at this point. We might have an issue with getting whatever is in that vault to surface if we do, though. But let's cross that bridge when we get to it. Do it!"

"All get clear, fire in the hole!"

With a small set of pops, the shape charges are set off, and the lift disappears from view.

"1,2,3,4,5 then a loud boom is heard. Gunny, that is ten floors down."

"Yeah, something is not right here."

"Bridge, we have a problem, the lift was not viable, and we released it from its braking system. We are sure that there is a total of ten floors below the main level. Please advise"

"Gunny this is Mika, the research team was only able to find a few references to the fourth sub-level vaults."

"Gunny, this is the Commander cancel special ops one, recall them and use them to scan subfloors. Though continue making way to subfloor four."

"Change to orders confirmed, Gunny out."

"Everett what do you have him doing?" asks Mika

"Mika, we can talk about it later. He is doing a special project for me. Please trust me on this." Replies Everett

"Okay"

"Gunny team two, we have reached our objective. Entering the building, we are faced with about fifty ships of various shapes and sizes. We assume there are also some fighters here as well."

"Awaiting orders Gunny."

"Group two received information is there a shuttle within that group?"

"Yes Gunny"

"Good, tell Bishop it is time for him to earn those fancy wings of his once more. I want your team to link with mine. Come to my location with that shuttle. I have an idea that we are going to need it."

"Yes, Gunny, we are on our way to you asap."

"Bridge, we are changing orders of team two; we will need their support at team one location. We have acquired another shuttle and will make use of it."

"Confirmed, Gunny, bridge out."

"Gunny, they dug into solid granite to create this shaft."

"I know it is easy to see they wanted to keep this place safe for a long time. Here is the fourth-floor; let us get some safe footing in the hallway, and then I will release the drones."

"Holy.... Gunny turns around."

"Fuck me! That is a vault door. Anyone have ideas on how we get into that?"

"Yeah, Gunny, shape charges are not going to open that door. Not in a million years."

"I have an idea, Gunny, in my bag of tricks I have some plasma rods. Those, when turned on, will melt the metal of this door. I just need to figure out where the locking pins will be at."

"Well, I guess you better get moving on that idea. I will advise the Bridge of what we are doing."

"Gunny, Ghost, here I have movement."

"Ghost, come again."

"I have movement."

"Confirmed you have movement, what do you see, Ghost?"

"It is hard to say might be something in an advanced camo-suit. One second, they are there next not. The rate of movement is slow and methodical. It is acting like a hunter on the trail of team two."

"Well, that trail will be cold as they are with my team now. But keep a close eye on the target in question. Remember, your weapons are hot. Keep me updated."

"Confirmed, Ghost out."

"Okay, teams, we have an unknown out there that Ghost has spotted; let's get this fucking thing going. Crack this bitch open now." Orders Gunny

"Stand back, boys, and things are going to get bright. By the way, don't look at what I am doing. It is bad for your eyes."

"Team two use one of the support vehicles and get it to the shaft and lower the winch cable. Let's also get some of those empty duffle bags down here; we are going to need them fast; I have a feeling something wicked this way is coming."

"Gunny pin one has released, I am searching for the other pins."

"Gunny, on the fifth floor, there is another vault." Says another soldier

"Keep scanning the rest of this damn building. If there is any information, I want it. Load up the transport vehicles with whatever we can find."

"Damn, I am good at what I do!"

"Mouse, you are the best little safecracker I know. You head down to the fifth floor and see what if you can open it up as well."

"Bridge, we are in the vault, we have a bit of a situation right now. We will be loading up the shuttle team two found, but that is not going to be enough space. So, we are going to load both of the transports to head back to the shuttles with the rest of the items from this vault. We have also discovered several other vaults. The Ghost has also seen a movement of some sort. It appears to be hunting team two who are combined now with team one. We have moved to a high alert stance." Gunny reports

"Gunny avoid other vaults focus on this one. We are sending two more shuttles to collect the transports and return to us. We will drop two more to make their way back to your location for evac. Stay safe and try not to engage unless necessary." Says the bridge

"Confirmed bridge."

"Fuck that, Ghost, if that damn thing starts heading our way, see if you can eliminate it."

"Yes, Gunny, my pleasure."

Within one hour the fault has been emptied

"Gunny"

"Yes Mouse"

"Vault two has been opened, and there is more down here."

"How much more?"

"Yeah, we will fill up the same amount again."

"Damn, that is not what I wanted to hear."

"Shuttle one,"

"Well, hello, Gunny! Are you on your way back to me?"

"Negative, we have a problem. I will be filling up the other two transport vehicles that are inbound. But there is still more information that needs to be collected."

"Okay, let me think on this one, and I will be in touch soon."

"Gunny, the transports are here to collect us."

"Negative load those up, and we will stack on the top of them as well. If we have to hump it some distance out, we will do it."

"Yes Gunny"

"Gunny, Ghost, the first hunter, has been joined by others. They are now leaving the husk's hanger."

"Are they heading our way?"

"Negative, they are going back to the airlock. It appears that they are going to start to track your team. I would suggest busting your ass, which means you are looking at max two hours until contact."

"Good Job, Ghost keep eyes on them."

"Confirmed Ghost out."

"Those seats we can rip them out to make more if it does not need to be in the transport get rid of it, do it now! Load those fuckers up!. We have inbound combatants, and we need to get moving" Yells Gunny

"Bridge, this is Gunny we opened vault two. There was more stuff stored in there as well. We have reloaded both the transports and are going to be hauling some out on our back as well. I am also informing you that we might have combatants inbound to our location."

"Confirmed gunny get out of there."

"We are moving out now, bridge."

"Woo boys I am back" screams out Bishop

Just as the shuttle lands, one of the transports is loaded, and the men unload the bags they were carrying.

"Go, Bishop!"

"Bridge, Bishop just returned and was loaded up. He retrieved the majority of the information we are still in the movement to evac location. Our ETA to evac point is one hour."

"Confirmed instructions Gunny."

"Shuttle one be ready for a hot evac of troops. ETA is one hour," The bridge instructs.

"Gunny, Ghost, they are one half an hour behind you now. I am running to keep up with them. Get moving fast if you can."

"Good eyes, Ghost."

"Get that transport moving to the Evac now we will haul ass!" ordered Gunny

"Gunny, I am setting you a different course that might get you to the airlock faster. Damn Gunny, they have picked up the pace, and are moving to fast for me to keep up with them. Find some shelter now!"

"Gunny to bridge find me a safe place; we cannot outrun these things."

"Gunny, give me an idea where you are at." Mika orders

"We are about two clicks out from the airlock" replies Gunny

"Okay that is not helping is there and buildings that look different," asks Mika

"Yes, there is a building that looks like a tesla tower that we will pass by soon."

"Okay I will have something for you in a second" replies Mika

Everett draws a Tesla tower

"Great turn left at that tower, then find the fourth house down on the right-side code is now in your tablet. Replies Mika

"Gunny, Ghost, my drone can see you, and they might as well you have five minutes until contact. Creating diversion"

As Ghost promised, five flares have launched and filled the sky from different locations of the city.

"Gunny, they are chasing lights get inside now!"

"We are inside now, get out of here, Ghost."

"Bridge we are inside the suggested location," says Gunny

"Good news then. Gunny, do as I say. To the right of the door, you entered is a security panel place the datapad near it with all luck it can be turned on" says Mika

"Okay, Mika, I am at it now."

"Security protocol alpha one," Mika says

"Mika nothing is happening," says Gunny

"SHIT" screams Mika on the bridge

Just then, a message appears on Gunny's heads up display.

"Can't move still watching your back no safe path to exit to evac. I will wait it out. They are heading back to you. Going dark. Ghost out."

"Shit bridge we have one man who is called Ghost who is trapped outside and is unable to make it to evac at this time. he has also gone dark."

"Confirmed Gunny" bridge out

"Gunny put the tablet next to the panel again Since I said it in English not my native tongue" Mika instructs

Soon the house comes alive and visible windows are now sealed up.

"Whatever you did Mika it worked" replies Gunny

"Great Gunny, let me be the first to say welcome to my family's home. You will be safe for about five hours. We will figure a way to get you out" says Mika

In a message to the Bridge, "Ghost to Bridge safe house is no longer safe; it is surrounded. They are aware that they are inside."

"Gunny, Ghost is safe, but your location is surrounded." Bridge out

"Mika, we have moved into your dining room; it appears. There is a message for someone on the table. I have translated it says, "I am sorry, Pookie" repeat. "I am sorry, Pookie," over."

"Gunny can you please save that, it was for me" replies Mika

"Ghost this is Shuttle one, check your O2 levels."

"Switching tanks now" messages back

Ghost sends a message to Gunny, "I think I have been found. It is searching for me but can't see me. It is about 1 meter away. It is not real, and it can't be real. I think it is speaking to me right now."

Gunny messages back, "stay calm Ghost what is it saying to you?

"I am not sure though the translator is working on it, if I could tell you what the boogieman looks like, then this is him. It is saying you do not belong here, stay, and die, leave now. It has moved off" Ghost replies

"Stay dark, brother, stay dark" Gunny orders

"I can't you did not see that damn thing. You did not see it! I am going to make a run for it. My active Camo should keep me alive. It could not see me." Replies Ghost

Ghost using his active camo suit stands up and starts to run for the side of the building in a race to make it to the airlock hoping to make it out of the dome safely and seeing the end of the top of the building that he is on. He can see that he will have to jump down to the ground level to continue his run towards the dome's airlock.

[The loneliness of the long-distance runner – Iron Maiden]

"Brother no" Screams Gunny

"Shuttle one this is Ghost I am running to the airlock get your door open I am coming home." Screams Ghost

"Open that damn door now" Screams Domino

"Gunners get ready; we have Ghost inbound, and he will be bringing the heat. Give him cover fire!"

Soon Shuttle one can see a running figure

"Bridge, I have eyes on Ghost; he is running towards us. Holy shit, what the fuck are those things are chasing him. Shuttle two lift-off now!"

Soon Ghost runs into the safety of the shuttle's shields and then is in the shuttle.

The dark figures rush the ship but are disposed of when they try to enter the shield.

Soon an Auditable scream is heard, *LEAVE!*

"Oh my god, yells out a woman on the bridge, it is a Wendigo." Shut up, yells the Captain.

"I am getting the fuck out of here, yells Domino. I have

not shat my pants since I was a kid, and I am not about to start again now."

"Domino, return to the ship asap," orders Gunny

"What the fuck do you think I am doing!" screams Domino

Soon the pilot named Bishop says over an open mic.

"They don't call me Bishop for nothing. Yea, though I walk through the shadow of the valley of death, I shall fear no evil, for I am your evac! In one hour, have your asses on the top of that building! So, say I and it is written and so it shall be!"

[Gangsters Paradise – Coolio]

"Bishop this is the Reaper, I've got left-wing my brother."

"Bishop, this is Hitcher, I've got your right-wing."

"Let's make it happen boys" replies Bishop

"Everett, what are they doing?" screams Mika with a look of terror on her face

"Mika, these are their brothers; they will not let them perish without doing all they can to save them. There is an unspoken bond that you and I will never understand as it is tested in the fires" Everett replies

"Mika, these are men of honour. Everett is completely correct. They planned for this, and they adjusted those plans because they are trained to think on the fly. These were my men, and I know them. They will come home." Replies the Captain

A deafening silence enters the bridge

"Bridge this is Gunny did Ghost make it safe to the shuttles?"

"Yes, he did."

"Was it Domino?"

"Yes, Gunny Domino evac'd him off-world."

"Good"

"Gunny, when Bishop arrives, you have to be on that roof. But there is a problem the security system will not allow Bishop to land; it will destroy his shuttle. That means you are going to have to shut it off seconds before he does land. Don't do it too soon I am concerned about the dark figures" informs Mika

"Thank you, Mika, and we got this; we are trained to do what is needed to be done. But thank you for looking out for us." Replies Gunny

"Listen up, boys" Gunny begins to give orders "We have one hour to get ready to evac through the top of this building. Mouse, I want you to make us a hole to get out but done blow it yet. I don't want to alert those things out there to what we are doing understood?"

"Yes, gunny, you can count on me."

"I knew I could, and then I want a charge to destroy the security systems so bishop can land it needs to be remotely controlled."

"Yes, Gunny"

"Bishop, Gunny, we are ready for your landing. Give us the go, and we will pop the roof on this place and shut off the security systems for you to hover."

"Understood Gunny"

"Alright, guys, we are going to do something for Mika to pass the time. I want you to go in sets of two to every room in this house. If you find something of value, grab it, bag it, and move on. We are not leaving this place empty-handed.

Next, whoever finds what looks like Mika's room will strip that room bare understood. Then whoever finds her parent's room will also strip that bare. This is a surprise for Mika, no one, and I mean no one says anything to anyone. I will tell Mika what we have for her."

Soon the men set off on their mission of kindness

Soon the parent's bedroom is found. There is a set of bones found in their bed lying next to a something in a bio-suit, the suit is still intact. Gunny is called for advice.

"Okay, I did not expect to find this. Red flag this room; no one touches the suit just in case it fails" orders Gunny.

The bones are bleached with time, still clutching the weapon. There is an obvious trauma to the left side of the head. It appears the person took their own life.

"Get everything else out of this room, but be careful around that suit." Order Gunny

"Gunny, a soldier, speaks up; we have something on a video screen downstairs that you might want to see."

As soon as Gunny enters the room, it comes to life. A screen turns on. While looking at the screen, a man's face can be seen.

"Mika, you should not be here; it is not safe. If this is you, please sit down; you deserve to know the truth."

The Gunny touches the screen to pause the message. On the desk is a note that was covered in dust that says "A note for Mika, a final goodbye" reads Gunny

"This is not for our eyes, pack the system up, and we will take it back to Mika." Orders Gunny

"Understood, Gunny"

"Alright, let's get into place Bishop just told me he is 10 minutes out from us."

"Mouse, is everything is a go?"

"Yes" Gunny

"Did we grab all we could in this place?"

"Yes, Gunny"

"Good now let's get our asses in place, this is going to need to be fast."

"Bishop, we are in place; all systems are a go, and packages are ready as well."

"Gunny, two minutes, do it now!" Bishop orders

"Pop the roof Mouse" Gunny orders

"Move, Move, Move here he comes. Pop security system."

"Get that shit on board" orders Bishop

CHAPTER 16

The First Death

"Alright, boys, you heard the man time to suck it up, pack it up and stack it up. Let's get it moving," yells out the Gunny.

"Gunny, I do not feel like I want to go back to the ship."

"Stow, the feelings soldier we have a job to do. Everyone that goes down goes back up we leave no one behind."

"Yes, Gunny."

"Good, let's get this shit in the shuttle and get it done. You there watch that crate we don't want any dust on that shuttle. Alright, tie everything down as your life depended on it because it does!"

"You there private, what where the fuck do you think you're going?"

"Gunny they are climbing the side of the building we need to go" Yells Bishop

"Gunny, I am not doing this as the soldier walks out the back of the shuttle."

"Bishop, we have a problem, repeat we have a problem abort lift off."

"Gunny this is Bishop, what the hell is going on out there?"

Gunny turns on his mic so Bishop can hear what is taking place.

"Private, we don't have time for this, and your team needs you onboard the shuttle."

"It is too late for me. I have made my choice."

"We need to leave it is starting to get dark, and we don't want to be here when that happens." Gunny tries to convince the young man

"Gunny, I can't do it. I can't see a reason to go back. I thought I could do it without my family. But it is not worth it."

"Soldier, we are your family now all of us on those ships are your family."

"No, Gunny, you are not my flesh and blood. My parents were all I had left, and they chose to face whatever came because they believed God would save them. He never came."

"That's right, and he left us alone. But you are not alone. You have us now come and get on this shuttle, and when we get back on the ship, then you and I can grab a beer. How about that just the two of us and a couple of ice-cold beers."

"I am sorry, but I am not coming," just then......

The soldier removes his helmet as his mates scream at him.

"No, what do you think you're doing."

"I can breathe the air look at me; if I die, then it is a good thing I don't want to continue without my family who chose not to be saved. I can't keep going without them. I am sorry, nothing it's worth losing them."

Soon signs on of the illness can be seen appearing on his face.

"Shut the door now, and he can't be saved" Bishop orders

"The creatures have stopped" another soldier yells out

"Look, they are watching him."

The illness begins to attack him with a vengeance that had been waiting lifetimes to find a new victim. They start to yell at him to put his helmet back on, but he ignores their calls and orders. In horror, his face begins to turn crimson red. Within minutes his skin starts to blister. Soon the blisters start to release.

"Fuck me," yells Bishop, "Seal the fucking doors!"

"Oh, it's so painful," the young man screams out, "but I am going home."

Bishop orders over the coms, "Don't anyone fucking move" As he starts to lift-off, "I fucking mean it."

"Bridge, we have a problem, and we are evac'n now. Minus one" informs Bishop

"Escorts here we come."

The soldiers watch in horror as the young man's skin begins to turn black, and he starts screaming in pain. Soon the soldier falls to his knees as his skin becomes white as snow and starts to flake off. It is exposing new pink skin that laid under the dead skin. Soon even it begins the same process all over.

The Gunny grabs control of the side cannon, takes aim on the soldier, and pulls the trigger. With one shot obliterates the soldier ending his cries of pain.

"Fuck me," as the Gunny slumps to the floor and screams, "Get us the fuck out of here, Bishop!"

As the ship starts to pull away, Mouse squeezes a handle, and the building implodes.

"No person's body should be left to rest uncovered."

The ship starts to lift off at full throttle and begins its journey towards home. Soon the remains of the soldier are covered in the dust of Mars.

"Bridge, this is Bishop; we are in-bound. Please have medical staff standing by"

"Bishop, this is the Captain what the fuck is going on?"

"Sir, Private Brooks just took his own life. He removed his helmet and stated he did not want to live without his family."

"Wasn't his family saved?" Questioned the Captain.

"No sir they were devout Christians and chose not to leave Earth due to religious reasons," Bishop replied

"Bridge, we also have confirmation that the virus is still alive. The way Mika tried to describe to us what it does. It is so much worse when you see it in person; her description does it no justice. It is one fast virus, sir; it wasted no time in attacking him." States Bishop

"Did you watch him die," questioned the Captain.

"No, sir, Gunny, sir, took responsibility and put Brooks out of his misery as he was screaming in agony and was going to die a pain-filled death. I think I just need to fly for now sir we will be docking soon enough" responds Bishop

The Bridge is silent; those that were standing now sit on the floor. People would cry if the shock of what they heard over the radio were not so great.

Within an hour, Bishop radios to the bridge.

"Permission to Dock"

"Permission Granted," orders the Captain

"Listen to me, please. I know that not all of you are soldiers. That what you just heard has shaken you to your core. It did me as well. We will see things, and we will experience horrors that we could have never been prepared for in many a lifetime. But I need you to get up, and I need you to carry on. So, do those men down there. There will be time to mourn, but that time is not now" Orders Everett

"Yes Commander" is heard on the bridge

"Captain you have the bridge" orders Everett

Everett walks into his office.

"You heard the Commander now is not the time to mourn." The Captain begins to issue orders,

"Get the Medical teams in place" that ship has docked; we need to get them into quarantine understood. I want all footage sent to the Commander's office. Get the cleaning crews to get everything they brought back cleaned up."

"Bridge private channel for Mika."

Mika walks into the office

"Hello Ma'am"

"Hi, Gunny, can I help you?"

"No, Ma'am, but my men and I have done something for you. You see, when we were in the house for an hour, we gathered everything we could find that might have had some value to you or your family. If we thought it was important, we took it. To bring it back to you as a thank you for all you did for our loved ones." Informed Gunny

"I don't understand Gunny why would you be so kind?" replied Mika

"We are all we have left, and we owe it to you. I wanted to repay you for everything, but I could never find a way to do so. So while you were meeting with all the pilots, I talked with the Commander. We had an idea to try to find your home; we sent out every single probe we could find on this ship to look for it. Then you ordered us right to it. I thought about how lucky we were. I sent a message to the Commander and told him we were back on plan."

"Gunny, he was in on it?" Mika started to cry

"Yes, Ma'am, I would not have done it without his permission."

"But there is something I need to tell you, and it is better if it comes from me," Gunny says as he swallows hard.

"Go ahead, Gunny."

"Ma'am, we found your parents' final resting place; they were together in the end."

"Thank you, Gunny, that means a lot."

"Ma'am, there is one more thing there is a data pad that we found down in what appeared to be your father's office. It is in one of the bags that we collected. I have given instructions that no one is to turn it on. It is a message from your dad to you."

"Thank you" Mika cries and the call ends

Get me the Commander and have him and Mika meet me in his office. Call the other Captains as well; we need to see what took place. The Captain turns and leaves the bridge through the Commander's office door. As soon as it shuts, he is greeted by Mika coming from her room

CHAPTER 17

Eulogy

Everett sits at his desk in his office, looking over the logs of the mission and trying to find a way to make sure that the soldier's death will mean something. Trying to make sense of the mindset of something that, in the end, makes no sense. His com alert rings,

"Yes," answers Everett.

"Sorry Commander I was told to alert you when the men were available to talk in the sickbay."

"Thank you, I will head there now" states Everett.

Everett turns off his data pad and as he leaves his office.

Mika says, "Everett, do you have, but a moment I need to talk to you."

"Yes, I do for you always" replies Everett

"Gunny told me what the special mission was. He told me what you two planned from the moment those ships landed. I have never felt so loved than I do at this point in my life. Everett, I love you so much."

"I love you, as well. Hey, I am going to the sickbay can you come with me. I think I need some support on this one." Asked Everett

The two of them Hug for what seems a lifetime. It is that type of hug that melts away the pain of life and replaces it with love.

Soon they walk towards the lifts, straitening his uniform. As he walks by his father, he is so focused that he does not hear his father. Soon they are in the lift headed for the Medical bay.

As the doors open, he is greeted by the Chief Medical Officer. Scanning the room, he makes his way to the Soldiers, not talking to anyone. As he arrives at the quarantine area, the soldiers stand naked and salute him.

"At ease, men."

"Get these men some clothes now. Treat them better than this, you understand me, doctor." Orders Everett

Mika places her hand on Everett's back to gently calm him

"Gunny, are you okay?" Asks Everett.

"I am doing okay," thank you for asking.

"Listen to me, don't fucking bullshit me, Gunny."

"You and I do not have time for pleasantries. I asked you a question, and I just want your complete honesty even if it is rotting in your gut," Everett demands.

"I am sorry, Commander I was, I mean...., oh, I don't know how I feel right now. I should have tackled him and dragged him on the shuttle. I could have done more, but I did not know if both suits would have held up in a fight on the ground. I watched that virus eat him alive. I had to shoot him to stop him screaming I never heard a man scream like that. It sounded like private Brooks was being ripped apart from the inside. I just could not let him suffer any longer. I saw that virus do that to him in seconds from him taking off his helmet to the time I pulled the trigger, but it felt like slow motion do you know what I mean? When I got to the gun, I did not even think twice about it; I just took my aim and pulled the trigger."

"Gunny look at me," ordered Everett.

"I can think of no more of an honourable act than what you were forced to provide. You ended his suffering at the end; that was what he wanted."

"But I don't think he was ready for it to hurt so much. You know Commander" replied Gunny

"Did you know him well?

"Commander, he was new to the ship, and I had not had the pleasure to even have a drink with him. I have never lost a man, and now I have not only lost a man. Someone, I did not even take the time to know."

You did not lose him; he was never really there. Sure his body was but not his heart that was left on Earth with his family."

"But I had to end his life. That is very hard to make it right in my head," states Gunny.

"I will have a good friend to come and talk to you. Then when you are ready, you come to see us at our home, okay?" replies Everett.

The Gunny smiles and nods.

Mika places her hand on the glass fingers outstretched, and Gunny does the same. Mika begins to talk. "Face to face is better, I have not seen what is in those bags as of yet but when I do open them would all of you like to come and hear about some of the items you rescued for me, please come. There are some very special moments in time in those bags, and I would like to share them with you all."

Smiles fill the room.

The Captain enters the sickbay

"Hello, Commander. Did you know my friend the Gunny has walked a path littered in the service? I trusted him with my life at one point or another."

"You take care of yourself, okay," states Everett.

Everett turns to leave the men after talking to them.

"Commander" the Gunny raises his voice

Everett turns around to face him.

"Thank you, sir, for coming and checking on my men and me."

"Gunny, every person on this ship is here because of my choices less than a year ago. It is my responsibility to uphold my choices. I hold every one of you as a member of my family. When you hurt or suffer, I will be there for you. Private Brooks will not have died in vain. I will make sure we remember him. I owe all of you more than you will ever know," states Everett as he stands straight and salutes the men.

Turns and walks over to the medical staff, "Get them clothes or face my wrath!"

"Yes, Commander," one of the medical staff replies.

He heads to the lift where Mika is waiting. "Let's go to the kid's school, please. I would like to read another book"

"Hmm, I will message ahead as not to surprise the teacher again. You know Everett, if you keep doing this, someone is going to think you enjoy it."

"I don't, and I hate reading" replied Everett

"Right, do you want to pull the other leg now." Mika smiled as she looks at Everett

"Okay, I enjoy reading to kids" Everett admits

"HA! Pay up big man" Mika turns to Yuri

"Did you just lose a bet to her?" smile Everett

"I have to cook dinner for you now, thanks, boss."

"Oh no, I am not being dragged into your bet with my love. Forget it, Yuri, you bet, you lost, you pay up. But bring your family as well. Your wife is a charm" laughs Everett

Soon they arrive at the school. Hello, Commander, to what do we owe this visit. Well, you know I like to keep a low tone and just come to read a book to the kids. Understood sir, why don't you all follow me. As they turn the corner, he is greeted by a packed Library.

Wow, the class grew.

"No Commander your reputation in reading to the kids grew" replied the teacher

"Well I guess it did and I better not let them down, Thank you," replies Everett

Everett walks over and grabs a book that he used to read to his children, Hooway for Wodney Wat by Helen Lester. Soon one by one, the children are all listening and laughing. Even the adults who are there with their children are listening as well. Reading the story and bring it to life for the children. Laughter is being heard, and love begins to fill the air. Soon the book is finished, and a complete family group hug takes place. Everett stands in the middle of all the children.

Then the children are sent back to their classes. As they all are leaving, Gabriel turns and rushes back to his dad.

"I love you dad thank you for reading that story it has been a long time. Are you okay?" Gabriel grabs Everett's hand and asks.

Everett leans over for another hug, "I am okay now, son, thank you for asking."

"I love you too, dad," says Gabriel as the hug ends, and he let's go, then walks off to class.

"Alright, everybody, lets' get back to work." With a smile a mile wide.

"Sir, I have to say a few things while we are heading back to the office. Can I speak freely?"

"As always, Yuri, I would hope that you always feel free to do so," replies Everett.

"Sir, what you did down in the Medical bay I have only seen leaders do when they want their press photos. Those men listened to every word that came out of your mouth from the moment you ordered clothes for them to the time you left.

Remember, I told you I would be an extra set of eyes and ears for you in case you missed something. Well, you did not miss something because you did not know it was not typically done.

Then I listened, and so did everyone else in the Medical bay when you talked about being a family. It resonated with all of us. We will not forget what you said down there. Then I saw you and heard what you said to all the children and how you lifted their hearts while they did not know they were raising yours. Whatever you do, don't change."

"Thank you," replied Everett. "I hope and pray that will continue to be a leader everyone looks up to and trusts.

"Sir, I take it that you did not hear your father as you were leaving?"

"No, my focus was on the men."

"He told you he was proud of you."

"Thank you, and I was so concerned about the men that I shut everything off. I did not know what I was going to find when I saw those men. We need to get back to the office; I need to make a call."

Soon they were back in Everett's and Mika's home. Everett walks straight over to his father, bends down and hugs his father. He stands up and straitens his uniform.

"I love you, dad."

Then he walks off to his office. Everett returns to his data pad, never noticing that Mika has been with him every step of the way and now watches him from the couch. Everett types erase and retype several times. Well, I think this is the best I am going to get. Taking a deep breath, he presses the commlink and selects ship-wide.

Can I have everyone's attention? Please, this is Commander Everett? A few hours ago, we lost someone, and his name was Private Brooks, to a horrific tragedy that could have been avoided. We sent a human-crewed mission to the surface of Mars to see if we could inhabit that planet. We were, however, greeted with the cold facts that we will miss Earth and those that chose not to be saved for whatever reason. Private Brooks was sent down to see if we could live on Mars. He was carrying such a burden that he was the only surviving member of his family. Private Brooks had not taken the time to talk it over with anyone and must have been feeling so alone. On the mission, this weight became far too heavy for him to bear, and he removed his helmet. His death was almost instant and also provided us with the information we needed about the surface of Mars. Though I will say that the cost he gave us this information was far too high a price.

I understand that we all carry a heavy burden being the sole survivors of humanity. But if this burden becomes a weight that you cannot take it, you need not take it alone. Talk to someone, and we have professionals on board who can help you work through what you might be going through. If you do not feel ready to talk to a professional, please take the time and talk to someone. Many of us can help with the weight that you might feel.

If you feel that you are all alone, you are not, this I assure you. Right now, we are all one big family. When one suffers, we all feel the pain and will support you. No one will ever replace that young man. We, who were his family and friends, will see him around the corner sitting having lunch with us. We will feel his loss in many different ways.

So, in closing, let us not forget this young man's choice to leave us. Instead, let us make a promise to ourselves that we will be our brother's keeper and be there for someone else. If that burden is even too hard for you to carry with them, find more people to help.

As your friend and Commander, I think I speak for all of the people on this ship when I say I am here for you. I love and care for you. I wish you all the best. Lastly, I would also like to say a farewell to Private Brooks, and you will be missed. I think this is an excellent time to have a minute of silence for those we have lost and for Private Brooks.

The ship goes silent in the dark of space.

Everett, after a minute, "Thank you for your understanding. Once again, I wish everyone you to know I care about you." Everett turns off the com and slumps back in his chair.

Mika sees the weight that rests upon his shoulders and

walks over and behind him and starts to Rub his shoulders in a loving gesture. Everett leans forward and rests his head on the desk, allowing her better access to his back. Soon he drifts off to sleep.

Hours later, Everett awakens to find he is in his bed. Wow, I must have sleepwalked to my bed. I don't remember getting here. Little did he know that Mika got Yuri to take him to their bedroom. Everett then stands up and gives a big stretch. Mika, thank you for the back rub. I feel amazing. Shit, the kids must be home from school. He rushes out the door, only to be greeted by a dark room. Mika steps out of their bedroom.

"Come back to bed; you have been asleep for a day."

"For a day really" a surprised look upon Everett's face

"Come back to bed, now" Mika looks at him

"Okay I know what that means"

CHAPTER 18

Revelations

"Where are the girls and Mika at?" Everett asks.

"Oh, Mika said, after this last week she and the girls were going to go do something for them. She wanted to have a girly night with them."

"Oh, no…. Oh yes, sir, the girls are growing up and wanting to do those types of things. Oh, okay, not a problem."

"Well there is one little problem" comments Yuri

"Oh yeah, what."

"They are at my home, and I am at your home tonight."

"Not a problem, we can have a guy's night in!"

"Give my dad a call and see if he wants to come over for some fun."

"Sorry, no luck on that your dad has a date tonight and is not expecting to be home."

"Okay, wow, the old guy is getting out more that is good."

"But Frank and the boys will be here soon too."

"Alright, do we have the food, this was my payment for the bet I had to cook for you guys."

"Damn Yuri, she is one smart woman."

"Oh yeah, she is a planner. By the way, they have dropped

off all of the bags from her home while you were taking your nap. Your office is a bit full.

"By the way, I bet you did not know by Hezekiah was going down to the sickbay every day at lunch to spend it with the men. I found that out today when Gunny stopped by with all the bags."

"I missed Gunny, why don't people wake me up?"

"Respect, sir, you have earned it."

Everett speaks up, "Okay enough about work I am home, and it is the weekend. I'll call the boys, and let's get a movie going and eat like pigs. Where did the bottle of whiskey come from?"

"The Gunny sir,"

"Let me guess while I was sleeping."

Dear Commander, Thank you. I will be waiting to have a drink together. Thank you for being there for me, Gunny.

"Well, son, that is a powerful statement from a good man. I hope you understand that."

"Yeah thank you, dad," I do

"I thought you had a date tonight."

"I did, but she forgot that Mika was stealing all of the women tonight."

"Yeah, thanks' Uncle. I get a break tonight because I don't breastfeed" Frank says with a big smile

"I am going to go place this bottle in my office," Everett says, walking down to his office.

To be greeted by Gordon in his chair working on a data pad.

"Hello Everett"

"Hello Gordon"

"I need to tell you something while you place that bottle."

"Okay, I am all ears."

"I am impressed with you. You see, in all my years in the service, I have never seen a top-ranking Commander rush to the side of men under his command when they have lost one of theirs. I don't recall any of them doing it without photos. Those men respect you beyond words, and you have my absolute respect. So, I have been waiting here to talk with you face to face. I am letting you know I am stepping down. I have sent far too many men out to die in my days. It has worn me to the bone, and I am not able to make those choices any longer."

"Gordon, I would wish you would reconsider I need your guidance" replies Everett

"No, you don't. You see that bottle that is telling you that you have earned the respect of a hard as a rock soldier. You respected and cared for them. You even cared for the young man who took his life.

You can, and you can do it. I know you were worried about it, but after what you did, you are more than ready. Take the helm look I have already talked this over with my staff and Roe they all agree that I should stay on as an advisor. But I am only going to do it in dire times. You are the Commander, and you need them to view you as their leader."

"Thanks, Gordon, it looks like we need to not only place this bottle, but we need to tell the staff."

"Everett, I am two steps ahead of you. I already announced while you were asleep. That I was retiring to help in the rose gardens." Okay, well looks like I am going to go out and enjoy my last meal before the chaos.

"What your wife is with Mika as well?"

"That girl moves so damn fast it makes my head turn. Good luck. You are going to need it. She sure does love you to bits.:

Everett walks over to Gordon and gives him a handshake. "Thank you for everything that you have done."

"Everett, it has been a pleasure now let's go and make Yuri earn his lost bet."

The two men laugh as they walk out of the office to a room full of men.

Everett walks into the living room and plops down into his favourite chair and lets out a sign followed by "Shit."

"What was that, son?" Everett's father asks.

"While I was sleeping, more changes are taking place."

"Well, I was talking with Gordon here, and I said I needed help at the rose garden."

"So, it was you're doing, dad?" Everett said pointing at his dad

"We just talked with you over my planned retirement." Gordon laughed

"Dad, that was not planned it was here ya go I am quitting."

The room fills with laughter

"Everett, it was one too many for me your dad and I had a few talks about it."

"Yeah, it is no big deal change happens, and I will deal with it. I am just giving you a hard time. Now let's get this movie rolling."

"What are we watching, guys?"

"Your son picked it out."

"Which one," asked Everett

Hezekiah

"Is someone going to tell me what we are watching?"

"Spaceballs"

As the night rolled on people fell asleep, Everett retired to the office.

"Hey son, his dad followed him in."

"Hey, dad."

"When you were asleep, Gordon came and saw me about getting some advice about getting out. I told him to rip off the Band-Aid; it will be difficult at the start. I know you, son, you were scared of the position as you have never been a military man. But not all leaders need to be Military, but they do need to be a leader of men. You have it in you to do it, and we saw it.

People know it was you that started this, and they want you to lead. I believe in you, son. Just keep doing what you have been doing, but now only accept it."

"I don't have any other choice, do I," Everett replied.

"Well, dad, I am not starting tonight."

The door com rings from the bridge,

"Crap," Everett says as he is about to get up.

"Sit down, son, and I'll get the door." Laughs his dad

"Well, my son looks like the troops are okay with you as well. Here is a bottle of Captain Everett rum for you."

"I don't even drink, and now I have two bottles."

"Son, these are bottles from the Earth that the men and women of the Military have given you. In the morning, take over the helm and announce to all the Military staff. Then thank them for their trust in you. That is all you have to do and get to work.

Then you need to have a drink with Gunny and the men who went down. But don't puke until you are out of his sight if you have to."

"Thanks, Dad, you are a real funny man...."

"Love ya, Son, get some more sleep."

"Mika, are you going to open any of these bags?"

"I need to start watching this data pad, but I did not want to do it alone. I am scared of what it might have on it. Then there is the issue that I will see my father again. I miss him so much the thought of seeing him again, but not being able to feel a hug from him breaks my heart."

"How about we do it together? Kids are at school, and I can set the do not disturb on the office."

"Okay, can we do it though in the lounge room. This is not a work thing; this is me and you thing."

"Yeah, let's go."

Mika takes the data pad and turns it on. In a short time a man's face appears, and Mika grabs her chest; it is her father.

"Hello, Pookie if you are watching this, you have somehow made it back only to be greeted by the reality of death everywhere you have turned. This place you once called home is no longer safe for you. I hope you were able just to take this tablet and leave. If not, then I am so sorry for what you may have found.

I remember the day you were born into our lives. You brought us so much joy watching you grow. Day by day, it was a never-ending set of wonders. The day you started at my old school was the best day in a long time. The war took so much from so many. But you had your plans, and you were going to find our ancestors ship. You stood tall when people called you a fool. Then you were kind when they had to eat their words when you found it. Your Mother and I felt so proud to be in your life as you became the lead engineer to the Mother ship.

The day you left to be on the Mother ship was the worst day of our lives. It tore us to shreds because we knew we would never hold you again. It was then it all started to go the wrong direction for so many families. I am so sorry, my child, we lied to all of you. We sent you away to that ship with the thoughts that we would be joining you someday. But the truth was it was just to save your lives. Our first big lie was that we had a ship that would bring us to you. I am sure if you have explored the city and the launch site, you would have noticed that the outside of the ship is all that was only meant to look like one. We did this so you kids would not lose hope and faith in the future. It was all done because we are the reason Mars has died, not our children, not you. We knew what we were doing, and yet we ignored the evidence until it was far too late. It took so long to let you go because the children from the other city-states were slow in reaching the last city, the main spaceport. So we had to keep sending you supplies to keep up the lies.

Then there were other lies. Once the illness started, the government labs were having the same issues as the private ones that the disease could not be stopped. We could stall it here and there, but it was far smarter than we gave it credit. I think it will outlive all of us in the end. Mars had the last word. Just after days, you left the surface of the planet and headed towards the ship. Your mother became ill, and with my contacts in the government, she was able to live a few more months, but she did not want you to know, so during this time, she recorded all the conversations with you ahead of time. Then a computer was set up to fake it so you could think you were talking to her. But it was an actor your mother picked out. She wanted you to complete your mission and survive. She made me promise that when she died, I would not tell you.

Mika begins to cry

"Mika, my love, just turn it off. Let their memories that you have with you be the last ones you remember of them."

"That is the problem, Everett; I think that while I was in the pod for so long, I lost some memories. I did not remember what he sounded like or even his face. I need to finish this.

"Okay, my love."

"I am so sorry for everything. I know this is a goodbye that you never wanted to hear. We were always so proud of you, and you filled our hearts with love, Pookie. I have recorded many files on this tablet, your even your mother's final words to you. As well as many files I stole in the last days from the hidden archives. I have also included all my research over the years. There are also a gem or two of all the photos we took of you as you grew up until the day you left.

Before I say goodbye, my lovely child, I need to get something off my chest, and I hope you can forgive me in time. That night you went to sleep I made sure that your sleeping pod was set to make you sleep for six months while the ship travelled to Earth. This was the deal I had to make to keep you on the ship from the last time you tried to come home. All of us who chose to stay watched you leave with hopes, dreams, and prayers in our hearts for you.

I am so sorry that I was too much of a coward to come

to the ship and be with you. But I needed to stay by your mother's side as I could not let her sleep for eternity alone, and I wanted to die next to my best friend. I have always loved you, Pookie.

But to be honest, this is my goodbye to you, my beautiful child. I am going to go now and rest with your mother.

The video ends, and then the files open for Mika to see. Mika finds her mother's name and starts the video.

"Hello, my little girl." Her mother's face appears smiling. After about half an hour, the video ends. Mika sits leaning against Everett's chest, crying as Everett strokes her hair. Hours pass as Jas, and the kids enter the home. Everett motions for people to be quiet. Niamh runs and grabs a blanket, then softly lays it on Mika.

Jas using sign language, asks Everett if everything is okay. Everett explains what has taken place.

"Tip Toeing children are like herding Elephants I have heard" Mika gently says

"I am sorry my love would you like to head to bed, I take care of everyone tonight."

"No, I am fine, and I am a parent, so I will get up and be one no excuses."

"Okay"

"Everett, I want to be your wife, like Jas is to her husband."

"Mika, okay, but you know that it is just a title."

"But Everett, I want what my mother had with my dad, and I want to hear that from your lips."

"Okay, when?"

"Sunday"

"This Sunday?"

"Yes"

"Mika, I love you with all that I am, but people plan these things out."

"I did it with Jas and everyone at the girl's night out. I was waiting for the right time to ask you."

"Okay, we just watched your parent's last goodbyes, and this is the right time for you?"

"They made me realize that love is the most important thing in all of creation. When it is right, never let it go. So, Everett, will you marry me?"

"Yes, yes now and forever, yes" Everett replies

Weeks have gone by, and the Wedding filled the park; everyone danced until the music stopped. Time moves forward in space differently. In some ways, people had forgotten that the year had passed since the loss of Earth. Routines created and followed time marches on.

"Mika, Mika, I was doing some reading in some of the documents your dad stole. I came across a thing called the Protection Protocol. But it is missing several references, and do you know what is meant by the Protection Protocol?"

"Oh yeah I do, I am going to be in trouble."

"Mika, I am not going to like this, am I?"

"I love you, and I am sorry it was so busy to this point, and I just simply forgot to talk about it. So, I left out a few issues and things. I did while I was alone or in my past."

"Fine, just tell me about it, and I will adjust."

"In my youth, I helped create the Protection Protocol; it is a released nanobot that can fight the virus. With a 100% cure rate and prevention rate even when the virus mutates."

"Okay, that is great, but I am sensing you are not telling me the whole story, are you, Mika."

"Well, Everett, there are two small problems with the nanobots. Those small problems were a bit distasteful to the government. The main issue is that at their height, they will self-replicate in the body to allow them to bond with all of the host's internal systems. But while that might not seem so bad. They can be as once they are in a person's body; they cannot be shut down, or the subject will die."

"That is not that bad for a first problem?" questioned Everett.

"Oh, I wish that was so they are machines after all, and if a strong enough electromagnetic pulse was to hit them, you're dead. There is no backup system, and I lived in a world of war followed by another war. Now, if everyone had the nanobots in them to fight the virus, think about it in weapons terms. What weapons could be created to wipe out the enemy quickly…"

"Oh well, I did not look at it that way. That cannot be all of it; keep going," says Everett.

"The next problem is age and health-based issues. We are amazing machines from the day we are conceived to about the age of 25; we are still being built. Then at about 25, we start to fall apart and die. I know that it is rather hard to look at life that way, but it is the bitter pill. So one of the side effects is that the nanobots slow this down to the point that it looks like you never will grow old. Remember, they see a problem in your body; they fix that problem. Have a weak spot in your heart; they fix it. But it is fixed with a nanobot always having to stay there, making sure it does not happen again. They also read your genetic code, and if something is not right, they will fix that as well if you have poor eyesight that will get fixed because it is not part of the code of your body to have bad eyes. Well, that change happens to everyone, glasses can be put in a drawer as they fix all infirmities and abnormalities a person might have."

"Wow like a fix-all for the human issues. How can that be so bad people would live a wonderful life.?"

"Everett, you are missing the problem. Dying is not natural to a machine that can only read a baseline code. So, it does everything it can to save your life. This was not what the government wanted to hear. Because that meant people would not die of natural causes. The machines see that the age of 25 is the best your body is at when it is healthy. So, they work hard to reverse the aging of a person. To bring them back to the age of 25. It will not happen overnight, but in time it does happen. Haven't you noticed that you feel like you have more energy these days since being on the ship?"

"Mika... What is going on? Do I have these things inside of me? I did not agree with something being put inside of me. You have no right to do that to me."

"Everett, I didn't; they are in the air of the ship. The moment you came on board, they saw you and said, look a new thing to fix. This was part of what the government did not like about them. They could not control them, and that meant no money was being made from them by anyone. That the government also did not like."

"Well, for those of us who are on this ship, it cannot be removed as the nanobots they are now part of the body."

"Okay, let us not worry about me right now and keep explaining to how they are in the air on this ship. When I was told no, I did something rather risky, and I injected myself with the first batch to show that they were not harmful. But no one listened to me on the ship. But I could see that they were working under examination and testing. But they were fundamental they could fight any disease that I tested them with."

"Okay, Mika, from where I see it, that is not a problem. They are amazing. I do not see where this all went pear-shaped. Except for everyone going back to 25."

"Everett, I come from a class-based society. The family is builders; they will always be builders, and they know what they are doing as builders. Now I am not a builder. I am a mechanical engineer who had to act like a builder to get my education. Then convince others that I also needed to be an engineer to build better things. I am also an inventor who thinks outside of the box. I got told so many times that I did not belong in that area, that I should just be happy at being a builder." No one liked to listen to me until I proved it, just like finding this ship. So, to prove it once again, I tried to create coup and takeover of the ship and single-handedly fly it back home. As you can see, I was punished to the point I out-lived all of them to meet you."

"Oh shit, I don't know what to say. I just don't have an answer for that. All I am left with is more questions." asked Everett.

"Everett, I have been left alone for a very long time. That is not always a good thing for a person like me. I build, and I test, and I then build some more. I have changed the nanobots so many times to make them better. To make them do more things. This ship has survived because of them. As I said, I am not a builder, so to have them build the ship, I don't think they can do that. So, what you see is what you get that they can do. I am healthy, and I am alive," said Mika in reply.

"But I see a problem with what you are talking about with them. You told me you could not have children. It should be part of your natural make up to have them."

"I completely agree, but it is not for me. It appears that it is not part of my genetic code. I am not the same as every other woman on this ship. My breast tissue is complete, but not that part, and it is just not there at all. I have spent years and years trying to fix that, but it can't be fixed because it is not in my code, and you cannot put parts into the code once the code is created. Editing a person is not as easy as fixing a person."

"Okay, so let's say a child who is challenged goes to bed at night, and will they wake up perfectly fine?"

"Once again, it does not work that fast. I am not sure as I could not test this on others as I have been the only one on this ship until all of you came."

"This is a lot to take in. I have so many people on this ship that are all going to be 25 for a very long time. How do I tell them that?"

"There are so many questions and problems with this. If a person ends up in space without a suit, will they live?"

"Hell no, they are going to die Everett; this does not make us superhumans. What it means is that you will have a healthy body for a very long time. Then if you leave this ship, the nanobots will slowly start to not self-replicate, and you will start to grow old."

"Why is that? Better yet, does that mean I can say the ship

is designed to keep us alive? Because if I can say that I might be able to sell this to everyone on this ship. Because right now I think that what I have to do. I have to sell this to people as a good thing. Now with age regression, what are we looking at in a timeline?"

"As I said, not overnight but not as long as it took them to get to that age."

"Okay, I can work with that. Now we come to an "us" issue here. Mika, for "us" to be a couple, you need to tell me these types of things. Because I have to say to others on this ship, I am the person that brought them all on board. I am responsible for every one of them, and I carry that weight on my shoulders," Everett said as he put his hands on the side of his head, running his finger through his hair.

"I can see this is stressful for you. You do that thing with your hands when you are stressed. It is your self-comforting technique, isn't it?"

"Mika, don't go there, please. I am stressed if you need to know. You see, I have gone from being a very simple man. I had a horrible wife and lovely children to a man who restarted his life. Who now has more children and a wonderful wife. I am no longer a simple man but a man who is in charge of thousands of people. If I fuck up just one little bit, people can die, or we all can die. I don't know anything about space, and I am not completely sold that any of us do. Mika, my love, I am going to go take a shower and try to relax."

"I'll shower, and all will be okay," Everett thinks to himself. As Everett stood in the shower, the feelings became all too much, and he was overcome. Tears are flowing down his face as fast as the water rushed over him. It felt like he was reliving

all his life to that point. He buckled under the stress and fell on the floor of the shower; broken-hearted laid as the water rushed over him and down into the drain.

Time passes, and Mika remains in the office, still sorting through bags and bags of memories of her family. When it dawns on her that Everett has not returned as he said he would. Mika leaves the office to go looking for Everett.

"Okay, I'll check the kitchen and the lounge room first. Maybe he is listening to some music that always calms his nerves down. Okay, not in here, maybe the kitchen. Nope, hmm, okay, taking a nap, I will go in there. Not in here is that the shower? Is it still running?" Mika thinks to herself."

"Medical staff to my quarters now! Mika yells in her commlink."

"Come on Everett are you there, wake up, I need you to open your eyes. Please open your eyes" Mika pleads with Everett in her arms; the shower is still going.

Soon Yuri and the medical staff rush in to take charge of the situation. Yuri takes Everett's limp body and places it on the gurney.

"Let's go I will move people out of the way" Orders Yuri

Mika still holding Everett's hand in hers. She can tell he is alive as she continues to talk to him. "Everett, I love you, and I am so sorry. Don't you leave me."

Soon the Chief medical officer comes out to the family who is waiting.

"Hello, he introduces himself. I have done all I can, and from what I can find, there is nothing wrong with him. He is just not waking up. So, I need to ask some questions. Has this ever happened before to him?

Both Jas and his dad say "Yes" at the same time.

"Great to know but can I ask that only one person talks at a time" instructs the doctor

"So, let's try this again, Bill, you have known your son the longest how many times has this happened?

Everett's dad begins, "When he was a kid, it happened a lot. He would get worked up for days over something, and then we would find him asleep on the floor in his room or somewhere. We would put him in his bed, and the next day he would be fine."

"Jas how many times have you seen this happen?" asked the doctor

"My mum was not a very nice person to him. He would get stressed and would take what she thought were naps. But looking back, they were more of this, I think. He would just sleep for hours then get up, and everything would go back to as it was before he was sleeping"

"Okay, Mika, it now your turn. Has he done this with you?"

"Yes, once when I asked him to help me save the people of Earth."

"So here is what I am thinking we are seeing. This is not a typical physical health issue like something wrong with the heart. I have already checked for that.

What it might be is an overload switch in him that when he reaches a certain level of stress, he has to have a time out. This allows him to sort out the issues that might be going on that are stressing him. It does appear that the more the stress, the longer it might take to sleep it off for the lack of a better way to describe what is going on.

I think it is best that we just let him sleep here, and we will keep him under observation. That way, if something changes, we can respond to that.

Before anyone goes into see him, his head does have a bandage on it due to the rather large bump on his head. But there is no need to be alarmed about it; the brain was not hurt or the skull itself.

Is there anything else I can tell you that might help you? No, okay, why don't the family head in to see him? Yuri, you can head home and take a break for a while. I am sure he will call you when he needs you again."

"I am family, and I will stay, get out of my way." Yuri says as he pushes the doctor aside, "After you, Mika."

Mika looks up at Yuri, "Thank you."

Yuri smiles back then tells the others to go.

One day turns into two, then to a week. As Everett wakes up to Mika's head resting on the bed. He can see Gunny and Yuri standing outside his room.

He starts to caress Mika's soft hair stroking it lightly. She sighs and slowly wakes up to feel his hand running through her hair.

She looks at him and begins to speak.

He stops her "Shhh..." Everett continues, "My head is feeling like shit. It happened again, didn't it? I am so sorry how long have I been in here this time?"

"Everett it is not you who should be sorry, I did not see that you were getting overloaded. Yes, it did happen, but not in a safe space; you were in the shower. It's been a week since you passed out." Mika tilts her head into his hand.

"I am so sorry. I need to work on telling you I am getting

overloaded. I am doing such a bad job at that. I did not even think it was happening. I am so tired, my love" Everett lets a tear roll down his face.

Mika, with all the love she has for him, wipes the tear away and puts it on her heart. "I will carry this one for you. Now you get some sleep, I am here beside you." she takes his hand and holds it until he returns to sleep.

[Make you feel my love – Adele]

The next morning Everett wakes up to his children in the room, Mika laughing with them as Gunny tries to read Dr. Seuss to them.

"Man, Gunny, and I thought I sucked at reading those books," Everett says as he laughs.

"Well if sleeping beauty is awake" he replies

The children run to Everett's side, and the hugs begin.

Doors to the Bridge open as Everett steps through. "Commander on deck."

"Knock that shit off on my Bridge." Everett smiles

"Good to have you back, sir."

"Good to be back."

CHAPTER 19

Exodus

Mika sits down and stares at a planet that was once her home. *"It seems like it was only yesterday that I was holding my father's hand, or my mother was brushing my hair. Then I blinked, and I was in school that seemed to go on for such a long time as a child, but it too was gone all too quickly. Next thing I know, I am saying goodbye to my parents at the spaceport. I did not know that was the last goodbye I would ever have with them. I am glad it was on such good terms. Looking below, I think it is time to go for us to face whatever lies for us in the dark of space.*

Are they ready to say their last goodbyes to what was once their hopes, dreams, and loves? It is still so difficult for me to sit here and think of it as well. It seems the magic of the Gods' are how we are attracted to them.

[The Last Goodbye – The HotDamns]

Mars was not a good God for my people; it turned us into something we were ill-prepared to see in ourselves. He was filled with hate and anger from the moment we set foot on him.

Poor Earth's God, she would have never known what hit her when they landed. Had she known that my people would be the death of her, she would have killed us first. Who could have blamed her? Will we find a new home again? Would that God be willing to allow us to earn our forgiveness? This is something that the people of Earth have not had time to ponder as much as I have.

For once in my life, I have someone who believes in me as much as my parents did. I am so blessed to wake up every day and be a part of this family. I wish my parents could see what has happened to their little girl."

Mika reaches for the office commlink. "Everett, can I meet you in the office."

Soon the door opens and in walks Everett, "Damn you are dressed, there goes that hope right out the window." He smiles at Mika

"I love you too. But I wanted to talk to you about the future of everyone on this ship. I was hoping that you could spare some time for that."

Everett opens his hands like a book, stares at them like he is reading them.

"Everett, what are you doing?"

He looks up and smiles, "Just a second, I am almost done."

Mika is looking at him with a concerned look on her face.

"Ah there we go, that is all done."

"Everett, are you feeling okay?" Mika says, still with a concerned look upon her face.

"Oh yes, my love, I am doing wonderful. You see, I have cleared my whole schedule for today just to be with you. That will give you and me some time just to be us and talk over whatever is needing to be done. I also wanted to spend some time with you as you cleaned out some of these bags and listened to your memories as you found places in our home for some of them. Then after dinner, I was hoping to go for a night-time walk in the park with you this evening." Everett smiled looking at Mika

"Everett, is there a catch her? Because right now, you are winning some major points with me." Mika looks at Everett, hoping that this is not a game.

"Mika, I don't play games with your heart. I am in love with you, and you matter so much to me. I have already cleared off my schedule just for you. I am surprised that you did not notice that I was not in my uniform as I walked in here."

"Oh Everett, you and so kind to me. I was in the zone, and I did not even see your lack of uniform. Would you mind if I got out of mine?"

"Can I help?"

"Can you catch me?" Mika says with a grin as she rushes out of the office with Everett close behind.

Over an hour later, the two return to the office "You cheated, Everett. There was no way you could have caught me."

"Oh, I know I am not stupid. I wanted "us" time, so I cheated big time" Everett laughed

"But I still love you. So let us get this stuff out of your office. As we talk about what we need to do for the future"

"Sounds like a wonderful plan. I have a few boxes that you can put things into so we can sort them where they need to go. Here is one for storage, another for important, and the last one rubbish."

"You thought all of this out."

"You bet I did, we need the office back, and time with you

is the bonus to cleaning. So, what did you want to talk about in regards to the future?"

"I want to change the name of the ship, and I want to name it EXODUS. Yes, I know that it has a historical Earth meaning, but it fits what this ship is and our goals."

"Mika, did you read the book? Because you know that in the end, Moses stayed in the desert and died."

"Yes, Everett, there is that dark part to the book. But we are not following the book to the letter; we are using the name as it shows a sense of hope at the end of a long journey into the unknown."

"Okay, I am glad you read it to the point that you understand what the name means. I can also see your thoughts on using it in such a way as to inspire us."

"So, can we do it? Oh my gosh, they saved all my childhood clothes. Those are going to the girls to see if they want them. My stuffed animal, is it okay to have it on our bed?"

"So, in answer to your questions, yes to the toy on the bed, please let me think about the name of the ship. Is that okay?"

"That is a deal, so Everett, I am not sure if you saw that I talked to everyone on the ship while you were in the medical bay resting. I took full responsibility for the nanobots and explained everything about them and what to expect from them."

"Mika, that was so impressive you planned that out perfectly. Having someone ask you questions, and you were answering them like a real confident leader."

"That was Gunny and your dad who set that up. Then they made sure I was ready for every question. I don't think I could have done it without those two."

"I know you better than that. So, don't sell yourself short.

"Oh, Everett, they saved my mother's perfume." She takes the lid off and inhales the scent. The memories begin to flow from her mother.

"Mom, what is that you are putting on? Mika, this is my perfume. I like to put it on when your dad and I go out to do something special. Would you like some? Yes, please, mom. There you go, you know it helps men not to forget you, don't ever forget that."

"I am going to put this in our room. Next, we need to stop looking at the dead. These planets will never be our homes again, and we need to let that rest and move on. Or else we will stay here in this space, never moving forward and learning from our past."

"I think you are correct. We will talk with the team on Monday and get an action plan together to move forward. I think Neil will be able to tell us our best path to get where we want to go. It might be like ripping off the Band-Aid as we watch our past drift behind us." Replied Everett

"Everett, why do of some them call me Ma'am?"

"It is out of a sign of respect, Mika. I am Sir, and you are Ma'am. As both of us are the Commanders of the ship, they will use Sir and Ma'am instead of saying Commander every time or when we are both in the same room."

"Oh, okay, that makes sense. It was just a bit strange as I kept thinking you know my name why are you calling me that. But you do know that you are in charge I am there to help you." Said, Mika

"Oh Everett, they got all of my Jewellery as well. Oh, I have to do something nice for all of them for being so kind to me."

"Everett, you know I don't care for that dinner."

"Can I take you for a walk the kids will go to bed, and when we get home, I will make whatever you want me to make?"

"Okay, I'll agree, but you are going to have to make it."

"Hey, did you know that tonight the park is turning down the lights and there is going to be some mood music? They have asked us to make an appearance and start this event. So, we need to get dressed up a bit for it. Sorry…"

"Wow, you are pushing it this night, you know. Let me go get dressed."

"That went well, dad."

"Thanks, Chris"

"I will get dressed in your guy's room."

"Chicken," says Gabriel as the children laugh

"No smart, I planned tonight out, and nothing is going to ruin it."

Later that night, as they are walking to the park, "After thinking about it, I will agree to the name of Exodus. Oh, I forgot it is your turn to put the blindfold on. I have done something special for you."

"Oh Everett, you had me get dressed up to have a walk in the park with you, and I did my hair as well and now a blindfold. That is going to mess up my hair."

"No, it will not. I will be gentle with you. Here we go. What is that scent?" Ever puts the blindfold on Mika and takes her hand, guiding her toward the entrance of the park.

"It is my mother's perfume; what do you think?"

"It pales in comparison to you, my love. But it is nice, and I like it; you should wear it more often."

As they walk, he takes care to guide her to where a seat was waiting. "Please, my love, sit down here is a seat right here." Then Everett leaves and walks away.

"Ma'am, you can remove the blindfold."

Mika notices that she is on the raised music stage sitting in front of a table set for two with dinner plates, candles, and flowers. There is a note on the table, "I saw return shortly." Soon a young woman comes out and sits down to play. As the music starts, Everett returns, holding a microphone and begins to sing.

[All Of Me – John Legend]

As he starts to sing, he walks over to Mika near the end of the song lowering to one knee to look into her eyes, finishing the song. Other couples in the park focus on their loved ones as well. A tear starts to fall when Everett finishes singing to her. With one hand, he reaches and takes the tear places it on his heart and says, "I'll carry this one for you," Everett says to Mika softly.

Mika reaches down and hugs Everett and whispers in his ear, "I love you as well." As they sit down and enjoy their dinner, the music plays throughout the night.

"Everett, have you been planning this for a while."

"Who me? Would I ever plan something like this? Never, it just magically happened." Everett laughs. "Yeah, I have been planning this for some time. Jenny, at the piano, has been working with me as a voice coach so I could sing the song you to correctly."

"But why did you do this? It is so magical and special."

"Mika, on Earth, we celebrate the anniversary of a couple being together. It was one year ago we moved in together and agreed we needed each other. So tonight, I wanted to do something that showed my love for you. To let you know that I have never been so complete in my life than I am at this moment."

The night continues as the lovers share some of their happiest moments while creating others.

Days pass by, and the hope of seeing the future for the human race does not look so easy. In the office, Everett and Mika are working on the plans for the future of the ship and her people.

"Everett, we need to get the navigation and research team in a meeting to look at getting us underway." Suggests Mika

"I think you are correct on that. I had been thinking the same thing, so this afternoon they are due to have a meeting with us. Luckily for us, we can use the office once more." Everett laughs and smiles at Mika.

"Everett you will keep, I love you so much."

"Everett, I am not completely sure that we are going to find a planet like Earth and anytime soon."

"Well, Neil, I understand the rules behind light and the distance it has to travel versus we making it in time to us the planet we find. Where can we even start looking, we need a goal?"

"Everett, how about we look towards Proxima Centauri, it would take nearly 20,000 years for us to reach it at the fastest Earth craft that we had built. This ship does not travel even that fast." Replied Neil

"Well, that is not completely correct. We have been learning about this ship inside and out. We can go as fast as light travel, but there is one rather large problem. We have as humans even come close to that speed of travel. We don't know what it will be like.' said one of the navigation team.

"So, we can do it?" inquired Mika

"Well, we can, but I would suggest until we fully understand its use we avoid using inside of solar systems. I think if we run into a planet, we might not like the results."

"Where are we going to go now that there is no place for us here," asked Mika?

"As the navigation team can I walk out on to the bridge and tell you to get us out of this solar system and on to our target destination of Proxima Centauri?" asks Everett

"Yes sir, we are ready for you to tell us that is what you want us to do."

Everett stands up without warning, walks out of the office and on to the Bridge of the ship. "Plot me a course to Proxima Centauri."

"Aye Commander, it has found a safe course and is ready" instructs the helmsman

Soon he is joined by everyone from the office. Mika walks over to Everett taking his hand in hers. "When you are ready, my love."

"Very well, let loose the sails and give me an open mic to the whole ship. To all aboard, it is time for us to take to the seas of space. We now enter our journey into the unknown."

Everett looks into Mika's eyes, Mika says "Where is this place at?"

Everett turns his head toward the view of space.

As they stood on the Bridge, Everett points into the darkness and says........

"Second star to the right, and straight on till morning."

-J. M. Barrie, Peter Pan